NRI: Now, Returned to India

Amar Vyas

Copyright © 2014 Amar Vyas

All rights reserved

ISBN:9781502318589

To My Parents- Aai and Baba

Acknowledgments

Author's Note

Chapter One: It's only for a Year	1
Chapter Two: The First Missteps	12
Chapter Three: "Look Ma…I Got Wheels!"	33
Chapter Four: Summer of Discontent	55
Chapter Five: Boys' Night Out	67
Chapter Six: It All Goes Downhill	77
Chapter Seven: Everything Changes	88
Chapter Eight: No One's Support	105
Chapter Nine: Alumina	109
Chapter Ten: Decision Time	114
Chapter Eleven: My Indian Dream Shattered	123
Chapter Twelve: Gyaani Baba Arrives	126
Chapter Thirteen: Mumbai-Hitting Rock Bottom	129
Chapter Fourteen: Déjà Vu	145
Chapter Fifteen: On the Move Again	150
Chapter Sixteen: How it All Began	155
Chapter Seventeen: The Job Search	163
Chapter Eighteen: Winds of Change	172
Chapter Nineteen: Pit Stop	184
Chapter Twenty: Mumbai Gone Right	206

Chapter Twenty One: No Wedding, Only Funerals   214

Chapter Twenty Two: The Benefactor   243

Chapter Twenty Three: Goofball   248

Chapter Twenty Four: Soulmate   254

Chapter Twenty Five: How Time Flies   265

Chapter Twenty Six: Off to America   275

Epilogue: Four Weeks to Go, Again   277

ACKNOWLEDGMENTS

Several persons have helped me in my journey towards becoming a published author. But first and foremost, I must thank my parents. Aai and Baba, I miss you. Moving to India for your sake began a transformational phase of my life, and it has made me a better person.

Aai in particular wanted to read my book. I did not want her to read a work in progress version. Today, the book is ready, but she is no longer with me. My sister, Dr. Monika has been another supporter, critic and guide in my journey from day one. Thanks also to the other members of my family who supported me all along. I would like to make a special mention of my uncle, Madhav Mama. His sage advice kept me going through some of the darkest phases of my life.

A big thank you to my in-laws, particularly my father-in-law, who has been eager to read this book. I hope his wait was worth it. I must also thank Col. Joshi and his wife and my dear cousin Anjali. I spent a week at their beautiful quarters in Hisar in Haryana in early 2013. Their hospitality helped me in re-starting the work on my book. A big thanks the hundreds of readers from the Return to India Forum- their encouragement has helped me reach this far.

I appreciate the contributions of the following people: Manoj Vijayan, who designed my book's cover, and Jayanti Solanki, who designed my website. And also to all the beta reviewers who told me from time to time what worked with my novel and what didn't.

Most importantly, I must thank my wife, Mrunal. She has been my biggest supporter over the years, and has taken a deep interest in my writing. In several ways, she is the reason why you are able to read this book today.

AUTHOR'S NOTE

Many NRIs, or Non Resident Indians, dream that someday they would return to India for good. For most NRIs, this dream remains far from being realized. But for others, it turns into a reality - either because they choose to relocate to India, or they are forced by circumstances beyond their control. Then there is another group of people who return to India with their spouse and kid in tow, only to go back to the foreign lands they came from and reclaim their NRI status. Living in India and getting used to the Indian way of life is not easy.

I moved to India in March 2008 with a simple goal in mind: I was going to spend a year with my parents and then move to Canada to get my MBA and start my life there. Fast forward to 2015, and I am still in India. During this period, my life has changed for the better.

From the time I was in the process of relocating to India in early 2008, I maintained an online diary at the Return to India forum (www. R2iclub.com), where I narrated my moments of joy, sorrow, anguish, and frustration. The support I received from this online community was phenomenal. Many of them liked my writing style and they encouraged me to publish my experiences as a book. Nearly 110,000 views for my posts gave me the confidence about my writing abilities.

Around July 2010, my wife suggested that I should start writing this book. One year later, she reminded me again. This time around, I took it more seriously. I started writing Now, Returned to India in November 2011, and it took me nearly three years to complete the first draft.

Other than the remote resemblance of Amol's character to yours truly, all other characters are neither based on, nor do they resemble any person I may or may not have known.

Amar Vyas

Bengaluru (Bangalore), March 4, 2015

PART I

Chapter One

It's Only for a Year

At each of the several dozen departure gates at O'Hare airport, the passengers form a queue to board a plane. There is no rush, no pushing, and no yelling. But at one particular gate, a huge crowd forms at the farthest side, from where it tapers towards the single entry point. One can practically witness a funnel in action. This is the departure gate for the Air India flights to India. There is chaos, but things finally fall in place. A first timer may experience shock and disbelief. For the repeat travelers, or for those who have stayed away from Bharat Mata, or Mother India for a long time, this is a re-introduction to how things generally work back home.

I was simply being re-introduced.

My journey from Chicago had begun with unexpected glitches. Once the boarding had completed, the main door of the aircraft would not close. This delayed the take off by an hour. Next, a malfunction in the plane's autopilot system added another thirty minutes to the delay. By then, the innumerable Gujju uncles and aunties had started munching on their khakras and theplas. The aroma of the food filled the aircraft cabin in no time. The family next to me offered me some of these munchies, but I smilingly refused.

A large Punjabi family near the rear of the aircraft had begun chatting in loud and excited tones. They were talking about a wedding that was going to take place in a couple of days in Amritsar.

I could hear seven or eight different languages all around me. I was in a potpourri, no, a bhelpuri of cultures. Someone had once told me that there were only two possible places where one could hear so many languages and witness a mix of cultures in a few hundred square feet of space. One of them was the New York City Subway, and the other was an Air India flight. I was definitely on the latter.

The plane had finally taken off two hours beyond the scheduled departure time. Things settled down and I was looking forward to a quiet and relaxing flight. But once we reached somewhere above the Atlantic Ocean, the live performances by the wailing babies began. The opening act was started by a little one who was just two rows behind me, and was wrapped in pink. She was shortly accompanied by the howling of a pair of twins who were seated somewhere on the far side of the plane. They created a stereo effect.

Before I knew it, two more wailers from the front of the plane completed the chorus, and the howling could be heard in home theater mode.

Much to my irritation, the live show went on, and on, and on. The babies seemed to be Energizer Bunnies in disguise. As if this was not enough, someone in the row behind me kept walking up and down the aisle. She wanted to use the loo, but all of them were occupied.

"Must be the theplas," I said to myself.

The scene around me was chaotic, and yet, it seemed so familiar.

I decided that sleep was my only escape, and took the route I preferred most on long international flights: two shots of whisky is the best way to enjoy a sound, relaxing sleep.

A helpful stewardess on a Lufthansa flight had once told me, "Try it if you like. I have seen passengers dive into a deep sleep for hours." I had followed her advice shortly after the flight had taken off from Frankfurt, and had woken up after the plane had landed in New York. It was the best flight I had ever been on.

This time around, sleep was hard to come by. All along, a voice within kept asking me, "Why are you on a one-way flight to India?"

I thought I had an answer, but that was far from the truth. I had left Chicago on a Friday. Three days later, I was going to start my new job in India. I was leaving behind a familiar lifestyle and heading into the unknown. Even the most irrational person would have thought that I was being foolhardy.

*

By early 2008, many members of the Indian Diaspora, also known as Non Resident Indians or NRIs, had started relocating to India in large numbers. Many of them were forced to do so because of the economic slowdown in Europe and North America. Only a handful had moved back by choice. Many people in India felt that NRIs only returned to India when they could not make it big abroad, or because they had been given the boot. In other words, many thought that it was only the losers who came back.

A friend had sent me a news article that read:

"The green pastures of the West are not so green anymore for many NRIs. India is witnessing the return of more and more professionals due to challenges such as a job loss or visa issues."

The article was dated September 2007, one year before the collapse of Lehmann Brothers.

My friend's message was clear: I should not return to India.

"Stay put in Chicago," a second friend had advised.

My cousins, Lalit and Shashi, had also moved to India in the last few years. Both of them had warned me, "Returning to India requires a lot of planning. Don't make an impulsive decision."

But somehow, my plans made perfect sense to me. I had merely put my future on pause mode. I planned to spend a year in India and then return to my life abroad. For the next one year, I would get to spend time with Aai and Baba, reconnect with friends and family, and understand what it takes to work in India. Following which, I would leave for Canada for my MBA. It all seemed pretty simple and logical.

My move to India was like a pilot project. That is, trying out an idea before a full scale launch. Any engineer or scientist would be able to relate to it. Retailers also do a soft launch of their stores before the grand opening in order to make sure all the systems are up and running. Software developers release work-in-progress versions of their product before the final release. They call it beta testing.

"We all learn by trial and error," I kept telling myself. I was to learn the hard way that my trial was in fact filled with errors.

*

"Air India announces the arrival of its flight AI 126 to Mumbai."

I was waking up from a very disturbed sleep, and was not yet coherent. Travelling on a sixteen hour flight had taken its toll.

I woke up wondering: *What am I doing here?*

"*Mumbai ke Chatrapati Shivaji antarrashtriya hawai adde par aap ka swagat hai,*" the announcement came in Hindi this time.

By now, I was a little more alert. I was home. Well, almost. Home was four hours away in Pune.

The officer at the immigration counter looked irritated. I figured he was in a foul mood because the late night shift was the busiest time for international flight arrivals.

I looked at his name tag; it read 'Nitin More'. Another *Marathi manoos*! I approached him and said, "*Namaskar.*"

"Passport please," he barked. I was to learn later that in an office or a social setting, Marathi folks *never* speak to each other in Marathi. The obligatory language of communication is English.

After scanning a few pages of my passport, he asked, "You were in India last month. Are you here for work or vacation this time?"

"I am going to work in India. My work starts on Monday," I told him excitedly.

He gave me a look of disapproval and said under his breath, *"Ek aur aa gaya."*

As far as I knew, as an Indian citizen, there was no restriction on me to work in India. So why did he make the snide remark? I had been asked similar questions every time I had returned to the United States. The immigration officers there would ask, "How long would be staying here?" Who is your employer? Where will you be staying?"

"You don't know how to fill this form? You did not write the date?" Mr. More's words broke my chain of thought.

"It is either the 15th or 16th of March today."

"Go and tell this to someone else," he barked again.

"I have no idea because I am not wearing a watch."

"Even mobile phones show time and date. Today is the 16th."

He had a valid point, but I had returned my Blackberry the week before, and had planned to buy a new phone in India.

It was evident that Mr. More was neither a big fan of small talk, nor a man of reason.

"Okay, thanks," I said, and I entered the date as March 16th, 2008. I did not realize at that time that March 16th would carry a special meaning in my life.

Half an hour later, as I headed towards the exit with my bags in tow, I noticed a sign which read: "Welcome to India." However, my true welcome was yet to happen.

Once outside the airport terminal, I waited for a taxi that would take me on the last leg of my journey.

*

The taxi service had sent an elderly Sardarjee who held a placard bearing my name. "Namaste Sir, I will take you to Pune. Please let me take your bags," he said as we began to walk towards the cab.

Considering his age, I told him, "It's okay, let me handle it."

The silver and blue cab seemed to groan every time the driver stepped on the gas. "How old is this car?" I asked him out of curiosity.

"Three years old hai ji. But you know how Indian roads are. And the traffic, of course," he was implying that there was nothing wrong with his taxi.

I made a mental note that my car needed to be both tough and sturdy. And looking at how others were driving, preferably one that was built like a tank. The taxi snaked through Dharavi, then on to Sion and finally towards Chembur.

"Ye cranes dekho. Poora sheher phir se bana rahe hain," he said to me as I stared out of the window.

I was impressed by the driver's keen sense of observation. The city did resemble a giant construction site. The lights mounted on the moving cranes had lit up the normally dull Mumbai skyline. The car slowed down and came to a halt as we approached the toll booth at the Thane creek bridge. Five minutes later, we had reached Vashi.

By now, the slow hum of the engine had begun to hypnotize me. I had almost fallen asleep again when a loud noise woke me up.

"*Accident ho gaya ji,*" Sardarjee said to me calmly.

"Are you okay?" I asked him out of concern.

"*Headlaat toot gaya. Raat hai, Pulis pakad legi. Mai doosri gaddi mangata hun.*"

We were involved in a multi-car pileup somewhere between Vashi and Belapur. I guessed we were traveling at 40 kilometers per hour when it had occurred. By the time I had stepped out of the taxi, some of the cars that were involved in the accident had already left the scene. A few others were being pushed to the side of the road. There were no injuries, but only bruised egos. Overall, it did not look like a cause for worry.

The taxi was hit from the front and the back, but only a headlight was broken. I was impressed with the Tata Indica. It was a car that was truly built for Indian roads, and I had found my battle tank. The Sardarjee driver did not want to drive the car in the night with a single functioning headlight, and had called for a replacement. An hour later, the replacement car arrived, and we were on our way again and I reached home in time for breakfast.

Aai, like all doting mothers, declared that I had become anorexic and said, "From now on, I will make sure you eat properly."

What I really needed right then was a hot shower. But there was a power failure, which meant that there was no hot water. The idea of a cold bath didn't sound very appealing, so I opted to grab a bite instead. I had barely managed to eat a slice of bread when I threw up.

I decided to take that shower after all.

In the evening, I went to Suman aunty's place to meet Shashi. Suman aunty is a large and gregarious person. Even strangers take a liking to her in a very short period of time. She has a tremendous sense of humor, and she is an excellent cook.

Her late husband, Milind Kaka, was a Professor at Mumbai University. He wanted to spend his retired life in Pune. "Pune is known as a pensioners' paradise," he used to tell us. Unfortunately, he was called upon to retire in a different paradise as soon as they had moved out of Mumbai.

As I sipped the super sweet tea, Suman aunty asked me the usual set of questions that I would have to face many times the coming days.

"How was your flight? What time did you reach home?"

I was hardly in a mood for a conversation with, but I told her about the car accident.

"You should go and pray in the Hanuman Temple on Paud Road. You were saved because He was there to protect you," Suman aunty interrupted me before I could speak further. This Hanuman Temple would form an integral part of my Saturdays in the coming months.

I was hoping that Shashi would show up soon. He was my friend, philosopher and guide. He was my biggest critic, but he was also the big brother I never had. As always, he had told me not to act in haste. And like always, I had not listened to him.

Shashi arrived half an hour later, carrying his one-year-old daughter with him. "Wait, I've got to change her diaper," he said before I would utter a word.

I watched in amazement as he literally finished the job in less than a minute. I had always believed that Shashi possessed only one skill, namely, opening cans of beer. Changing diapers was very unlike him. But I had also heard that fatherhood changes people, and Shashi's act had just proved it.

"Welcome back," he said as he hugged me. His words brought me back to reality. I felt like he was saying, "Welcome to the jungle."

"You look different, I mean... *good*," I said to him as we sat down.

"Yup," Shashi replied. He had always been a man of few words. I sensed that a drink was out of question.

Shashi had gained a few kilos. He looked under-slept, and his hair had grayed. The Shashi I knew used to be quite a character, and a far cry from the person who was sitting in front of me.

*

It was summer of 2004. We had met at Lalit's place for a cousins' reunion. Lalit was the eldest among us. He lived in St Louis and worked with the leading brewer in town. It also ensured that there would be an almost unrestricted supply of beer at his place. Lalit was moving back to Pune at that time and we were supposed to help him with the move.

I had driven down from Chicago, while Shashi had flown from Atlanta. Instead of helping Lalit, we had finished two dozen cans of beer in a couple of hours' time and were wasted. Around midnight, Shashi wanted to smoke a cigar, so the two of us had stepped out. As he lit up his cigar, he had asked me about my work. By the time I could reply to his question, we had reached the swimming pool.

"I want to go for a swim," Shashi had declared.

Before I could stop him, he had stripped down to his underwear and dived into the pool. The cigar was still in his mouth. A few minutes later, he had stepped out of the pool in the buff. "My underwear got wet, so I put it to dry," he had said, pointing to a black fabric that hung on the fence.

By now, I was worried that someone would call the Police, so we made a hasty retreat to Lalit's apartment. I had managed to collect his clothes in the process.

On our way back, Shashi shouted, "The cigar is wet. I cannot smoke it!"

It was obviously time for him to go to bed. I was thankful that we didn't get arrested that night. The hum of the air-conditioning from the neighboring homes had drowned the ruckus that Shashi was creating. Somehow he had managed to wake up at dawn and collect his underwear from the poolside. "I didn't want to leave any evidence," he admitted later.

*

Today, I could see that the Shashi I knew had changed. Rather, lots of things had changed about him.

*

Before going to bed, I tried to watch TV but could not figure out why the hosts on every channel would first say something in English, followed by its Hindi version.

"Please stay back while we take a short break. *Milte hain break ke baad,*" an overly made up and seemingly bubbly young girl spoke on some channel. Almost immediately, the loud jingle of a commercial began.

I shouted, "Why do they say the same thing in two languages?"

"Maybe they speak in English to cater to the South Indian folks?" Aai meant well, but her point was practically irrelevant. There were more regional language TV channels than the Hindi ones, and the non-Hindi speakers would naturally prefer to watch those channels. But I was hardly in the mood to argue and turned the TV off.

Tomorrow was going to be my first day at work, and I needed to rest. As is, I was not happy to learn that the sofa in the living room was going to be my bed for the next several nights. Aai and Baba liked to carry their worldly possessions with them wherever they went. As a result, the bedrooms were overflowing with boxes and furniture, and there was hardly any space left for me to sleep.

As I lay on the uncomfortable sofa, reality hit me. I was back home in Pune. As I wondered if things would work out as planned, I consoled myself by saying, "It's only for a year."

Chapter Two
The First Missteps

"Wake up. I have made tea for you."

Baba's voice was the last thing I expected to hear after a restless night. I thought it was a dream.

"Wake up, Amol," Baba's words rang in my ears again.

"What time is it?" I asked, opening my eyes.

"It's five-fifteen in the morning. Get up," he commanded.

"Baba, I am not a tea drinker. I prefer black coffee," but my complaining had no effect.

"The tea is getting cold. Get up...Now!" Baba shouted.

Baba had always been an early riser. It was a habit from his younger days when he was growing up on a farm. More than half a century later, he still liked to have his tea early in the morning.

Before his retirement, Baba would wake up at 5 AM and leave for work by 9. How he had managed to spend four hours getting ready for work, day after day, was a mystery to me. Aai, on the other hand, had always been a late riser. In Baba's book, she was a *Suryavanshi*, or someone who woke up after sunrise.

*

An hour later; I stepped out of the house for a walk in the park next to where we lived. That's when I heard a voice calling my name.

"Amol!" It was Lalit. As he came up to me, he asked, "What are you doing up so early?"

"I have been up since five-thirty!"

"Jetlag?"

"Baba," and I told him what had transpired in the morning.

"Welcome home," he laughed, and began to tell me what life in India was all about. After a while, he realized that he had engaged in a monologue for too long.

"*Accha*, listen. I have to go now. But *shaam ko* Lata is going to make Paav Bhaji," Lata Vahini was Lalit's wife and was known for her culinary skills.

"I'll be there, thanks!" I used to call Lata Vahini as Lata V; and I was not going to miss her signature dish.

It had been nearly two years since I had last eaten Paav Bhaji. I had driven twenty miles to Devon Avenue in Chicago, which was almost the home for the homesick Indian. Sukhadia, the restaurant where I had devoured the dish, had a friendly Gujju uncle at the cash counter, but not-so-friendly fellow customers. The unpainted walls of the restaurant had crates of Thums Up stacked up against them. The scene presented simplicity and vintage that reminded me of the Irani hotels in Mumbai.

*

By eight, I had showered, shaved and had my second cup of coffee. Dressed in neatly ironed khaki pants, a light blue shirt, and brown leather shoes, I stepped outside the house and walked up to the nearest auto-rickshaw stand.

"Dhole Patil Road," I told the auto-driver. It was the first and the only time that my commute to work would be so effortless.

Fifteen minutes later, we had reached Karve Road, and were heading towards Deccan Gymkhana. Traffic was slowly building up, as was the heat. As the auto-rickshaw neared the intersection with Law College Road, the driver switched on some loud, irritating music. Some things never change, I thought to myself.

During my college days, anyone who played loud music would be instantly labeled a rickshaw-wala. Those were the days when the music composer duo of Nadeem Shravan and singer Kumar Sanu were the rage. They had this new addition to their songs, called Jhankar Beats. For some unfathomable reason, the auto-wallas liked them the most.

"*Awaz thoda kami kara,*" I said to the auto-driver to turn down the volume, as he turned left from Karve Road on to Deccan Gymkhana. But he was not willing to yield.

"*Saheb, ye navin song Lai hit hai. Vaishali Sawant singing hai.*"

It did not matter to me that someone called Vaishali Sawant was singing, and her song had topped the charts. Which charts, I did not know. All I knew was that a woman with a very shrill voice was narrating the story of a hen that was running away from someone.

It was a shame that Marathi music had not evolved beyond its fascination for birds. In the late 1980's there was this song about some parrot that had fallen in love with the neighbor's mynah. One could hear it all over the place. That was nearly two decades ago. And now, the parrot had been replaced by a hen.

But the woman's singing seemed melodious compared to the cacophony I could hear around me as the auto zigzagged its way from Jangli Maharaj Road towards the Engineering College building, and then inched its way past the RTO Office towards the railway station.

Along the way I began to see some familiar signs. There was a building on the left where one went to submit the papers for a U.S visa application before the pilgrimage to the U.S. Consulate in Mumbai. Little beyond that was a left turn near a Pizza shop which led into a lane. At the end of this lane was my destination: City Tower Building.

The journey to the office had lasted nearly an hour and I was late for my work on the very first day.

My office in Chicago used to start at eight, but I would always reach by seven-thirty. If I had to go to the construction site, I would leave home by seven and would talk to a few suppliers and foremen as I drove. That gave all of us an hour's head start to get ready matters that could make or break the day's work. I thought it was a good practice, and I should continue it here in India.

But it would soon dawn upon me that people in India preferred to come late to work and stay late in the office.

*

Surprisingly, everything seemed very quiet as I entered the City Tower building. An office complex should have been buzzing with activity by now. I was equally surprised to find that the only other occupant besides myself was the elevator attendant.

"Third floor, please. KMM ka office," I told him.

I felt sorry for the attendant. He had to perform one of the most thankless, brain- numbing jobs in the world by spending and entire day in a six foot by six foot cab, pressing buttons, and going up and down the same shaft several times.

As we reached the third floor, the elevator came to a halt with a jerk. "Thank you," I told the bewildered attendant, who was probably not used to being thanked.

I walked down the hallway and turned left. One month ago, I had the most frustrating time in this office: I had spent a long time waiting for Paresh. Today, I was going to work with him.

I tried to open the glass door that would lead me inside. It was locked.

"Sir, *aap ko KMM jana hai? Woh to Nucleus Mall chale gaye.*"

I turned around to find a skinny lad talking me. He was wearing a dark brown uniform which bore the logo and name of some company called SKS Securities. His name badge read Balwant Singh. What irony, I thought. Parents should think twice before naming their children. The guard's name was Balwant, which means a strong man, but the poor guy wouldn't even be able to defend himself should the need arise. But I was not here to debate on how parents should name their children.

Apparently KMM had moved their office to some place called Nucleus Mall, but he did not know where this mall was. The trouble was that I didn't know either.

"*Unko call karo Saheb,*" Balwant walked away with these words.

Nobody had informed me that the office had moved. I did not know where Nucleus Mall was, nor did I have their new phone number. I called Paresh right away, using Baba's cell phone that I had borrowed this morning. His phone was switched off. I was left with no choice other than to locate the new office on my own.

"Nucleus Mall," I told a group of auto drivers who were sitting outside the building. None of them responded. They were sitting beneath a tree in a circle and were busy playing cards. I could also see a pile of money in the middle. Something told me that they would not be very keen on leaving their current money-making activity for another one. The former required good luck, while the latter needed hard work. It was the latter that they were shying away from.

An hour later, I finally found a ride and a driver who knew where this mall was. Like every self-respecting auto-wala, he had also put on some loud music.

"*Ye Tashan picture ka gana super hit hai,*" he told me. The song in the previous auto had been *Lai Hit*, and this one was *Super Hit*. Both were played so loudly that my eardrums hurt.

I reached Nucleus Mall around ten-thirty, and walked up to the front desk of KMM's office. There was a burly guard and a petite woman behind the desk. The guard's name badge read Chotu Ram, another shining example of a mismatch between a person's name and their personality. But I was beyond contemplating such things.

"Hi, I am Amol Dixit. I start work here today," I told the girl who was busy messaging on her cell phone. It was amazing how she managed to type on that tiny keyboard.

"I am sorry we have not been told that someone will be joining today," she replied coldly.

"Miss, this is frustrating. Nobody informed me that you guys had moved here, and I had a terrible time finding this place. Now you tell me that there is no mention of me joining. Can you please check with the office manager?"

The girl was irritated by now. Her phone had buzzed three times as I was speaking. Probably her boyfriend had sent her messages that she needed to respond to urgently. She ignored me and went back to her texting.

I called Paresh on his cell phone again, but there was still no response. That's when I remembered then that I had Manpreet's number. He was my point of contact with HR, and the only other person I knew in KMM. I heard a busy tone when I dialed his number, and was about to call him again when my phone buzzed.

"This is Amol," I said, answering the phone.

"Amol, where are you? This is Manpreet."

"I am outside the office in the reception area of the new office. Nobody told me that you guys had moved."

"Then ask them to let you in," Manpreet remarked.

"They are not letting me enter!" I replied.

"Wait. Let me do something about it," he said, before hanging up. The phone at the reception desk buzzed. The girl answered it.

A couple of minutes later, she looked at me and said, "Please have a seat. Someone will take you inside."

I shook my head in disgust. I was hired as a Project Manager, but my treatment was worse than that of a kid straight out of college.

*

This was so different from my first day at work at Vojak Construction. I had arrived a few minutes before eight AM, but the office was already alive with activity. The friendly receptionist had welcomed me with a smile and said, "Welcome to Vojak Construction, Amor." She had mispronounced my name, calling me, Amor. But knowing that Amor means love in many languages, I took it as a compliment, and smiled back at her.

Within minutes of my arrival, Jim Vojak, the owner of the

company, had come to meet me and had walked me to my desk.

"Leave your stuff here. I will be right back, and then lets' go and meet the folks," Jim had told me in his commanding voice.

Someone had placed a card on the desk which read, "Welcome to the family."

There was a box next to the card which had my laptop, a box of business cards, my security badge and a mobile phone. They even had placed some T-shirts, a hard hat and some stationery: every minor detail had been taken care of. While I was going through the goodies, Jim's voice boomed on the public address system in the office.

"This is your Captain speaking. I am very happy that Amol has joined us today. In a few minutes, let us all meet in the cafeteria. Little Lilly has ordered pizza for all of us."

I was surprised. There were over a hundred people in that building. A pizza party at work for all of them would have cost lot of money and time. What a way it was to welcome a new employee!

Over the next four hours, I had been introduced to everyone in the company, right from the directors to the project engineers. The environment was so informal, relaxed. During my interview with Vojak Construction, I was told that Jim Vojak believed in working hard and partying harder. That day I had witnessed it first hand.

As I was lost in these thoughts, I heard someone say, "Good Morning. Sorry about the confusion. Please follow me."

A woman who was draped in a green and yellow sari was addressing me. I followed her into the office, and began to wonder: *Looks like people do not like to introduce themselves here. Is this the culture of this company, or is the work culture in general like this in*

India? Only time will tell.

Time would teach me many more things about working in India.

I was led into a large meeting room. The woman disappeared, and a server clad in a white jacket entered. He asked me, "What would you like to have Sir? Tea or Coffee?"

"Black coffee, please." I replied, and noticed that he was wearing gloves that were supposed to be white in color, but now were almost yellow with stains. I wondered when he had last washed those gloves.

A few minutes later, another woman walked in. "Good Morning, I am Sudha, your HRBP. Welcome aboard."

HRBP was a new word for me. I would learn later it meant 'Human Resources people who caused Blood Pressure to rise'.

"Good morning and thanks. What does HRBP mean?" I asked.

"Oh! I am the HR business person. I will be the point of contact for all the HR issues for your business unit."

Before Sudha could tell me more about her role, her cell phone rang. "Yes, he is here with me. The forms are on their way. We should be done by 1 PM," she told the person on other side.

The wall clock showed that it was 11 AM, so I would have to spend two hours in this room. It was going to be an interesting day.

"That was Manpreet. He is talking to Paresh. Someone should take you to the project site after the joining formalities have been completed," Sudha said with a faint smile.

That's when it dawned upon me: I had not asked during my interview where I would be working. It was one of the many questions that I should have asked. In the days to come, I would have to pay a heavy price for not doing so.

A few minutes later, Sudha handed me a bunch of papers that looked like some sort of forms. My ten page offer letter seemed like a pocket book compared the Encyclopedia that was in front of me.

"Never sign any paper without reading it first," Baba and Aai had taught me and my sister Natasha when we were growing up.

Remembering that lesson, I dutifully set about reading every line of every page in those forms.

KMM's HR had sent me a checklist of sorts with the offer letter. That list had mentioned that I was required to carry four photographs with me on the joining day. The list in front of me said that I was to submit eight of them.

The first form required me to attach a fitness certificate. During my days at Vojak, I was used to submitting fitness certificates for cranes, excavators and other construction equipment.

"Mr. Dixit, you are officially a construction vehicle," I said to myself, and smiled at my own private joke.

Two hours later, I was less than half way through the paperwork. By now I was filling information for insurance. They needed information like date of birth, employment history, and known ailments.

What amazed me most was that almost every form required a photograph. "What is this fascination with photographs in India?" I asked myself. The rate at which they were asking me for photos, I would need at least a hundred copies very soon.

*

"Hi! Are you done?" Sudha asked me as she entered the room.

"Not quite. I have to complete this set," I said, pointing towards the pile of papers on my left-hand side. I had split the paperwork into three stacks: forms that were completed, those I was working on, and the ones that were yet to be filled.

"Oh! How come it has taken so long?" she asked again.

"It's a lot of reading," I remarked.

"Don't bother reading the forms. It's standard stuff. I am sure you know what it says," she shrugged out of frustration.

"The fact is that I do not know what is written in them, and therefore I am reading every single word."

"If you could just sign them and get them ready by 1:30 PM, it would be great. I have a lunch meeting to attend. Anyways, Rajesh will be here shortly."

"Rajesh?"

"Rajesh Tickoo. You haven't met your teammates so far? How about Ashok ji, your project leader?"

I shook my head and started to fill the forms again. The next form asked my employment history. KMM already had my resume, and they obviously had seen it, and probably even run a background check on me before making me an offer. So what was the point in asking me for the same information?

I would learn later that people in India submit resumes that run into several pages, which makes the job of HR very difficult. They have to read these long documents and then copy the information on to the employment forms. Out of frustration, HR folks had passed this burden on to the applicant.

Even though I only had a one page resume, it was futile to fight a system I was not familiar with. So I simply wrote 'See attached resume.' With that, I started completing the rest of the forms.

My concentration was broken when I heard a voice, "Sorry *yaar*, I got delayed. The traffic was bad. By the way, I am Rajesh Tickoo."

*

I noticed three things about Rajesh. First, he was short. Second, he practically epitomized the word rotund. And third, his face had a broad smile. I had a feeling that we would get along well. A few minutes later, we were in his car and on our way to the project site.

"So you have returned from USA. How long did you work there?" Rajesh asked me.

"I was there for nearly a decade," I replied.

"So when did you come back to India?"

"Yesterday."

"Oh!" Rajesh was surprised to hear my reply, but continued, "I was in the Philippines and Singapore for four years. I am a PMP."

I almost heard him say, "I am a Pimp!" If Rajesh was trying to solicit a customer for his side business, I was the wrong guy. But I realized that he meant the Project Management Professional certification. I also sensed that he wanted to narrate his story first.

"Great. What type of projects were you involved with?" I asked.

Rajesh was pleased that I had taken his hint well. "I used to work with Sembawang. You know, building jetties, refineries, and the likes"

"Great!" I said. "So tell me about our project here."

"*Yaar*, it's an interesting project. A Mumbai based developer called the Apogee Group is working with a local builder to build a project called Village Market, which is located near Hadapsar on the eastern side of Pune. This will be one of the largest projects of its kind in the country. On 30 acres of land, they will build shopping and entertainment area, offices and a hospital. Totally, they will build 50 lakh square feet of building space. That's five million square feet for you. Our team will manage the project." Rajesh was proving to be a storehouse of information.

"So what exactly does project management mean in India?"

"The usual things like coordinating with consultants, managing the tendering process, making recommendations to the clients, sending reports and things like that."

"So who manages the actual construction work?" I continued my questioning.

"Oh! That will be the contractor's job," he replied, and went on to describe other aspects of project management. By the time Rajesh completed his monologue, I realized that the job was certainly very different from what I thought I had signed up for. This was a paper pusher's job, whereas I was a man of action.

Paresh had told me during my interview that I would be the project manager for a very large project. To me it had meant that I would be heading that project. "The contract has not been signed, so I cannot tell you anything else," he had said. I had been lured by the idea of working in Pune and living with Aai and Baba and signed up.

I had made a huge mistake.

But this was just the beginning of a series of disappointments.

"Where's Paresh?" I asked Rajesh.

"Paresh will visit the project site on Saturday for the weekly meeting with Ashok Desai, our team leader."

"And how big is our team?" I asked him again.

"There will be six of us. Three, including myself, already work from the site. You are the fourth, and two more will join next month once the office is ready."

I was used to working out of construction trailers and sometimes even my car, so not having an office was not a problem. But what Rajesh said next sounded alarming.

"For now, we all sit in a meeting room," he added.

"What about phone, laptop and Internet?"

"You will get them in a couple of weeks' time. It is standard procedure."

By now, we had driven past the Race Course and were on the Pune-Sholapur road. Only one lane of the six lane highway was operational due to the construction work.

"The construction work you see here is for the BRTS, that is, Bus Rapid Transport System," Rajesh remarked, and continued, "Some traffic consultants had sold the idea to the city leaders that a dedicated lane for public transport buses would be the perfect solution for the city's traffic problems. The consultants had even taken a few of these leaders to some cities in Europe to show them how the system works. Now, the Pune Municipal Corporation has become a believer in BRTS."

Looking at the shabby manner in which the work was going on, I thought that the BRTS would only provide a fig leaf to the otherwise exposed transportation system in this city.

Ironically, my current job would also provide a fig leaf for my career. I had accepted the job thinking that I would be working with Kevin Mervin Moses, a Chicago based real estate consulting company. I had worked with them when they were developing a mall on the south side of Chicago. But KMM were investors in that project, while they were project management consultants here. That made all the difference.

I recalled what Rajesh had mentioned, *"Paresh will visit the project site on Saturday for a weekly meeting with Ashok ji."*

"Rajesh, what's with this weekly meeting on a Saturday? Why does Paresh want a meeting on a weekend?"

"Amol, my friend, this is India. Construction goes on seven days a week. And we work six days a week, *yaar*."

By now, it was evident that I had not asked the right questions during my interview, and I was about to pay a very heavy price for my mistake. My dreams of spending a quiet weekend and quality time with Aai and Baba would not be realized. My plans of meeting friends or exploring new places around Pune, including driving to Lonavala on a lazy Saturday afternoon, seemed like a remote possibility. So far, I had only worked five days a week throughout my career. And I really, really valued my weekends.

I was jet-lagged, hungry, tired and now full of remorse. I wanted to go home and fly back to Chicago, but that was not a choice anymore because I was committed to staying in India for one year.

The air-conditioning in the car provided little relief from the afternoon heat, and in a lame attempt to console myself, I repeated my mantra: *It's only for a year.*

*

Ashok Desai, or Ashok ji, was in his mid 50's. Rajesh had aptly described him as 'a man with a receding hairline and an increasing waistline'. Ashok was a loud, short-tempered person. He was a civil engineer who had studied in England.

"I worked abroad for several years before returning to India in the mid- 1980's. Those were interesting times then," he told me when we met for the first time.

"I had no experience of working in India. The project site where I worked was fifty kilometers away from my home. I would take two hours each way, and that too after changing three buses. One year later, I took up a Government job with Bombay Municipal Corporation. Fortunately, I know Marathi very well. Being a Mumbaikar Gujju helps." Ashok said with a sense of pride.

"A Mumbaikar Gujju?" I was a bit perplexed.

"Yes, a Gujju from Mumbai is different from a Gujju from Gujarat," he declared emphatically.

I could feel a sense of pride and a hint of arrogance in his tone.

As far as I knew, a Gujju from Mumbai spoke in the same tongue as his northerly brethren. However, a city lad and his upcountry cousin would utter *"Kem cho?"* in different dialects.

"You go to Gujarat; you will understand," Ashok advised before I went to meet the fourth and final member of the team.

Sachin Nair had a thick set of hair that could easily require an entire bottle of Parachute brand of oil. Looking at the shine in the hair and the strong aroma of coconut oil that filled the air, he probably *did* need an entire bottle.

Sachin had recently finished his decade long tour of duty in the Gulf, where he had worked as the head of design for a plumbing contractor. For Keralites, or Mallus as they are affectionately called, working in the Persian Gulf countries is almost a non- negotiable rite of passage. He was also our resident skeptic, and was not at all impressed by Apogee Developers.

"Mark my words," he said, "these people will throw us off the project once they have learnt our systems and methods. I would be surprised if we last more than a year." His prophecy would be tested in a few months' time.

When I returned to our makeshift office, I realized that we were sitting around a table in a room that was smaller than my office in Chicago. This place would continue to serve as our office throughout the summer. The project plans that I was so keen to see would not be ready for nearly two months.

I was surprised. "We are getting paid for doing nothing?"

"We have mobilized at the site as per our contract, and lets' leave it at that for now," he replied, not willing to say anything further.

Instead of sitting in the room and getting bored to death, I began to complete the rest of the forms that Sudha had given me. I was required to open an account with HSBC for my salary. I already had a HSBC account in the United States, so I thought that opening an account in India with them should not be a problem. After a while, I was tired of providing the same information over and over again.

"It is 6 PM, time to go home," Sachin declared, and added, "I can drop you to the nearest auto rickshaw stand."

*

Almost every auto-driver refused to take me to Kothrud, which was at the other end of town. One driver demanded twice the money. "*Meter ka double*," he told me in Hindi.

I recalled an old trick from my college days, when I used to split the journey, that is, take one auto to a halfway point, and take a different one from there. One of the auto drivers readily agreed when I asked him to drive me to the railway station. My plan seemed to have worked: there was no demand for extra fare. The rickshaw driver snaked his way through the crawling traffic. An hour later, I was sitting in another auto which would take me to Kothrud. It was 8 PM by the time I reached home. The trip back home had cost me two hundred Rupees and taken nearly two hours. I had also forgotten Lalit's invitation.

*

My first week at work flew by faster than I had thought. For most of the day, we would sit around the table in the makeshift office, walk around the project site, or have several cups of Kadak Meethi or dark and sweet tea.

Ashok would spend nearly the entire day in meetings with the developers. Rajesh would be on the phone nearly all the time. And Sachin would draw caricatures of the people he knew. I sometimes wondered why he was wasting his talent sitting here in this office.

I recalled what my friend Rohan had told me while he was driving me to O'Hare airport the week before.

"Watch out for your first month at work when you go back- you will have no work to do. You will not get a computer or even a phone, nothing. I had moved to India in 2002 to work with the largest software company in India at that time. But they had not given me a workspace or a computer for the first six weeks. I used to sit at a desk that wasn't even my assigned location. Somebody was on leave and I was merely a squatter. When I asked my group's VP about this, he had simply told me that my desk and computer would take time to arrive. He had given me books on Java programming and some manuals to read. It was a waste of time. I left within six months and never went back to India."

I wrote about my experience to Rohan, and he replied, "Some things haven't changed in India."

*

By Saturday, I was desperate to talk to Paresh. After reaching the site around nine AM, I learnt that Ashok, Rajesh and Sachin had gone to the Nucleus Mall office for a team meeting.

I wondered. "Why didn't anybody bother to inform me?"

It was an all-hands-on-deck meeting. I had not received the notification because my two weeks of 'standard procedure' had not been completed. But *somebody* could have informed me.

The company had not provided me with a cell phone so far, but Rajesh and Ashok had my home phone number and also Baba's cell phone which I was using at present. They could have at least called me. But all this thinking was of no use.

By the time I reached the office, it was eleven A.M, and I was late by an hour. The meeting had ended, and a group of people were chatting in a corner of the meeting room.

I saw that Rajesh was listening attentively to a man who sported a neatly trimmed silver goatee.

"Here comes Amol. Amol, meet Ganesh ji. He will be joining our team from Monday."

"How was your first week?" Ganesh asked as we shook hands.

"Kind of interesting, everyone wants to know who I was, and why I have returned to India. It is as if I am a new exhibit in a museum, or a new animal in a zoo," I replied with a smile.

Ganesh smiled back at me. He looked like a seasoned construction veteran. His arms and neck were tanned, rather, burnt by days of working in harsh sunshine. He reminded me of my uncle, who was a civil engineer himself and had spent his career building roads for the state government.

"I did not know that we had a meeting today," I said to Rajesh once Ganesh left us to meet others.

"The meeting invite was sent to everybody. How come you didn't get it?" Rajesh asked me in a surprised tone.

"Because I don't have a computer, or email access, or a phone, for that matter," I replied, trying not to show my irritation.

"*Arey yaar*, I wish I knew. *Nahi to call kar deta*," Rajesh remarked casually. But he knew my situation very well. And had he genuinely cared, he would have called me.

"Where's Paresh?" I asked him, trying not to lose my temper.

"He left a few minutes ago to attend an important meeting."

I reached for my phone and called Paresh, but his phone was

switched off. "I can't reach him!" I said and looked at Rajesh for help.

"Did you try his new phone number? Wait, let me call him."

"I didn't know that his number had changed."

But by then, Rajesh nodded his head several times. He spoke into phone, "Yes, that's great, thanks, thanks..."

He was grinning from ear to ear when the call ended. "*Yaar*, he will call you on Monday. By the way, the bonuses have been very generous this year."

*

It was 7 PM by the time I reached home that evening. As I entered the house, Aai asked me, "How was your day?"

"Fine, but I am tired of the commute," I replied coldly.

Aai could sense the irritation in my reply, and left me alone.

That night, I decided that it was imperative to buy a car. My first missteps had caused me enough troubles.

Chapter Three
"Look Ma...I Got Wheels!"

I am going to buy a car today!" I declared over breakfast on Sunday morning.

"Which car are you going to buy?" Baba asked out of curiosity.

"Probably a used car that I can drive while I am in India. In a year's time, we can hire a driver to take you around."

Baba continued his questioning, "Where will you buy it from?"

"I don't know, and I'll have to figure it out. In the US, there were options like Craigslist and the local newspapers, but I used to prefer buying a car from a dealership. I would shortlist a few cars that I liked, and note their vehicle identification numbers. Then I would go to Carfax.com, look up the car's ownership and title histories, and make my selection. Payment was partly by cash and the rest by loan. Banks would issue the loan in a couple of days' time."

By the time I had finished my narration I could see that Aai was thoroughly confused.

"But we have nothing like this here in India," she said, and added, "I think you should talk to Lalit or Shashi. They bought their cars almost together last year."

Aai was right. It was better to talk to someone who knew the lay of the land. And that someone was Shashi. I called him a couple of times, but as usual, he did not answer.

That's when I decided to dial Lalit's number. "In India, the only car worth buying is a Maruti Suzuki. It is good value for money, has a great network of service centers, and the spares are cheap. Plus, the cars have good resale value. It is important for you because you are planning to sell the car next year," he advised.

Sell the car next year. I hadn't thought of that at all. Fresh from the experience of selling my car in the United States, I was not keen to undergo that pain and suffering all over again so soon. But then I recalled my commuting troubles over the past week, and came back to my original decision.

"What do you drive?" I asked Lalit.

"A Maruti Swift. It's a good car."

"What about an Indica?"

"It's good if you plan to operate a taxi service for a call center." Lalit had degraded my battle tank with his remark.

"What about a used car?" I asked him.

"I would advise you against it. Title histories can a problem, and sellers usually do not keep maintenance and service records. Some cars may even have been involved in accidents that might have gone unreported. Here, we do not have used car dealerships like the CarMax that you used to build. But hey, why don't you come over? There is a used car shop near my house. We could go and check it out after we have lunch together."

*

Lalit had just moved into a shiny new apartment building in Karvenagar, which was not too far from where we lived. The building did not have a working elevator yet, nor did it have an access road. I wasn't even sure if the building's firefighting system or emergency lighting, if any, was working. I could not understand why a developer would hand over an incomplete building to customers. Moreover, why would the municipality allow people to start living in an under construction building? And, most importantly, why would people rush to live there? I hoped Lalit would be able to enlighten me on this.

The trouble was, that he lived on the seventh floor.

"I need the exercise." I told myself as I started my climb. "Climbing stairs is also a good way to build an appetite." This was the second reassurance I offered myself.

The first flight of stairs was conquered in no time. The second took no time either. By the time I reached the third floor, I began to realize the downside to climbing stairs on a hot day. My shirt was soaked with sweat by now.

By the time I reached the fourth floor, I was huffing, puffing and panting. My legs had begun to ache and my back was hurting. To motivate myself, I imagined settling down comfortably on a chair near the air-conditioner with a beer in one hand. Fifth and the sixth floors were behind me, and there was only one more floor to go. As the number of steps reduced to three, two and finally one, I reached the seventh floor.

Three minutes and ten seconds after I had started my climb, I rang the doorbell to Lalit's house. There was no response. Tired of waiting, I knocked on the door. The door was opened by Lalit this time. He had a finger on his lips, indicating that I should keep quiet.

"The electricity board disconnected supply this morning because the builder hasn't paid the bill," Lalit said to me as I entered his house.

"What builder, and why hasn't he paid the bills?" I asked.

"A builder develops a building project." Lalit replied, and

continued, "You should know... you come from the industry."

"In my un-informed world, a developer conceives the plans, gets the funding and approvals, and hires contractors to build. He also markets the project. A builder is a new term for me." I replied.

But Lalit was not impressed. I began to imagine what a builder looked like. He would be a dark, short man clad in a short-sleeved safari suit. In one hand, he would be carrying a leather pouch, with a gold wristwatch adorning his thick, hairy wrist. One cell phone would bulge out of his front pocket, and he would carry another phone in his free hand. A pair of sunglasses, with a golden frame and green lenses, would be resting on the bridge of his oily nose.

In contrast, a typical builder in the United States would be a tall, muscular man, wearing a pair of jeans and a T-shirt. He would be a balding person probably in his forties, someone who had been working on job sites since his teens. With advancing age, he was adding more calories than burning them, as evidenced by a beer belly.

While the two contrasting images ran through my mind, a streak of salty sweat ran into my mouth. I realized that I was hot and miserable, and was standing in the hallway of Lalit's house.

"Hey, come and sit," Lalit said to me as he realized my discomfort. The red upholstery of the couch complimented my face very well, which had turned red due to the heat.

"Beer hai kya?" I asked, finally settling down. To me, it was a rhetorical question. Lalit *always* stacked beer in his fridge.

"Nahi." Came his reply.

"What?" Lalit's reply had stumped me. Imagine the disappointment of a diehard cricket fan who has decided to skip work in order to watch an India-Pakistan match at home, only to witness Sachin Tendulkar get out on the very first ball. I kind of felt like that.

"We are back in India, Bhai. *Special permission needed for beer...*" Lalit smiled and winked his left eye.

I vaguely recalled that there was a rule from 1930s that required a person to obtain a permit in order to consume alcohol. It was one of the many legacies from the British Era.

"Where do we get the permission from?"

Lalit replied with a smile, "Home Ministry."

That's when I realized what he was trying to say. Lata V. had said no to the beer. "We can always go and get some beer from the store near the petrol pump," I responded.

The wine shop had existed for several years in that area. During my college days, my friends and I were its regular patrons. We used to jokingly call it a can of Kingfisher beer as KFC, because that fast food chain was yet to enter India back then. The late 1990's was an era when ATMs and cell phones were a rarity and a can of chilled beer was a luxury.

But today, I was not so much motivated that I would walk in the hot sun and trek up the seven flights of stairs again. Moreover, the beer from the store couldn't be put in the fridge to chill.

"So, are you planning to get the beer?" Lalit asked me.

"Water will do," I replied, just as Lata V. entered the room.

Seema Kaku, Lalit's mother and my late aunt, had insisted that her son should marry Lata. She used to say, "One should marry a fair woman. That way, the children would be born fair." Unfortunately, she wasn't around when Lalit and Lata had a son, because ironically, Gopal was as dark as the God after whom he was named.

Seema Kaku's theory had failed in her own grandson's case, but I was sure that she would have an explanation for that. "Oh! Gopal is dark because he was born around *Amavasya*," she would have said. Apparently, children born during the dark phase of moon were darker than those born around the full moon night. I had often wondered whether her theories held ground only in India, or whether there were more exceptions- Scandinavia, for example.

Lalit had hardly stayed at home when he was in the United States. Now, he practically worked from home most of the time. He was a consultant for many of the breweries that were located in Aurangabad, which was only a few hours' drive away from Pune.

Lata was a religious person, even to the extent of being called orthodox. Since her return to India, she had started teaching Sanskrit at a neighboring school. Sixteen years of marriage had added a boy and a girl to complete their family. As the TV advertisements used to say back in the day, theirs was a '*Chota Pariwar, Sukhi Pariwar*' – or a 'small family is a happy family'.

I recalled Lalit's finger-on-the-lips sequence and asked Lalit, "So, why did you ask me to keep quiet when I entered?"

"Ganga is not well," he said even before I could finish speaking.

"Which means just the four of us for lunch? Where's Gopal?"

It was Lata V's turn to speak this time. "He is away at his friend's place. And I am sorry, there is no lunch. No gas to cook. With no electricity either, I cannot prepare anything."

It was my turn to run out of gas. Lalit could have at least

informed me in advance. But for a strange reason, he had become a penny pincher ever since his return to India.

"A phone call costs one Rupee a minute and a SMS costs the same," he had once told me. In his book, the price of inconvenience caused to others was much less than the worth of his Rupee.

"Ok, lets' leave for the car dealership then." I suggested, resigning myself to the situation.

*

Five minutes later, I had left Lalit's house with a piece of paper that bore the address and phone number of Royal Automobiles.

Lalit had chosen to stay at home to answer the door, take phone calls, and make the afternoon tea, provided the electricity was back. He had practically become a neutered Labrador; one who was warm, friendly, and waiting for a command from his master. Or in this case, the 'Master' was Lata V. Gone was the Pit Bull that I used to know. Shashi had become a diaper daddy and Lalit had been neutered. I had known them to be men's men when they were in the US. Somehow, India had changed them. I began to wonder what would happen to me if I stayed beyond a year.

Shaking my head to shrug off these thoughts, I looked around. Kothrud had changed quite a bit over the past decade. What was once a narrow dirt road leading to a hamlet called Azadwadi had now become a four-lane road, which led to Azad Nagar and the new subdivisions that lay beyond.

I thought it best to ask for directions, but the road was empty, with only a few stray dogs, an occasional cow, and a few birds. It was ironic. Pune was a city of four million inhabitants, and yet, the street was deserted. I eventually reached Royal Automobiles around 2 PM.

It was closed.

*

"I do not deserve this," I said aloud as I entered my house an hour later. The five kilometer walk in the heat was hardly worth it.

"How was your lunch?" Aai asked.

"Didn't have it..." I replied and added, "Ganga wasn't feeling well, and they had no lights or gas. I wish Lalit had informed me."

"That's the Desai family for you." Baba said as he entered the room. At sixty-five, he needed a cane for support. His nearly toothless mouth was an unpleasant reminder of the ill effects of chewing tobacco. He had visited the local barber recently and his hair was cropped. But the most visible feature was the child-like smile on his face. This was one quality I had inherited from him.

The Desais were related to us from Baba's side, and he always seemed to have a problem with them. As he settled down in a chair, he said, "By the way, the phone was ringing every now and then while you were away. It was nearly impossible to sleep." Baba handed me the phone as he finished speaking.

The cell phone was a relic compared to the Blackberry I was used to. This three-year-old LG phone was about five inches long and a couple of inches wide. Its screen occupied a third of its front face, and the key pad was nothing remarkable. But the phone could do three things very well: it could receive incoming calls, make outgoing calls, and its alarm clock could put any rooster to shame. For the past week, Baba had reluctantly let me take this phone to work. On Sunday, he had asked me to return his prized possession.

I checked the missed calls log. Rajesh had called me twice, and

Pangulal had called me three times. There were a few other numbers that were unfamiliar to me, I chose to ignore them.

On the first day at work, I had asked Rajesh for his number. "I will give you a missed call. Then we can add my number in your phone," he had suggested.

But when he saw the phone I was carrying, Rajesh was aghast. "Amol *yaar*, what are you doing with this old phone? After all, we are in India, and a cell phone is not just a phone, it is a fashion statement. You are known by the phone that you carry. And for a US returned person like you, this old phone is a no-no. But let me save my number in your phone for now." Saying so, he had pressed a few keys in the phone and handed it back to me. The screen had displayed the words, 'Rajesh Work'.

Seeing my surprised look, he explained, "In India, people have more than one cell phone numbers. I have two myself, and my wife has two as well. The best way is to save them separately. Look."

He had shown me a few entries from his phone's address book. In reality, he wanted to show me his iPhone.

I failed to understand why Rajesh had called me on a Sunday. After all, he had not called me yesterday when it had mattered. I chose to ignore his calls.

*

Pangulal was next on the list of callers. He was my best friend, my brother, and my partner in crime...or rather, several crimes.

"Why don't you answer your calls?" He asked as he answered the phone. It was typical of Pangulal: cut and dry, and to the point.

"I had left the phone at home," I replied.

"Whatever. Namita and I are going to a Maruti showroom to test-drive a car. You can meet us at JM Road at our usual place."

"Great. But what's a showroom?" I asked, surprised.

"In America, they call it a car dealership. See you at six."

*

Pangulal had spent three years in Australia before he had fallen for a girl and followed her back to Bangalore. They had to elope in order to get married. I knew the story, because I had managed the show from Chicago. Two of my friends had traveled from Chennai to Bangalore to be present as witnesses, their travel was paid for by me. For all my efforts, Pangulal had not expressed one word in gratitude. We did not believe in thanking each other.

But the bigger issue was why Namita had chosen to marry Pangulal in the first place. She was a quiet, shy, level-headed person, and was a Lawyer who worked with one of the Big Four audit firms. Her father, Sanjay Garg, was a very successful Lawyer, and her mother was a well-known artist. Namita was the younger of the two girls. Her elder sister had married a musician.

*

True to our tradition, Pangulal and I met at Surabhi, a nondescript eating joint on Jangli Maharaj Road. This place was our hangout during college days. We ordered our standard menu: coffee, followed by masala dosa.

Namita had a glass of lemon juice. She was still recovering from the excesses of their recent second wedding; a traditional wedding which was reluctantly arranged by her reluctant parents. As we worked on our dosas, Namita narrated stories of their wedding. I was least interested in the irrelevant details that she was telling in an excited tone: the color of the clothes that Pangulal was wearing, or how the food was too spicy. I rued that I was not able to attend my best friend's wedding both the times. My parents had filled in for me on the second occasion.

Namita stopped her narration and asked me out of the blue, "By the way, what is the story behind the ten thousand Rupees that your parents gave us as a wedding gift?"

"Namita," I said, "It is just one of those things that friends promise each other. This goes back to the time Pangulal and I were in college. We cruising down Karve Road on Pangulal's motorbike. Ahead of us, a wedding procession was led by a band. The party had created the obligatory traffic jams. As Pangulal steered his motorbike through this circus, we noticed a sign that read, 'Joshi and Lele Families welcome you.' I was amused by the entire *tam Asha*, and asked Pangulal why did people spend so much money on weddings?"

I took a pause and continued, "He did not know the answer, but had said 'Don't know, but the rents for the halls are high.' Out of curiosity, I had asked him, 'How much is the rent, anyways?'"

Pangulal smiled as I narrated this incident from our college days.

I looked at him, and continued, "Pangulal had replied, 'I don't know. Ten thousand Rupees, maybe?' That's when I had told him, 'Bhai, don't worry. I will pay the ten thousand when you get married.' To which, his reply was, 'And I would be happy to return the favor.'"

I saw that Pangulal, like me, had become nostalgic. Good old times, those. Ten thousand Rupees was a tidy sum in 1996. And for a twenty year old college kid back then, it was a lot of money. Those were the days when a cup of tea cost two Rupees, the chai and sutta ritual could be completed in less than a fiver.

Namita's voice broke my chain of thoughts. "So you gave us ten thousand Rupees for that reason. But hall rental is much higher these days; I think at least ten times that amount. Twenty times, if we talk about Mumbai or Delhi."

"Namita, your point is valid. But what we had agreed to was a fixed sum. There was no adjustment for inflation or addition of interest." Over the years, Pangulal had become a smooth talker, if not a smart talker.

"You should have asked him for ten thousand Dollars as a wedding gift for us," she remarked.

"We had no plans of going abroad back then." Pangulal replied, and I nodded in agreement.

Namita continued, "But both of you did end up going abroad. Amol, now you have no plans of staying back in India. But what if you end up doing exactly that?" I nearly choked on the *Sāmbhar*.

*

A few minutes later, we were at the dealership. At best, it looked like a very well- maintained car garage. As we entered, a young lad came up to us. He was clad in blue jeans, a black shirt, and a yellow tie.

"Hello Sir, can I help you?" He seemed the least interested in saying anything more than that. He was probably the owner's son, or someone who was working there just for the money.

"We would like to test-drive a Swift," I told him.

"I will be right back." He said. A few minutes later, he returned with a clipboard with a few sheets of paper in one hand and a pencil in the other. "I am sorry we only have one car today that you can test drive. All others are out. Please come with me."

"What car is it?" Pangulal asked, as we began to follow him into the parking area. "It's a Zen Estillo," the lad replied.

Pangulal frowned and looked at me, indicating that this car was not worth considering. But I ignored him. Our small party walked down the dimly lit hallway, past a row of cubicles, and finally down a short flight of stairs into an open parking area.

The car was purple in color, and it bore MH 14 registration plates. Pangulal burst out laughing. "You get the whole package. This is a must buy."

Namita did not understand why he was so excited. The salesman sounded confused. "It is a good car," he remarked.

I had seen only one car in the United States whose shape could not be described in easy to understand terms. It was the Pontiac Aztec. These cars had such a poor demand that the car makers had no other choice but to offer the steepest discounts possible. The Zen Estillo was a car in that league. If its shape was an absolute turn off, so was the purple color. Moreover, it was too feminine for any self-respecting man's tastes. A biker chick earns cat calls and whistles, but a man watching a chick flick is often made fun of. The Zen Estillo was the chick flick of cars. But the main reason to stay away from the car was its MH 14 registration.

You see, there are two kinds of bad drivers in India. There are those who simply don't know how to drive, and then there are those who hail from the Pimpri Chinchwad area, the twin industrial towns located west of Pune. The drivers from this area have absolutely zero sense of driving. They honk their horns loudly on an empty street. They show a turn signal for the left side, and turn right instead. When they drive, they occupy nearly two lanes. The white stripes that separate the lanes are exactly in the middle of the car, just like an aircraft's nose wheel on a taxiway. These driving traits are universal, irrespective of the make or vintage of the car, or the age or the gender of the driver.

While in college, quite a few Premier Padminis, Marutis and an occasional Mercedes Benz that drove on streets of Pune bore the dreaded MH14 numbers. Pangulal and I would ride our motorbikes with extra caution if we noticed a vehicle with these license plates.

There was no way I was going to even sit in that purple car, let alone test-drive it.

"No thank you," I told the young lad, and hinted to Namita and Pangulal that we should leave.

"Wait! Let us at least check the car out." Namita said, as she opened the door and took the driver's seat.

"Step in," she said. We had no choice. Her dutiful husband sat next to her. I tried to fit myself in the incredibly cramped rear seats. The salesman sat next to me. Almost immediately, I stepped out.

"What happened?" Pangulal asked.

"This is not what I like. Listen, why don't you folks carry on with this? I think there's still time. I will head over to the Tata dealership on Tilak Road," I said, hoping to find a car that was to my liking.

"Too bad, you are going to miss out on the experience of a lifetime." Pangulal remarked as we said our goodbyes.

*

Fortunately, I found an auto-rickshaw as soon as I stepped out. Ten minutes later, I was standing in front of Pandit Motors, the dealership for Tata Motors. The guard at the gate asked me what I wanted. It seemed that businesses in Pune had a fetish for employing guards who invariably prevented potential customers from entering.

As I entered the showroom, I walked into a large hall that displayed six or seven vehicles. They carried names such as Safari and Indigo; and there was an advertisement for something called Dicor technology. It was supposed to be the best thing to have happened to cars since the launch of the Model T. And then there was a car called Xeta. I began to wonder what had happened to the good old Indica.

I asked a young girl who was sitting behind the reception counter, "I need to buy a car. Who can I talk to?"

She looked at me and pointed to her left. I walked into the office area and asked a middle-aged lady who was struggling with the computer monitor that occupied more than half her desk.

"*Namaskar*. Can someone tell me how to buy a car here?"

The woman was irritated by my interruption. "Please go to the reception desk. They will call someone."

"Madam, the ladies at the reception asked me to come here. I am a walk-in customer; the least you can do is to have a salesman talk to me." By now, my patience was wearing out. The place was hot and stuffy. The air-conditioning was turned off, probably because it was nearing the closing time.

I was to learn later that companies, both large and small, Indian and multinational, would spend millions of Rupees in building fancy offices, only to realize that they were simply too expensive to maintain. As a result, they would look for ways to reduce the operating costs. Turning off the air-conditioning was the most common way of doing so. This malaise of cost-cutting would eventually spread to malls, theaters, restaurants and even hospitals.

The woman at the desk picked up the phone and spoke to someone, *"Kamal la pathva."*

Kamal happened to be a youngish lad who was about five feet tall, and his shirt pocket was stained with blue ink.

"Yes?" He asked me as he looked at me. I began to wonder if he was a waiter in an Udupi restaurant in his previous job.

"I am looking to buy an Indica," I told him.

"Which one, diesel or petrol?"

In the United States, I had always driven cars that had petrol engines. Diesel cars were a no-no, unless one drove some of the expensive European luxury cars.

"Petrol," I said. He looked at me with disbelief, perhaps thinking that I was out of my mind.

Over the next few days, several people would give me a similar look of surprise and shock. "There is a new Indica petrol version, it is called Xeta." Kamal said to me.

"Perfect, what are its features?" I asked him.

"It depends on the model. There is the GLS, GLG and the GLX, they all come with a variety of features. The car you see here is the GLX. It is the top end vehicle."

I opened the door and sat in the driver's seat. The car was indeed designed for taxi drivers to ferry passengers from call centers. The console was basic, the dashboard made of cheap plastic, and there was no music system. It felt strange to sit in the driver's seat of a right-hand-drive car after so many years.

"Does this car have ABS?" My question startled Kamal.

"I am sorry?" His reaction told me all that I needed to know.

"What about airbags?"

This question left him equally startled. "Sorry sir, there are no such features in this car."

This was turning into a WYSIWYG moment: what you see is what you get. To me, disc brakes and airbags were basic safety features. But I decided to engage Kamal anyways. The more the questions I asked up front, the better. It was bitter a lesson I had learnt after the mistakes I had made during my job interview.

"So what is the difference between the top-end model and the next best?"

"Sir, you get power windows for all the doors in the top-end model, and there is an accessories kit."

"What's the price difference between them?" I probed further.

"About twenty five thousand Rupees."

"Twenty five thousand Rupees for two power windows and accessories? What if I buy the next best, and get the kit and windows installed separately?"

"In that case, Sir, it will cost you eight thousand Rupees more."

Kamal was getting uncomfortable by the minute.

"Okay, I like that option. I would also like a test drive," I said.

"Sorry Sir, it is closing time. Can you come on Tuesday? We are closed on Mondays."

Good old Pune, I said to myself. Businesses here remain closed on Mondays, afternoons, and of course on holidays. And they also open late, around 10 AM and close by 7 PM.

*

It was eight PM by the time I reached home that evening. My daylong weekend was over in no time.

*

As soon as I reached my workplace on Monday, I saw that Rajesh had already made himself comfortable in the office and he was busy looking at his laptop screen.

"*Yaar*, I called you several times yesterday. You didn't pick up the phone," he said.

"I had left it at home. By the time I saw the missed calls, it was late in the night."

"That's okay, no issues. *Accha*, listen. Ganesh bought his car from the Tata dealership. I think he bought a Fiat. But he said that there is a salesman by the name of Prashant. When you go to the dealership, ask for Prashant. He will help you."

I thought to myself, "Had I returned Rajesh's call yesterday, the trip to JM Road and my poor experience at Pandit Motors could have been avoided."

On Tuesday morning, I went to the dealership again, walked

up to the front desk, and this time asked for Prashant.

The girl behind the desk told me, "You may please sit in the waiting area."

The waiting area was a smallish room, with bare walls that were painted in white, and there was a long sofa that was draped in dark blue faux leather. A news channel on the TV was informing people about the upcoming cricket tournament called Indian Premier League. But cricket was not on my mind at the moment.

In a few minutes, another youngish lad walked in and said, "*Namaskar*, I am Prashant."

"My colleague Ganesh referred me to you."

"Yes, Sir, he called me yesterday and told me that you would be here today."

It was strange. I had never met Ganesh till Saturday, and yet he had gone ahead and called Prashant.

"Can you come with me to the sales area please; which car would you like to buy? We have the Indigo and the latest Safari Dicor. Both have great diesel engines. We offer attractive financing."

"Thanks, but I am looking for a small car, maybe an Indica with a petrol engine. And I would be making the payment in full."

Prashant was surprised. He had not expected me to say that I wanted to buy an Indica. But to me, that car was field-tested, and I was not willing to pay an insane amount of money on a car that would be worth less than half its current price very soon.

"Sir, there is a heavy rush for buying Indicas, but let me see what I can do. We are heavily backlogged because of the festival season. But if you make the payment today, maybe we can arrange for something. Please follow me."

I walked into the sales area again and sat next to a small desk. At the sales desk to my right, another salesman was talking to a family of three— husband, wife and their son, who was probably six or seven years old. I overheard their conversation, or at least bits of it. It went something like this:

"The car will cost you Rupees five lakhs. Taxes and duties will cost you extra. Are you planning to finance it?" The salesman asked the husband.

"Yes," the husband replied.

"That's okay Sir, no issues. We have financing facility available. Can you tell me where you work?"

"I work with Wipro."

The next questions took me by surprise.

"May I know your annual income?"

"Three lakh a year," came the man's reply.

The salesman smiled a wide smile and called someone. "Raman, get three cups of tea, and a cold drink for our young customer."

Something didn't seem right to me. This man was willing to buy a car that cost six hundred thousand Rupees when he only made three hundred thousand a year. And he was willing to take a loan for making this purchase, for which the dealership was serving him tea and cold drink. On the other hand, I was willing to pay the full price of the car, but was hardly getting any attention. But it was obvious: the family next to me was meted out VIP service because the dealership stood to earn a commission on the loan. This commission alone was worth several times the margin they would earn on the car, and that meant big bonuses for the sales staff. My chain of thoughts was broken by Prashant. He said, "I have brought the paperwork, shall we proceed?"

After nearly an hour, we had haggled over the price and agreed to the down payment amount. Several minutes later, the paperwork for the car was complete and wrote a check for forty thousand Rupees. The rest was to be paid on delivery. I wanted the car to be delivered on April 6th, Gudi Padwa day. It was one of the most auspicious days according to Baba, and it also marked the beginning of the New Year in Maharashtra. I was not a big believer in rituals, but gave in to his demand. After all, I had relocated for Aai and Baba's sake.

April 6th was three weeks away, but Prashant was still noncommittal. "I cannot commit to the date, but I will try."

I asked him out of curiosity, "What is the interest rate for loans?"

"Fifteen percent. Are you interested in financing?" he asked.

"No, I was just checking. Thanks."

At fifteen percent rate of interest this family would be paying more than two times the price of the car over the next five years. A car whose value would depreciate the moment it left the dealership. The news of credit bubbles in the United States had probably not yet reached India.

Baba woke me up early in the morning on April 6th. "We are getting the car home today," he said, unable to conceal the excitement in his voice. It was a moment of joy for many reasons. For years, my parents had spent nearly every major festival by themselves, and today I was going to celebrate Gudi Padwa with them for the first time in twelve years. Lalit suggested that he could drive the car home from the dealership, and I had agreed readily. Around noon, the four of us; Aai, Baba, Lalit and I, went to Pandit Motors in two auto rickshaws. I had never seen such a mad rush at a dealership anytime in my life. We were asked to wait in the sales area when we entered.

"We have a large number of deliveries. Over one hundred people are taking their new cars home today." Prashant said to me. I was one of those hundred, and so was the family who had taken the loan. Several hours later, I had the car keys car in my hand. Lalit took the driver's seat, Baba sat next to him. Aai and I sat at the back. Aai and Baba were happy because their son would drive them around in Pune. Almost everyone from the mechanic to the guard at the exit wanted some money or *Baksheesh* from us. It was a legacy of the British era, one that served no purpose in current times. In Pune, they called it "Chaay pani", or money for the proverbial tea and water.

"Why is everyone asking for money?" I asked.

"Let it be. It's goodwill," Lalit replied. I thought it was extortion.

Half an hour later, the car was home. And before I could say "Look Ma... I Got Wheels!" the car was in the body shop.

Chapter Four
Summer of Discontent

It was a Tuesday evening when the twin accidents occurred. There is a traffic signal at the intersection between Pune-Sholapur Road and the road that leads to Magarpatta Township. I was waiting at this traffic light when two trucks hit my car.

The first truck came from the left and smashed into the passenger side door, jammed the door at the frame, and broke the side-view mirror. As I stepped out of the car to confront the truck driver, the second truck came and hit the car from behind. That impact broke the rear fender, tail lamps, and the windshield.

By then, the traffic light had turned green. The first truck sped away before I could note down its number. The driver of the second truck also began to drive away. I did note the number from its license plate. The trouble was that the front and the rear license plates were different. I could see a group of traffic cops on the other side of the street. They were looking in my direction. Finally, one of them walked up to me and asked what had happened. Then, he looked at the car and remarked casually,

"*Aise to hote hi reheta hai.*"

The traffic policeman was not interested in noting my complaint. He had simply told me that things like this happened every day, and that I should go home.

"*Mazya jawal truck cha number ahe,*" I said, showing him the paper on which I had noted the truck's license plate number.

"*Police Station la ja. Amhi traffic wale,*" the policeman

remarked as he walked away. Though he had advised me to go to the Police Station, he had not told me where it was located. It took me two hours to find the Police Station and file the report.

The car was damaged but drivable. I was pleased with my choice of a battle tank, but battle tanks were costly to fix.

Aai was shocked when she saw the car, but said, "Are you all right? I am glad nothing happened to you."

Baba simply remarked, "This is not America. You should learn to drive more carefully."

"Baba, yes, I made the mistake of stopping at a red light. I used to make that mistake in America also. There it is called obeying the law." But my words had no effect on Baba.

A few minutes later, I tried to call my sage counsels— Shashi, Lalit, and Pangulal. Only Lalit answered my phone. "These are merely teething troubles. You will have to learn to live with Paplus," he said in an attempt to console me.

"Paplus?" I asked.

"Paplus are the last minute surprises. Don't worry, you will get used to them." His words were hardly reassuring. I was not looking for sympathy, but was looking for advice. And I did get a lot of free advice that day.

Next day, I called up the insurance company and told them about the incident. The customer support representative told me, "Sir, please take the car to the repair shop near the Parvati hill."

The manager at the body shop looked at the damage, and began noting down the repairs that needed to be made. Fifteen minutes later, while he was still scribbling on his notepad, he asked, "Do you have insurance for this car?" When I nodded in the affirmative, he wrote the estimate as sixty thousand Rupees.

"What if I don't want to pay through insurance?" I asked him. "In that case, it will be forty five thousand, half in advance."

I called the insurance company again. They responded, "Sir. It is very unusual for a car to get involved in an accident within the first week of purchase. Your policy has not been activated in our system yet, but rest assured, your claim will be honored. In the meantime, you can pay for the repairs up front and claim for reimbursement." *But the accident was not my fault, and I was* not going to pay for it.

*

While the car was in the body shop, I thought of focusing on the other tasks that demanded my attention. Opening a bank account was becoming a top priority. The account executive at the HSBC branch insisted that I should open a regular salary account.

"I am sorry Sir, we cannot open a NRE account for you because you will be getting your salary deposited in Rupees. A NRE, or a Non Resident External Account, is an account used by the NRIs to send their foreign currency back to India, which is then converted and saved as Rupees. One can repatriate the money in foreign exchange, and make the deposit in Dollars, but one cannot deposit the money in Rupees in a NRE account. The only choice left for you is to open a regular salary account."

"You may be right, but this does not help my case. I have not received my salary, and for the company to pay me, I need an account with your bank," I protested.

"I can give you the account opening form, Sir. Please fill it and hand it over to counter number 6. We would also need a copy of your PAN card." She said, as she handed me the form.

"What is that again?" I asked.

"A PAN or Permanent Account Number card, is a card that bears a number which is needed for tax purposes. It can also be used as an identity proof."

"Miss, I do not have a PAN card, and I need my account to be opened urgently. I am already a HSBC customer in the United States. Why do I have to fill up all this paperwork again?"

"I am sorry, these are the rules," she said and left.

A few days later, I received a call from the bank.

"Good morning Sir, I am Tejas, your account manager. There are some technical difficulties with the opening of your account. But, in the meantime, there is an insurance plan that I would like to discuss. We have some of the best ULIP products."

"My friend, I am trying to open the bank account so that I can get my salary deposited. Let me get some money first, and then we can talk about investments," I replied.

"We can offer you a personal loan, if you are interested."

I hung up the phone. The next morning, I went to the bank and walked out with my checkbook and ATM card. My account had been activated after three hours of persuasion, threatening and finally an angry altercation with the branch manager.

*

"It is time you get re-Indianized." Shashi said to me that evening when I went to meet him.

"I am trying, Shashi. But there are only a few things that I am used to by now."

"What do you mean?" He asked.

"For example, I am no longer amused when I see boys and girls go to a McDonald's for a date."

"So you are used to some things. What are you not used to?"

"I see that a lot of people have a habit of shaking hands every now and then. They shake hands with anybody and everybody, including the ones they meet every day. When the folks at my workplace come to the office, the first thing they do is to go around and shake hands. I have stopped wondering what has happened to the good old Namaste."

Even though Shashi was not interested, I continued, "The loo is probably the only place where people do not shake hands when they meet. And then I wonder how many of these hand shakers wash their hands after going about their business. I have started carrying a bottle of a hand sanitizer in my backpack for that reason."

Shashi asked me calmly, "Amol, does it really matter?"

"Maybe you are right. It shouldn't," I replied.

"You need to appreciate that things here are different."

"Okay." I conceded. "But above everything else, it is really difficult to get used to the fact that every single task takes long hours of waiting, multiple follow-ups, and cajoling or even threatening."

Shashi looked at me and said, "When we were growing up, we had learnt that S*aam, Daam, Danda, and Bhed* are embedded in our culture. If you recall, *Saam* means using reason to convince somebody to see things your way. *Daam* means paying someone in cash or in kind for getting the work done. That would also explain why corruption is so deeply rooted in India. *Danda* refers to using threat or the use of force, legal or otherwise, to get the work done. And *Bhed* means simply to close the door on the person or the entity one is dealing with, and look for alternatives."

"I get that. But *Bhed* will not work, correct? There is only one agency for getting the PAN, one option for opening a bank account, and one option for getting the insurance work done."

"Yup," Shashi replied as we parted ways.

*

The last week of April dawned, and so did my birthday. Ashok offered to drop me to the half-way point from my home.

"So, are you getting used to the life here?" He asked me as we left the project site.

"Kind of, though I am still struggling with my insurance and a few other things. I still need to follow up with the post office almost every day to see if my boxes have arrived or not."

"Don't worry, things will fall in place. Till then, make sure you build up your patience levels. Learn to meditate. You know, I used to blow a gasket every now and then during my first few months in India. Like you, I hadn't worked in Pune either."

"I was here during my student days. This is the first time I am working here, or in India for that matter," I replied.

"You will get used to it. Pune is a nice city, though I think it has grown too big for its breeches. I find the people a little arrogant and rather unprofessional, but compared to Mumbai, every other city in India would seem unprofessional."

As I got out of the car, he said, "By the way, Happy Birthday."

"Thanks," I replied, and began my hunt for a ride back home. Half an hour later, as I was about to sit in a rickshaw, I realized I had no money to pay the driver.

"The last time I loaned you some money, you were in college. It is shameful that you are asking me for money even today," Baba said to me when I reached home. The whole neighborhood had probably heard him. He had also forgotten that it was my birthday.

After paying off the auto driver, I sat down in the little corner that I could call as my space in the house, and the day's events ran through my mind.

"Get ready, did you forget that we are going out for dinner?" Aai said as she brought me a cup of coffee. Looking at me, she asked, "Is everything okay?"

"Aai, I do not deserve this."

"These things happen. They will get resolved in no time."

"I am not complaining, Aai. I am not upset that the whole neighborhood could hear Baba. I had to break my own rule of not borrowing money from him."

"Is the coffee too sweet for you?" Aai asked, in an attempt to change the topic. I took the hint.

"Please don't add sugar the next time," I said with a smile.

Before we left the house, Baba handed me an envelope and said, "Happy Birthday." The envelope contained a life insurance policy. As I read it, my eyes fell on the words, Twenty Five Thousand. I thought that Baba had paid twenty five thousand as premium for the policy, which meant that the policy covered me for at least five hundred thousand Rupees.

"At least I am worth more dead than alive!" I said to myself. But a deep frown formed between my brows when I read the words, 'Sum Assured', next to the 'Twenty Five Thousand'.

"Baba, what is this?" I asked him.

"I had purchased this policy for you the day you were born. The papers had gone missing, but I found them recently. I thought you would like the gift."

"But Baba, the coverage is only for twenty five thousand Rupees!" I nearly screamed.

"It was a lot of money when you were born," he replied.

"Thanks again, I really appreciate it." I said with a resigned look. There was no point in arguing. He was looking forward to the dinner, and he had told me on several occasions the day before.

And for the first time after many years, my birthday celebration did not involve any partying or drinking, and dinner was a simple dosa. The evening had ended on a quiet note. Only if I had the car to drive us back home, it would have eased my frustrations.

*

I woke up the next morning and called up TATA AIG and gave them an earful for taking so long to settle my claim.

"Don't worry Sir, the payment will be made today, I can assure you that you will be able to drive your car home today itself." The customer service representative told me. My next call was to the body shop.

"Your car is ready, and your insurance claim has been settled. You can come any time after 1PM and take your car. You have to pay four thousand, five hundred Rupees," the manager at the repair shop informed me.

I was merely following the traffic rules by stopping at a red light, and still had to pay for the damage caused by others. I remembered the traffic cop's words, *"Aise to hote hi reheta hai..."*

I now turned my attention to my unpaid salary, and wrote to Manpreet and Paresh.

"Gentlemen,

I have been working with you for over six weeks, and till today, I do not have a phone, a laptop, or an internet connection. I have no salary, and no news of insurance or my relocation allowance. This is not the kind of treatment I expect from a professional organization like KMM."

My email set off a series of phone calls, emails and SMS'es. Manpreet wrote back and assured me that all things would be taken care of by the end of the week.

Paresh called me and said, "You sounded very upset, and I can understand. HR said that your details were not entered into PS."

"PS?" I asked.

"PeopleSoft," Paresh replied, and continued, "But don't

worry. Your check will be ready by the end of the day. You can collect it tomorrow and deposit it in your bank account."

"Paresh, why can't someone from the office deposit the check into my account? The bank is literally next door to the office. It will take me nearly three hours to come to the office, deposit the check in the bank, and return to the jobsite. Not to mention it will cost me two hundred Rupees each way for auto fare. Who will pay for that?"

But Paresh had disconnected the call by the time I had finished speaking. It was his way of avoiding any confrontation.

The next day I collected my paycheck and went to deposit it in the bank. As I looked at the amount, my thoughts went back to my first and only paycheck in India till that day. While in college, I had worked as an assistant in my neighbor's advertising firm. I was the happiest person on earth when they had paid me one thousand Rupees for my work. Today, the amount had grown a hundred fold, but my happiness hadn't.

*

By the middle of May, things had begun to settle down on the work front. Much against my wishes, I was made the design manager for the project. At first, the building plans came in one's and two's. Soon, the trickle turned into a stream, and by the end of the month, the stream had turned into a flood. I barely had any time to complain.

Every day, Sachin, Ganesh and I would spend time pouring over the drawings. And then we would discuss what needed to be done to develop the schedule and also the cost estimate. These discussions invariably happened over tea. And that's when the *chai and sutta* ritual came back into my life. We would step outside the office, buy our cigarettes from the tea vendor, and light up. Five Rupees per cigarette was easy on the pocket. This apparent ease had turned me into a smoker again even before I had realized.

*

I also learnt the hard way that all the *chais* and *suttas* in the world would not help me overcome my challenges with paperwork. The source of my latest frustration was the health insurance policy.

One day, Rajesh said to me, "You should go to our office and meet Sudha. Your insurance papers have arrived."

Sudha handed me a package that contained the policy and three cards. They had the usual errors and omissions. Errors, because they had mis-spelt Aai's name and changed her gender. Seeta is a very common Indian name, and it typically implies that the person carrying this name is a female. But the insurance company thought otherwise. They had sent a card which read: "Mr. Sitaram Dixit, Male, 60 years. Relationship: Mother."

Omission, because the paperwork did not include Baba's card. It was as if he did not exist in their system at all. There was no mention of him anywhere in the policy documents.

But what really took me by surprise is that out of nowhere they had made me a father. The third card read: "Mr. Abhay Yadav, Male, 10 years. Relationship: Son."

I knew by now that throwing a fit was of no use, nor would any screaming be helpful. I wrote to Sudha instead.

"Dear Sudha,

Thanks for sending me the insurance papers and the cards. I have the following comments about them:

a. My father's name does not appear anywhere in the paperwork. I can assure you he is very much alive. I had provided you his details along with his photographs to support my statement.

b. My mother's name is Seeta and not Sitaram. I have known her to be a female all my life, and it is surprising to know that the insurance company thinks otherwise.

c. Most importantly, to the best of my knowledge, *I do not have a son*. If this is something that was discovered during my background check, then please do let me know. I would also appreciate if the details of his mother are provided to me. The laws are very stringent when it comes to child support, and I have no intention of breaking them should it turn out that I am indeed the child's father. I hope you realize the gravity of the situation. Your help would be greatly appreciated."

Half an hour later, Sudha called me back. She assured me that the matter would be resolved ASAP. But by now, I had understood that in India, ASAP meant *As Slowly As Possible*.

I dreamt that night that I was nineteen again, and was dating a certain Ms. Yadav. On a rainy night, we both were traveling on a motorbike, and were getting soaked to the skin. A few minutes later we had reached my home, and that's when our lips had met.

Just when things were heating up in my dream, I heard Baba's words, "Amol, your tea is ready..."

Chapter Five
Boys' Night Out

There are social butterflies, and then there are social caterpillars. Social Butterflies are admired and their photos are often featured in Page 3 columns. In contrast, social caterpillars have the 'eww' factor, and they are ignored, derided or even despised.

By mid-June, I had turned into a social caterpillar. I would head out to the gym in the morning, would spend the day at the site office, and return home by eight in the night. This went on for six days a week, and it was killing me. I was desperately missing a social life.

Almost all friends and family lived within a two kilometer radius from my home. Baba had three siblings, and two of them had settled in Pune. Aai had six sisters and three brothers, most of them lived in Pune as well. And the list of family and friends was endless.

It was a great feeling at first, but it began to get intrusive after a while. I would step into a store and meet an aunt who was also shopping there. A visit to the barber could mean running into an old friend. And going to the park would involve meeting a cousin or two. They all had the same set of questions to ask:

"Are you getting used to life in India now?"

"How does it feel to work in India?"

"Are you planning to stay here or go back?"

But the most common question would be "Now that you are back, it is time you settled down. When are you going to get married?"

Had it not been for Aai and Baba, I would have preferred to live in the eastern parts of the city, maybe in Kalyani Nagar or Koregaon Park. Those areas had a much younger population. Kothrud and its vicinity was a different place altogether; with a dense cluster of buildings, crowded streets, and ageing residents.

Kothrud had very little to offer on the social scene, and I had no option left other than to visit the nightclubs that were located on the other side of town. But almost every place had a very high cover charge for single males, or stags as they are called. The cover charge at even the trashiest club in Pune was a few thousand Rupees. In contrast, even the busiest nightclubs in Chicago did not charge more than fifty Dollars. In Pune, the drinks in clubs were over-priced, the food was tasteless, and the staff was arrogant.

Very often, I was the oldest person in the room. The under-25 folks thought I belonged to a different generation. They would talk about Shahid Kapoor and Ranbir Kapoor. They equated social networking with Orkut, where one's popularity was judged by how many testimonials had been written for them. For them, Facebook was a novelty, and LinkedIn belonged to people from a different planet. In the malls, or the newspapers, or on the TV, everyone talked about the IT and BPO boom. Test cricket was ancient history, and most cricket fans thought that One Day Internationals were passé. T 20 cricket was the rage. Smartphones were yet to become commonplace and Nokia ruled the phone market. I was in a very different India in 2008.

I also realized that Pune had changed a lot in the past decade. Gone were the days when one could go for a quiet, peaceful drive from Law College Road towards Pune University, and then back to Kothrud via Pashan. The very beautiful University Circle had been replaced by a hideous flyover that had worsened the traffic situation.

Once, I even tried going to Chandni, the shady bar near our college. Chandni offered solace to the saddened heart, be it due to a rejection from a girl, or failing in the exams. Different students had different excuses to visit this place, but the remedy was the same: Old Monk and Thums Up. But now, bars had stopped serving Thums Up, and Coke simply did not make the cut.

It was not long before I stopped visiting such places altogether. I felt like a relic from a different era. It was time to try something new.

*

While I was struggling with the lack of a social life, two incidents made me realize that there was no point in trying to reconnect with old friends. The first occurred when I met Nayan.

Nayan was not a close friend, but during our college days, we had shared a few times of joy and sorrow at Chandni during our college days. I had tracked him down and he was very happy to hear from me.

"Why don't you come down to my studio?" He asked me when we spoke over the phone. Nayan had set up an interior design studio, which was located near Fergusson College. I went to meet him one evening after work. I was impressed as he showed me around his office. Over a cup of tea, we caught up with each other's lives.

"So Amol, how do you plan your vacations?" He asked me out of the blue. "I am asking because I have an idea to share. It will take an hour or so to explain..."

Half an hour later, I walked out of his office. Nayan was trying to sell me vacation rentals. He had joined a multi-level marketing scheme and had thought that parting with a few thousand Rupees would be child's play for me.

I had always been wary of these multi-level marketing schemes, be it Amway, Quixtar, or their cousins. I had stayed away from people who were engaged in such businesses.

Nayan thought that I was loaded, like all NRIs are expected to be, but he was sadly mistaken. It was his problem if he thought that I had an unlimited capacity to spend in Rupees. The fact was that I was simply trying to live off the money I made in India.

That day, Nayan lost more than a business prospect; he even lost a friend.

The very next day, Vidyut also voted himself off my list of friends. His email had come as a pleasant surprise, but its content was anything but pleasant. It read as follows:

"Dear All,

I want to share a story with you, a tale of treachery, a story of betrayal, and a story of how my so called friend nearly ruined my life.

It all began one evening in March 2006. I was in Chicago, and had decided to pay him a visit. No names shall be mentioned here, because I do not want to insult you, my true friends, by uttering expletives. Yes, his name is an expletive in my book now. We had met after fifteen long years. He was a friend from my schooldays. At least then I used to think that he was my friend.

Over a bottle of Rum, he laid a trap for me. He had told me that Geeta was in town. I had a crush on Geeta since my school days, and she was my first love. So when he told me that she had just fallen out of a relationship, was alone and miserable, and needed a shoulder to cry on, it seemed too good to be true.

However, mine turned out to be a long-distance relationship, and soon things became difficult. The next year was hell for me. One day, I was insulted by Geeta's parents. There was only so much I could take. Sadly, I had to cut the cord. Thankfully, today I am married to someone with whom I share unconditional love.

But this villain had set me up just because he wanted to impress Geeta's roommate. I am marking that cunning villain on this mail. If you see a name in this email that is not familiar to you that will be his. I want him to know that he is no friend of mine."

As I finished reading his email, I felt that he was Julius Ceaser and I was Brutus.

*

Vidyut was a friend from my schooldays. We had lost touch over the years, and he had showed up at my door two years ago.

"I am happy to see you, my friend," he had told me.

We had spent the evening catching up with each other's lives over a few drinks. That's when I had told him about Geeta. This part of the story was true. The rest of it, however, was not, except maybe the part that I liked Shivani, who was Geeta's roommate.

I began to wonder what I had done to damage his relationship with Geeta. I was no longer in Chicago or even talking to Geeta since my return to India. I wrote to her to find out what had happened, but she never replied to my email.

Shivani, on the other hand, wrote back, "A friend of mine told me that Vidyut has also moved to Pune, and he lives somewhere in your neighborhood. Apparently he saw you at the local grocery store one day and he came to know about your return. He holds you responsible for his break up, and he wanted to get even. I read the email he wrote to you and his other friends. It was quite shocking"

*

The Hanuman Temple on Paud Road was the same temple that Shalu aunty had asked me to visit when I had met her on my first day back in Pune. It is situated in a neighborhood that was dominated by old folks. Somehow it became my duty to drive Aai and Baba to the temple on Saturday evenings, where they would meet their friends and catch up with each other's lives.

Before my return to Pune, they would visit the temple only once a month. But now, Baba had begun to demand that I drive him to the temple every Saturday. He would get ready and eagerly await my arrival from work. Aai was equally happy to meet her friends, even though she did not show it.

"Baba, it is a Saturday evening for heaven's sake. I do not want to drive again in the traffic. Paud Road is crowded at this time of the day. Moreover, I do not want to make this temple a regular entry in my calendar. I would rather go to town side," I had protested.

"No, we will go to the temple. It is the only time we get to meet our friends," Baba had replied sternly.

"I understand, Baba. But there are only old people."

"What's wrong with old people?" Aai had protested, which further weakened my defense.

"There is nothing wrong, Aai, except that I should not be there with you. You guys talk about grandchildren, arthritis, and angioplasty. The place smells of Iodex and Tiger Balm, while I would rather smell Chanel and Lancôme. You also discuss how this person passed away and how old age is a punishment. It is too depressing."

Baba was angry because I had touched a raw nerve. "We all talk reality. Even you will grow old someday, then you will realize."

"But Baba, try to see things my way. You have a group of about thirty people, and all of you are over sixty. When I am a part of this group, it makes me a sixty-year old as well. Remember school level mathematics? Sixty times thirty is eighteen hundred. Add to that my age. Eighteen hundred and thirty divided by thirty one makes it fifty nine. So there you go! If I spend my Saturday evening with old folks, I will have no energy left to meet anybody my age." But my protests had fallen on deaf ears.

"Have you come here to go partying, or have you come here for our sake?" As always, Aai's words had sealed the argument.

And soon, I was the designated driver whenever Aai or Baba would go to any of the countless social events. A wedding here, a birthday there, a puja at someone's place, or some other engagement that I was least interested in. Aai and Baba's social life blossomed while mine shriveled and shrank during the summer.

I reminisced my time in Chicago. Things were different there.

*

My Saturday evenings in Chicago would mean an obligatory visit to a nightclub or a movie, or just hanging out with friends. During summertime, I would play softball with the folks at work. During the dark, gloomy and cold winters, bowling was a great way to beat the blues. For two years in a row, ours was the noisiest and the most disorganized team in the league, but we had made it to the finals both the times. Had we played a little more seriously, we might have won.

After the game, we would go to the bar across the street. It was a crappy bar that served cheap drinks. The highlight of the place was that the waitresses wore shiny, glowing pink and green bikinis. They were a sight for sore eyes during the cold and gloomy winter nights.

*

"Sunday afternoons are not working out for me," I said to Lalit and Shashi when we met one day. "Afternoons are too early."

"I agree. The ladies are not happy with this time either," Shashi remarked in agreement. The ladies in question were Shashi's mother, wife, and daughter, respectively. How he managed to live with three generations of very demanding women was a mystery to me. Maybe that's why he wanted to blow off some steam.

We would meet on Sunday afternoons for an hour at an innocuous place called Shabri on Karve Road. There was nothing remarkable about this place, but it was close to where all of us lived. Shabri was a five-minute walk from Shashi's home, and likewise for Lalit. For me, it was a fifteen minute walk or a five minute drive.

"How about Saturday night?" Lalit suggested. "If we meet by nine, we will get the time that's needed. Amol, you coordinate."

And so began our boys' nights out. Every Saturday afternoon, I would send out a text message which simply read: "Shabri at nine?" The recipients of this message would be Lalit, Shashi, Mandar and Nikhil. Mandar was Shashi's friend whom I had met recently. Nikhil was my nephew, but he was nearly my age and was more like a friend.

Everybody would reply to my message within half an hour, except Lalit. He would only reply if he was not going to meet us. His explanation was, "Why waste a message if you know I am coming?"

By 7 PM, I would drive Aai and Baba to the temple, and we would reach home by 8.30 PM. Over the next fifteen minutes, I would grab a few bites while receiving an earful from Aai. She told me one such evening, "I do not like this. You should stop going every time."

But her words had no effect on me. I simply told her, "Aai, everyone needs an outlet. The earth has a system of volcanoes that act as valves to release the pressure that builds inside. Similarly, pressure cookers and even factories have pressure release valves. My time with the Boys is my venting mechanism. Without it, I would go mad."

I began to look forward to Saturday nights. By nine-fifteen, our first bottle of Old Monk would be consumed, and the discussion turn to one of the usual topics: wine, women, life in Pune against life in America, or our plans for the future. In short, we would discuss anything and everything under the sun.

It was during one such meeting that Nitin asked me, "So what will you do if you do not go back?"

"I am not staying here. By this time next year, I will be in Ontario..." I replied.

"Tu ab shaadi kar, aur India mein hi ruk," Shashi remarked.

He had just suggested that I get married and stay back in India. As much as I hated him right then, he was annoyingly right most of the time. He was not only a keen observer; he was a logical thinker and could make convincing comments. He was our Mr. Spock.

Shashi was older than me by four years, and my life had followed his life's footsteps to a great extent. He had completed his engineering degree in 1995; I had graduated in 1998 from the same alma mater. He had left for the US in 1997 and I had followed him there one year later. Shashi finished grad school in 1999 and I completed mine in

2000. Shashi had returned to India in 2005, and nearly three years later, I was drinking with him here in Pune.

But here was the troublesome part. Shashi got married in 2006 and his daughter was born a year later. This meant that it was time for me to get married within a year from now. No, that was not possible. A year from today, I was going to be in business school. I was planning to marry Nandini, the woman I loved, shortly after my MBA. And I was definitely not going to stay back in India.

"Bravo!" Lalit's remark broke my chain of thoughts, and all of us raised our glasses to toast. It was a full house for the Boys' Night Out, and it was my turn to pay.

Chapter Six
It All Goes Downhill

The next morning, I saw an email message that made my day.

"Hi Amol,

Hope you are doing well. I wanted to tell you that I will be visiting Mumbai in early August. It would be great if we could meet. I really want to talk to you.

Love, Nandini"

Nandini was a doctor and a very smart one at that. She was easy on the eyes, had a great sense of humor, and was fun loving. In other words, she was the whole package. She lived in Canada, somewhere in the suburbs of Toronto. A couple of years ago, she had visited Chicago for work. A common friend had introduced us, and we had clicked right away. Over the next few weeks, we had met several times and enjoyed several memorable moments together, including a visit to the Field museum, taking the riverboat tour, and watching a movie at Grant Park during their summer screenings.

On her last night in Chicago, we had met at the Kingston Mines Club on Halstead Avenue. The place was known for live bands and one could enjoy some of the best blues as the artists alternately perform on two stages. It was a pretty crowded and loud place, not the best place to have a conversation. But we had talked for hours and had stayed there until closing time. We had shared everything right from her interest in the theater to my love for the outdoors. We had kissed as we parted.

I had fallen in love with her that night, and knew that I wanted to marry her. She had hinted on more than one occasion that she reciprocated my feelings.

*

There are two parts to a hike. The first is the climb to the summit. The second part is the descent. A hike is considered successful when one completes both the parts safely. The downhill journey can be particularly treacherous and lead to a Humpty Dumpty moment or two. Or, as it happened in my case, several Humpty Dumpty moments. My downhill roll began after my meeting with Nandini.

*

While planning for the trip to Mumbai to meet Nandini, I realized that I had not traveled out of Pune since March. That was nearly three months ago. As these thoughts crossed my mind, I noticed that it had started to rain. The monsoons were about to set in.

Nandini was going to stay at her cousin's place in Dadar along with her parents and her brother. By that time, Mumbai had begun to face the fury of the monsoons. I took a bus just in case the rains flooded the city and damaged my car in the process.

I met her on a Sunday morning. She was wearing a white kurta and blue jeans, and was standing beneath an umbrella. A light rain was soaking the tree-laden street near Shivaji Park. She looked very beautiful. I had brought her flowers, the ones she loved. The setting was as picturesque as it was romantic.

We went to a nearby coffee shop to catch up on our lives and talk about our future. Then she asked me if I could travel to Goa the following week.

"We have planned a family holiday in Goa. It would be great if you can meet my mum and dad and the rest of the folks."

Somehow a trip to Goa during the monsoons did not make sense to me. But I realized that Nandini was not inviting me to enjoy long walks on the beach, or to sit under the sun and enjoy the cool breeze. Her invitation had a different purpose altogether.

The trouble was that my six month probation period had not yet ended, and I could not take any days off from work. Moreover, the airfare and the hotel stay at a week's notice were going to cost me nearly half-a-month's pay. But these matters would have kept only the rational persons awake at night.

I went to meet Ashok and told him that I needed three days off. His response was in the negative. "No way. Absolutely not. First of all, you know what the policy says. Secondly, the design is picking up pace, and I have been told that some major design changes are expected next week."

But I insisted, "Ashok, I have to go. It is important; otherwise I would not have asked you. The same policy you are referring to also states that the leave can be granted under exceptional circumstances. And trust me, this is an exceptional situation."

"Talk to me later. I have something important to do right now."

Rajesh accosted me as soon as I had stepped out of Ashok's office, and asked what was wrong. I told my story.

"*Arey*, just tell HR that somebody close in your family has passed away. Then you will get your three days' leave, no questions asked. I once used this excuse when I needed to go to Jammu urgently. A man's got to do what a man's got to do."

Rajesh was trying to be helpful, but I did not want to lie to get my leave approved. It was simply the wrong thing to do. I was going to tell them the truth, and was determined to make a case for it. I would go to Goa whether they agreed or not. The consequences of my action could be dealt with later. With this resolve, I began to look for flight tickets.

"*Yaar*, there are very limited direct flights from Pune, and they are very expensive. I think you should fly out of Mumbai. This would increase the travel time, but you would save a few thousand Rupees. Try Spice jet or Indigo airlines," Rajesh suggested, and continued, "but don't book online. Call up a travel agent. Here, call Shahi Travels, I use them all the time." Rajesh was helpful as ever, and I was both irritated and thankful that he was around.

Over lunch, Ashok asked me why I wanted the time off. I told him about Nandini and the visit to Goa.

"You know, you are one screwed up person. You are a NRI from America who now works in India, and has a Canadian girlfriend. By the way, I overheard what you were told…to fake somebody's death to get the leave. Why didn't you use that excuse?"

"That's not how I operate," I said to Ashok.

"Good. So here is what I am going to do. I will let you take those days off. We will worry about the reasons later. HR will not be pleased to hear this, nor will our client. But go ahead, and let us hope things will work out for you. All the best."

*

I left for Mumbai that Thursday evening. The heavens had opened up, and the bus cruised its way through the pouring rain during the entire four-hour journey. Sleep was hardly on my mind that night as I stayed at my uncle's place that night. I was anxious, excited, and worried at the same time about meeting Nandini and her family in Goa.

The rain was loud enough to keep me awake. I had barely fallen asleep when the alarm clock went off. It was 5 in the morning; and my flight was at 7.30 AM. As I was getting ready to leave, I received a phone call from the airlines. They informed me that my flight had been rescheduled due to bad weather and new takeoff time was 1 PM.

It was six in the evening by the time I finally reached the Park Hyatt in Goa. Nandini was waiting for me in the reception area when I arrived at the hotel. As the shuttle from the airport to the hotel drove up to the paved circular porch, I could see her sitting in one of the dark leather chairs at the entrance. Behind her, the sun was peeking through the dark clouds. As I stepped off the bus, Nandini walked up to me and we kissed. My long journey was worth it.

"You are late. I have been waiting for you all day," she said, as we walked towards one of the cottages which would be my living quarters for the weekend.

"I'm sorry. The flight got delayed. I know it has been a long wait for you, and I am exhausted."

"Not so soon, dear. We meet over dinner in half an hour."

Over the next twenty minutes, I had shaved, showered, and had put on the best attire I could come up with: a beige jacket, a dark green shirt, and blue jeans. I wore my black shoes, though they did not match the clothes. Baba had asked me if I wanted to wear cufflinks. He was known for his taste for fine dressing, but unlike him, I had no idea how to put them on, let alone sport them with aplomb.

The humidity was killing me; and I was already beginning to

sweat and feel miserable. But the occasion demanded that I wear the best smile possible. As I entered the dining area at 7 PM, I noticed that Nandini's family had already made themselves comfortable in one corner of the room. They were all dressed in casuals.

Two men, probably in their early twenties, sat on one side of the table. They had to be Nandini's brother and cousin. The duo was watching the cricket match that was being telecast on the TV screen at the far end of the room. There was a large, dark-skinned man and a petite woman sitting on the opposite side of the table. And next to them was Nandini. She was wearing a black blouse and a white jacket, the same dress that she had worn when we had last met.

As I walked up to the table, she looked at me and smiled.

"Mum, Dad, this is Amol," she introduced me to her parents.

Over the next hour or so, I listened to discussion that ranged from ice hockey versus cricket to the latest Bollywood movies. Nandini's brother and her cousin, though engrossed in the cricket match, were enjoying the Scotch more than the game. Nandini's mother was munching carefully on something that looked like a salad. Nandini was fidgeting with her fingers and alternated between staring at me and her parents. I was hungry by now. It was nearly eight-thirty when Santosh, Nandini's father, finally spoke.

"We should move on to the main course, both for the food and the conversation. So young man, you lived in the US but have a Canadian Permanent Residency. How did that happen? And why did you do it?"

"Sir, one can apply and complete the process from the US. The process took me a little over a year," I replied.

He seemed to be pleased when I had referred to him as Sir, and smiled. I paused for a few moments, and continued,

"As for the second part of your question, why Canada? The reasons are complicated. To me, Canada seems to be a better option over the long term."

"So you like cold climates?" Santosh continued his questioning.

"I don't mind the cold."

"India is hardly a cold country. The only thing common between Mumbai and Toronto is that they both have 35 degree weather for a few months, but it is 35 degree Celsius in Mumbai and 35 Degree Fahrenheit in Toronto. Its apples and oranges," he commented.

I had always believed that Canada also followed the metric system of measurement; in other words; kilometers for distances, and Celsius for temperature. But I did not see any point in correcting him.

"So how do you explain that?" Santosh growled. He resembled a Policeman who was questioning a suspect in a murder case.

"I am okay with warm climate, but that does not mean I want to live here forever," I replied.

"How would you explain that?"

"It's complicated."

"Is there anything at all that is simple and straight-forward?"

"Yes. I was selfish and I only thought about myself for many years. That is no more the case. I am in India because of Aai and Baba. And I am here in Goa now because of Nandini."

Santosh seemed disinterested in my reply and continued his

grilling. "So you moved back for your parents?"

The food on my plate remained un-eaten, because I had lost my appetite by now. I took a sip from the glass of water, and spoke. "There was a time when I did not want to come back to India. But then Aai and Baba started ageing and began to take turns going to the hospital. First, there was Baba's heart surgery, then Aai's kidney troubles. I ignored it all at first. My friends and family were there to support them, and I did not feel the need to visit them. But then, the guilt set in. I started sleeping with the phone next to me, just in case I got a call informing me of what I feared the most. I would wake up with a scare even when the alarm would go off in the morning. This went on for nearly two years. Then one fine day, I came to visit them in Pune. A month later, I had returned with a plan to spend a year with them."

Santosh nodded as I finished my narration. Then, he looked at me and asked, "Quite interesting. But why only one year?"

"It seemed like a reasonable period of time."

"And what do you plan to do next?"

"Sir, I plan to go business school for one year starting April next year, following which, I plan to work in Toronto. And I would like to seek your permission to marry your daughter."

At this point, Santosh announced, "This meeting is over."

As he rose, he motioned to his wife and the two men. Nandini also left without saying a word and I was left alone at the table. They had all left without saying goodbyes. Maybe her father had not liked what I had said, but I had told them the truth. I could have been more diplomatic about it, but the end result probably would have been the same.

The air conditioning or the TV in the room did little to help me go to sleep. By 2 AM, I had made my second cup of coffee and lit my fourth cigarette. Three hours later, I had walked up and down the beach several times. By dawn, I was exhausted. As soon as I reached my room, my phone buzzed. It was Nandini.

"Hey, meet me at the gym in fifteen minutes. We need to talk."

The gym was on the far side of a large building that also housed a spa, a small but functional library and a large playing area for the kids. As I entered the gym, I could see that Nandini was its only occupant and she was running on a treadmill.

With a beach nearby, why would she want to use the gym? But this was not the occasion to ask this question. When Nandini saw me, she slowed down and said, "Hi! You look like a train wreck."

"And you look beautiful."

"Come on, what are you waiting for? Hop on. That way we can talk and work out at the same time. Then, we will head into the town. I hear they serve excellent fish and masala cashews there. And I am dying to try the Feni."

I was hardly dressed for using the gym, but I climbed on the treadmill next to hers. In a matter of minutes, I was breathless. I had gained several kilos since my return to India and combined with the smoking, my fitness level had tanked considerably. I could sense that Nandini was not impressed.

"You have not been taking care of yourself." She remarked.

"I haven't slept for two nights in a row," I replied.

After the workout, we met in the lobby at ten. The rest of the morning was spent exploring the nearby areas, shopping, and finally we had lunch. The fish was edible, but the Feni had a strong stench. One sip later, I put it away. Nandini seemed to enjoy the drink. The masala cashews were the only thing I could eat, but I remembered my struggle in the gym, and chose not to eat any.

"So what do you think about my folks?" Nandini asked as she finished her Feni.

"They are nice people. But I don't think your father liked me."

"Nonsense. In fact, he loved it that you told him the truth." She replied. Her words should have brought me a sigh of relief, but something seemed out of place. She wanted to say something, but was struggling to get the words out of her. I had the same feeling as we met over the next two days. She spilled the beans on Sunday night. "Amol, I have to tell you something."

I prepared myself for the news. Her parents had objected to us being together. Worse, she was seeing someone else.

"I have thought a lot about this. I was looking forward to us being together in Canada, but you left for India all of a sudden without even informing me. I was hurt, upset and felt cheated. You took such a drastic step and you did not even ask me."

Nandini's tone and her words were becoming harsher.

"I really liked you, but now I am not sure if I feel the same way about you as I did before. You took such a drastic decision without even informing me. You acted by yourself, and that is a problem. Today, it is India. Tomorrow, it can be something else. This is not what I would expect from my boyfriend or spouse."

Everything that she had said was true. I had not told her that I was relocating to Pune, and was responsible for the mess I was into.

"Amol, are you going to say something?" She ordered.

"Nandini, I want to hear what you want to speak first," I replied.

She spoke almost immediately, "So this is what I think we should do. I want to see how serious you really are about us. If in seven months' time you are not in back in Canada, I will know that our story is over. On the other hand, if you do return, then let us see if we can start our relationship all over again."

A minute later, I was left sitting alone in the beachside shack. Nandini had put me on a waiting list just when I thought I had a confirmed place in her heart.

I spent the next day drinking Feni in the same shack, and I had lots of fish to go with it. In the process, I did not realize that it was almost evening. My return flight to Mumbai had flown several hours ago without me on it. The next morning, I went to meet Nandini. The clerk at the front desk informed me that her family had checked out the previous evening. I wish I had stayed sober. At least I could have seen her one last time and said goodbye.

The ticket for the next day's flight was very expensive, but I had no choice. I was unshaven, tired and badly hung over when I reached Pune on Tuesday afternoon. And I smelled of Feni. By the time I reached the office in the afternoon, Ashok was seething with anger. It was all going downhill for me.

Chapter Seven
Everything Changes

I was late for work on the very day that the design for two of the buildings had changed significantly. The buildings were originally designed as squares with circular domes at the top, and the columns for these buildings were originally laid out in a grid. Now, they columns had been changed to a circular pattern to match the dome they would have to support. This called for significant changes to all the drawings, which would take many months to complete.

The challenge was that the bid documents had been released merely two weeks ago, and the contractors were in the process of putting their bids together. It was now nearly impossible to develop a new schedule for the construction, timelines for ordering the material, and a cost estimate for this project. The bid was likely to get postponed by several weeks as a result of these changes.

"*Yaar*, we were all worried about you. What happened?" Rajesh asked me in the evening.

"Nothing," I replied, not wanting to talk about my situation.

"*Accha*, Paresh called me just now. He wants to speak to you."

Paresh answered his phone on the third ring.

"Amol, I have looked at the drawings for the mall. It is an interesting design. I think the idea of having anchor tenants towards the end of the building is very common in the US, isn't it? They have the largest space and they draw the customers to the mall, right?"

"Yes," I replied. Talking to him was the last thing I wanted to do.

"I understand the food and beverage or F & B areas, and also back office and maintenance areas. But one thing is confusing me. I see that over forty or fifty spaces are labeled as Vanilla Stores. Why do they need so many ice cream shops in the Mall?"

I did not know how to react. "Paresh, a vanilla store is a small store that can sell anything from beauty products to clothing and from shoes to books. These can be standalone stores, or a part of a chain of stores. Unlike the anchor tenant or F & B areas, which are located in specific areas of the building, a vanilla store can be located anywhere within the remaining space," by the time I had completed my monologue, Paresh had disconnected the call.

*

Over the next few weeks, I concentrated only on my work. It was a good escape from what had happened in Goa. Aai and Baba had asked me repeatedly about my visit. So had the Boys, and also Rajesh, Sachin and Ganesh. Ashok was still not talking to me.

Fortunately, the project site finally had a field office, and we had moved into the new location with much fanfare. As I started looking at the designs, the scale of the project began to dawn upon me. Constructing Five million square feet of building space is a large project by any standards. This area is twice the size of the Empire State Building. In India, nobody had executed a project like Village Market before. There were plans for even bigger malls, but they would not see the light of the day for several years.

The Apogee Group wanted first class features but was only willing to pay third class prices for them. As a result, Village Market was turning into a poor man's Las Vegas. I hit my first roadblock over a tunnel that was planned between two buildings. The Architect had proposed that the tunnel would have glass walls, which would form an underground aquarium of sorts. Apogee's marketing department had also designed a campaign around this idea, which was titled, "Experience shopping, Singapore style."

But Apogee was willing to pay only one fourth of the amount that the suppliers had quoted for this work. The problem was that these systems had to be imported, and they were expensive because the installation work was a laborious process. After several weeks of deliberation, Apogee finally dropped the idea. Instead of a live aquarium around the tunnel, the shoppers would get to see murals with images of fish. This was a far cry from Singapore style shopping, and the marketing campaign was quietly put to death.

I had failed to see why this tunnel was so important to Apogee. This silly idea had taken up nearly a month of everybody's time. Most of this time spent on long and often unproductive meetings, and instead could have been used to focus on more pressing matters at hand, such as getting the municipal approvals for the project. But the developers had a fetish for developing an Iconic project, and were very keen on presenting this project as a statement rather than a building. During the next few months, several ideas such as the tunnel got discussed, beaten to death, and eventually were dropped.

There was a time in India when movie theaters had only one or two screens. Such theaters existed in many cities even in 2008. These theaters were housed in smallish buildings, and could only seat a few hundred persons at a time.

In contrast, Village Market was supposed to have a 40 screen multiplex, which could seat over ten thousand people at its peak. This raised another question: how would so many people enter and exit this building? The sheer number of cars would create a huge volume of traffic that would come and go out of the Village Market. But nobody except me seemed to be worried about this problem.

As I was pondering over this matter, I called up Fayaz, the traffic consultant. "Don't you think we need to rework the parking system? There is only one entrance and one exit planned for cars in the theater building. I do not see any service entrance for the trucks to carry in food or take out the garbage."

"You are right," said Fayaz. "However, I was told that there was no need for a service entrance. The deliveries and garbage collection could be handled during the night. Between us, I do not think that they want to spend money on the service areas."

The frequent changes in the building drawings had also pushed the design behind by several weeks. I had initially believed that the design team was slow to catch up to the changes. But soon, it became evident that Apogee themselves were responsible for the delay. They would call up the designers and make some change or the other, and not bother to inform me about them. For Apogee, many of these changes were minor. For example, they had planned a swimming pool on the third floor of one building. Two weeks later, they moved it to the second floor of the same building. Another week later, the swimming pool was moved to a different building altogether. With each change, the structural, plumbing and electrical drawings would all have to be altered. Even a minor change in the location of the swimming pool required over fifty drawings to be changed, each one of which required several hours of time for the redesign.

"What a bunch of jokers," I said out of frustration during one of our weekly Saturday meetings with Paresh. Ashok simply raised his eyebrows. Rajesh began to fiddle with his phone. They both were trying to hint that I should keep quiet.

"These are very smart and capable people, Amol. They must have taken the decision to make these changes after thinking through the process. There must be some valid reasons for them to do so. They are reacting to the market conditions. I had several case studies in my MBA which dealt with such situations. Many other projects which have met a similar fate," Paresh's reply was hardly convincing.

"Paresh, this is not business school, this is life. Apogee simply *cannot* make up their mind on several matters. They wanted to build a hotel but now they want an office building at the same site. They are planning a hospital in place of a movie theater. This is not Lego, Paresh. Recently, they have simply started reducing the number of floors in each building. It will not be long before entire buildings will be chopped off from the project. This is not how professional real-estate developers work. If these guys really knew their stuff, they should have realized that the economy was going downhill before they launched this project."

But my words had no effect on Paresh. "There are some other things that I cannot discuss with you right now. For now, just go with the flow," he was frustrated by my remarks.

Paresh knew that we had a problem, but the management of KMM wasn't really interested in our woes. The project management group wasn't really a money maker for the organization. That title belonged to the brokers. Our group merely supported the business, so our problems weren't really worth their time.

"It is no different in other countries, or in many other professions in this country, Amol," Ashok said in an attempt to convince me. He was speaking to me after several weeks.

"I know, but at least in the US, people respect each other's personal time and rarely call over the weekends. But here, it seems people just work and then do even more work. What is the use, Ashok? We Indians work during our festivals because the clients abroad do not celebrate either Holi or Diwali. And we work during Thanksgiving because it is not our holiday. We work on 15th August, and also on 4th of July, and Independence Day of every other country. Isn't this slavery?" I asked him forcefully.

"You have too much of a NRI in you. Give it some more time. Things will start making sense." I could see that Ashok was irritated by my remarks.

Sachin was just as bitter as I was. "We consultants are responsible for delivering the project, but we hardly have any authority. We are the worker bees, who work their butts off in order to keep the Queen Bee happy. The construction sector is going downhill, but there is a lot of noise in the media whenever a new project is launched or when a multi-million dollar investment is made by a foreign fund in this sector. In reality, there is more activity around the drawing boards and in meeting rooms than on the construction sites."

*

By mid-September, very few of the cranes that dotted the skyline could be seen moving. To me, that was a warning sign. I voiced my concern to Ganesh.

"Oh, it's because of the monsoons," he remarked casually.

"Ganesh, it has to be a different reason. It is a clear day today, and no contractor would spend thousands of Rupees every day in paying rent for the cranes and not put them to use."

"There are other things that you probably don't know. Come, lets' go to the tapri."

"What reasons?"

"At each site around us, either the developer has run out of money to pay the contractor, or the project has run into trouble with the Government. A typical project requires around thirty different approvals, and many developers start the work without getting them. They stop the work when the government inspectors find out."

A few days later, I asked Ganesh about another issue that bothered me. By now, the tapri had become the preferred venue to discuss such matters.

"Ganesh, I worry about the life of the construction laborers. If their working conditions are bad, then their living conditions are even worse. They live in makeshift homes that resemble slums. These so called labor colonies are often located a few kilometers away from the project site. Every morning, we see over two dozen buses bringing over a thousand laborers from these colonies to the construction site. And every evening, a second batch of a similar number of laborers comes for the second shift. Some from the day shift work in the night shifts also to earn more money. Isn't that illegal?"

After listening patiently to my concerns, Ganesh replied, "Amol, there is a huge demand for construction laborers. There is literally no manpower available to work on sites. We need nearly three thousand laborers to work here every day, seven days a week, in order to get the work completed on time. And we work in two shifts because we are short of manpower. We need at least a thousand extra hands, but we cannot find them. I know of many contractors who send out one or two trucks every morning to the railway station. They have agents who go with these trucks, and they pick up anyone and everyone who is willing to work on the construction sites. These laborers work for a week or two, and then they are lured away by the contractors who are working on the projects across the street."

"I was not aware of this." I confessed, and added, "I am amazed by how much the construction sector here depends on manual labor."

"Machines are expensive to rent, but labor is cheap. Unfortunately, most of the laborers are unskilled, so the overall productivity is very low," Ganesh remarked.

"Ganesh, I was used to building large retail stores from scratch in six months' time. But here, nobody talks about a construction schedule in terms of months. Everyone speaks in years. And even then they nobody is certain whether the project will be completed on time or not. Things are indeed different here."

"You will see bigger problems in a few months. The signs of slowdown are evident, but the prices of land, labor and material are all going up day after day. Steel costs nearly twice as much compared to just a few months ago, and even concrete is getting costlier. Somebody blamed the Beijing Olympics for the high steel prices the other day, because a lot of steel used in construction of slabs in buildings is imported from China."

"I don't believe this. Isn't it likely that the Rupee has fallen and that is causing the prices to rise?" I asked him.

"In India, the prices of cement fall during the monsoon season because construction is slow. But the months of August and September this year have seen some of the highest prices in recent years. Because of the demand, the cement distributors have an order backlog that is running into several weeks. There is talk of importing cement from Pakistan to meet the local demand. You should be happy that work is going on this site in spite of all these problems."

As we walked back from the tea stall, I noticed that a boy was carrying two cans of water that were hooked to either side of the bicycle carrier. He looked under-age and underfed. As he struggled to push the bicycle up the ramp, half the water spilled out of the cans. The ramp led up to a stack of bricks where a man and a woman were trying to build a wall of sorts. They were assisted by a boy and a girl who were carrying a brick or two. Child labor was still rampant at construction sites in India. It was a Wild, Wild Waste.

*

By end of September, the depreciating Rupee threw the project off-track. The budget for the project got affected every time the Rupee fell against the Dollar, and this was turning into a daily phenomenon. The very smart and capable people that Paresh had referred to went into a penny-pinching mode.

A week before the Dussera festival, Rajesh accosted me as I entered the project office and said. "Amol, let's go and have some tea."

This was unusual. Over the past six months, he had never asked me to accompany him for tea. And by now, I had learnt to be cautious of anything that seemed unusual.

We walked out of the office towards the tea stall Rajesh ordered tea for us. As we started sipping the piping hot tea, I noticed a mild sunlight that peered through the clouds. It was a pleasant site, though the sun's rays offered no respite from the slight chill in the late monsoon air. In a couple of weeks' time, the famed October heat would start baking the earth again.

"*Yaar*, Paresh called me and said that you were upset with how things are progressing. This is India, *yaar*, things like this happen. Take it easy. It will all work out in the end."

"Rajesh, I am not concerned about what has happened so far. I want to know how long we will stay on this project. Sachin had said March. My guess is April," I replied.

"*Yaar*, that is too far out into the future. The immediate worry is whether we will get paid or not."

This was news to me. "They are not paying us?" I asked.

"Shh...we have not been paid for the past three months. Apogee does not have the money. They cannot even pay the cement and the steel suppliers."

"Looks like Apogee Developers have turned into Apology Developers," I said sarcastically, and asked, "So what happens now?"

"We just keep working as if nothing has happened. And I will keep chasing Naresh about the payment. But it is looking bad, *yaar*. He told me the other day that they have made a mistake by hiring us, and that our mobilization advance is far more than the value we have delivered so far. Now, they want us to work for free for one year. He also wanted to know what you were up to."

"What do you mean?"

"He said that ever since you came back from Goa, you have hardly sent him any updates."

"Rajesh, what is there to update? The design team is demoralized with all the changes, and they are not too excited about the latest revisions."

"*Arey*, I know all that. But you should go and meet Naresh at 10

AM today," he said as we walked back to the office.

*

Naresh was the right hand man of Apogee's Managing Director. He was short, portly, and irritating, and he was the quintessential 'Yes' man. I had avoided him like the plague so far, but today I had no choice. I was asked to wait when I went to his office.

"Sir is in a meeting. Please wait," a young lad at the front desk told me. I sat waiting for nearly two hours.

Finally, Naresh walked out of his room and said to me, "It will take a few more minutes."

The few minutes turned into another hour. The whole incident reminded me of my job interview earlier in the year. Had I walked out of the interview that very day, none of this would have happened. But it was too late to think about the past. By now, I was not only tired of waiting, but also hungry. Naresh had stamped his authority very clearly by now. He was the paymaster, therefore he was the boss. I was a lowly consultant.

"Sorry to have kept you waiting. How are you?"

Before I could reply, Naresh interrupted me and rang the bell for the office attendant and asked me, "Would you like tea or your black coffee?"

"I am fine, thanks. I would rather avoid any coffee before lunch," I replied, trying to control my anger.

"Don't worry about the lunch. We will go out and have it together. Do you mind non-vegetarian food?"

"I will prefer vegetarian, though if you want to have non-veg that should be okay with me."

"Very well then, let us leave. The driver will bring the car."

One of the perks of being the right hand man of the boss is that one gets to travel in fancy cars when the boss is away. As we stepped out of the office, a silver Mercedes pulled up in front of us. As we sat in the car, Naresh told the driver, *"Chala."*

Atithi is a small restaurant located a few kilometers away from Hadapsar and it is known to serve spicy *gavraan* Kolhapuri chicken. I was to learn later that the closest cousin of gavraan chicken was the free range chicken which had become quite popular in North America. I ordered daal and roti. After Naresh had wolfed down the chicken, he asked me, "Would you like some beer?"

"No thanks." For me, drinking during working hours was a no-no. After 5 PM, it was a different story altogether.

"I will have a Cannon 10000," Naresh told the waiter as the plates were being cleared. He now turned his attention to me. "So Amol, I wanted to meet you for a reason. You see, we have a problem with one of our other projects."

"What is the problem?" I asked.

"We have provided two lifts in each of the four wings of an office building. You call them elevators in America. The vendor is confident that two lift cars will be enough. They used some software to calculate this number. But the Town Planning Department is not convinced. According to them, we should have a minimum of three elevators in each wing. And you know what that means. We will have to redesign the shafts, the hallways, reduce the area of the office spaces, and the likes. I cannot go back to the investors and tell them that they will get spaces that are smaller than what we had promised them. If it was a residential building, it would not have mattered. We would have simply redesigned and gone ahead with the construction. But the investors in this building are people in very high places, you know."

"So how can I help?"

"Well, you were in America, You must have learnt something different. I am sure there is something that you can do to help us." The tone of his voice suggested that it was a demand rather than a request. But his other projects were none of my business.

"Let me talk to Paresh about it." I said.

"Oh don't worry... it was Paresh who suggested that I should talk to you. He had called me yesterday about payment and a few other matters," Naresh said with a smile.

*

I spent the rest of the afternoon thinking about the situation but could not decide. In the end, I told Ashok about my dilemma.

"Amol, you should listen to the guy who signs your paycheck. In this case, it is unfortunately Naresh. So look into his problem if it is legitimate. You can say no if you feel otherwise," he advised.

The next day, I looked up the design code for the section that dealt with elevators. The elevator supplier had sent me a copy of the software that they had used for their calculations. This software program was a black box. One had to input the data and the program would throw out the result.

The sales person himself had no idea how this software worked. It was no wonder that the Town Planners were not convinced with the calculations. The next day, I pondered over the matter, and had my eureka moment around noon. I opened a spreadsheet on my laptop and began to enter data into it. By 4 PM, I emailed my work to Naresh.

He called me back within five minutes, and asked, "How did you get this result?"

"Why, is there a mistake in my work?" I shot back.

"No, I have the general manager of the elevator company sitting in front of me. He has been in this business for twenty years, and this is the first time he has seen anybody use a spreadsheet for these calculations. He wants to know how you got this answer."

Ten minutes later, I answered the question in his office. "I used the building code book."

"I don't understand," the general manager said.

I replied, "From what I gather, the calculation for the number of elevators that are required in a building is based on several factors and a few equations. The factors include the number of floors, the height between two consecutive floors, the number of persons on each floor, and other such details. The equations give two important values. One is called waiting time, and the other is called round-trip-time or RTT. Waiting time is the amount of time in seconds that a person has to wait for the elevator to arrive after pressing the call button. Depending on the type of the building, it could be between 45 and 60 seconds. RTT is the time required by the elevator to start from the lowest floor, reach the topmost floor, and then make its downward journey. The RTT also includes the time required for opening and closing of the elevator doors and the time taken by the passengers to enter or leave the car. I am sure you are familiar with all this."

Before he could speak further, I continued, "This is similar to a train journey. At each station, the train stops, the doors open, and the passengers enter or leave the train, the doors close, and the train resumes its course. Based on the RTT and the waiting time, the calculations showed that the building needs 1.9 elevators. Two was therefore the right number, as was calculated by your software."

Once I was done talking, Naresh looked at the general manager of the elevator company, who nodded in acknowledgement.

"Very good. Can you come to the Town Planning office tomorrow? Madam has asked us to meet her," Naresh remarked.

The Madam in question was the Deputy Town Planning Officer. She was earlier posted in Latur, a town known for producing politicians as well as students who scored very high grades in the State level high school exams.

"I don't know this high-rise business. The biggest project I saw before this was a ten thousand square foot mall in the district. It had three floors. I don't understand what you have done here." The officer said as we sat in her office.

"Ma'am, let me show you what the code says," I said.

"Don't show me the code book. I know it inside out."

Knowing the code book inside out was one thing, knowing how to interpret the code is a different matter altogether. But this was not the occasion to engage in that debate or highlight this fact, so I said, "Ma'am, please hear me out. The assumptions and the formulas in the spreadsheet are exactly the same as what the code says."

"Let me see..."she said, as she pulled out a pair of glasses from their case. Then she nearly buried her head into the computer screen. Her graying hair indicated that she was nearing the end of her employment with the Government of Maharashtra. For the next several minutes, she asked me to try every possible combination that could change the result.

"What if we increase the number of floors? What if the area of each floor changes? Are you sure the speed of the elevators is okay? What if we reduce it by one meter per second?"

"Madam, this is good work." The man from the elevator company said, and continued, "I have verified it myself."

"Are you sure? Wouldn't it be more beneficial to you if it you had to supply three elevators instead of two three?" The officer asked.

"That is true madam, but why should we sell more lifts than are required? After all, we cannot take our customers for a ride."

I smiled at his reply. It was a sincere remark, but ironic: the elevator company did not want to take its customers for a ride.

"Okay, I am convinced, but attach a copy of this sheet in your application, and email me this calculation sheet. I will show it to Sir. He will be happy to see this. He is very computer savvy, you know."

The 'Sir' in question was the Chief Town Planning Officer. I made a mental note to write-protect the sheet before sending it to her. I was sure that not even the computer savvy 'Sir' would care.

As we walked out of the Madam's office, Naresh received a phone call. "Ho Saheb, it went well. Madam is convinced with two lifts."

As we returned to the project office, Naresh said, "Ask Rajesh to come and meet me."

Rajesh almost ran out of the office when I gave him the message. With his short and portly figure, he literally resembled a ball that was rolling on the ground. Ten minutes later, he came back with a big grin on his face. He was talking on the phone as he walked past me.

"Paresh, we got the check. Yes, I will go to the office and hand it over to accounts right away."

"Amol, *yaar*, I don't know what you did but Naresh was very happy. He gave me the check as soon as I entered his office," Rajesh said to me as he prepared to leave.

Naresh had every reason to be pleased. I had just saved his company several million rupees.

*

The next morning, Rajesh entered the office with a grim look.

"Why the long face?" I asked him.

"*Yaar*, the check bounced. Now Paresh has asked me to write up an explanation on this matter."

Naresh had pulled a fast one on us, and there was nothing we could do about it. The say, everything changes with time, but some things in India do not seem to change at all.

Chapter Eight
No One's Support

As 2008 came to an end, so did the prospects of the Village Market project's survival. By October, the project was losing one floor every week. In November, the hospital building was dropped, and in December, the office building was also gone. The project was reduced to two buildings, a hotel and a mall.

As January 2009 entered its second half, Paresh called me one day and said, "Amol, there have been some changes. You should start coming to the office from now."

Rajesh filled me in on the details. "*Yaar,* we have been given the boot from the Village Market project."

"It happened sooner than I expected." I commented.

"I think Apogee have gone into panic mode after the Satyam scandal and seeing how the stock market and the economy are doing. Ganesh and Sachin will stay on the project till the end of May. I will help Ashok in recovering the money that Apogee owes us."

As a consultant, sitting on the bench is never a pleasant experience. As a non-billable employee, a consultant is no longer an asset, and in times of slowdown in the economy that means trouble. I had to keep myself busy, or pretend to look busy if I had to remain employed. But to me, this was not a cause for worry. My immediate priority was to start planning for Canada. But I hardly had a day's time to think about it when three incidents shook me up.

KMM had finally reimbursed me for the expenses that I had incurred while moving to Pune. They had paid me the three hundred thousand Rupees as promised, but had credited that amount as a special allowance. Payroll had promptly deducted a third of that amount as tax. I called up Paresh and Manpreet to ask them what had gone wrong. As expected, Paresh pleaded ignorance about the matter.

Manpreet also did the same. "I am sorry, I cannot do anything, we have out-sourced our payroll processing to Carlton Trust, and so you will have to talk to them."

The folks at Carlton Trust had no idea what I was talking about. Their email was a one-line reply, "We have made the deductions as per the applicable tax rules."

I called up Sudha and told her what the matter was. "They have deducted tax on my relocation reimbursement. This was my own money. How can anybody think that reimbursement is an allowance?"

"I am sorry; I cannot help you in this matter. Maybe you should talk to your Chartered Accountant about this," she replied. The events over the next few months made me forget to follow up with the CA.

Two days later, I met Pangulal at Surabhi. He told me something that I was completely unprepared for.

"I am leaving for the United States in a month's time. Namita has been transferred to Boston." His tone suggested that he was not excited by the idea.

"Good for you, though I am in a fix. The year has gone by sooner than I expected. Now, a part of me wants to stay in India, even though things are not going well on the work front. I need your help in figuring out what to do next," I told him.

"Sorry cannot help. I only have a few weeks to wrap up things and leave."

My friend, guide and philosopher was no longer going to be around when I needed his help.

The final blow came when Nandini sent me an email with 'Happy New Year' in the subject line. I opened the email in excitement. Her email was brief.

"Hi Amol,

Hope all is well with you and your parents. I wanted to wish you a Happy New Year and send you this update.

Regards, Nandini."

I opened the attachment. It was a wedding invite: Nandini was getting married on February 14th, 2009, Valentines' Day.

I was an emotional wreck by now. Fortunately, it was a Saturday and the Boys would come to my rescue. But for the first time in nearly nine months, my 'Shabri at Nine' message received replies that said 'Sorry', 'No' and 'cannot'. Even Lalit had spent a Rupee to say that he would not be able to come.

*

I wanted some fresh air in order to think about my future, but Aai and Baba were reluctant to go to the temple.

"It's too cold outside," Aai had told me. Ever since they had been through a spell of health problems in October, they preferred to play it safe. Aai and Baba had to be hospitalized around Diwali. I and my sister Natasha, who had traveled from the US to spend Diwali with us, had looked after them. Now they both were very well, but were nervous about their health.

I thought it was ironic. Had they really cared about their health, they would have stopped eating the oily food that the doctors had asked them to avoid, taken their medicines on time, and Baba would have stopped chewing tobacco. I shrugged these thoughts away as I asked Aai and Baba to sit with me. It was time to talk to them.

"Aai, Baba; there is no point in me continuing in Pune with all the changes at my workplace. I learnt today that Nandini is getting married in February. It has made me realize that I've paid a very heavy price for my return to India. Also, my company has deducted one third of my relocation money as tax. And by the way, Pangulal is also leaving for the US."

I had given them the latest news updates in a single breath.

Baba was quiet for a very long time. Aai burst into tears. "All of this happened because of us, didn't it? You came here for us, and you lost Nandini. She was such a nice girl. I really liked her." Aai's words of sympathy would have meant a lot to me. But the two of them had never even met before, so how would she know that Nandini was a nice girl? I did not get a chance to ask this question to Aai, for she had gone to the loo for the third time. When under emotional distress, Aai preferred to seek solace in the toilet.

Baba finally took a long breath and asked, "How much money do you need for your MBA, and how are you going to pay for it?"

"Baba, I need around seventy thousand Dollars and I am planning to apply for a loan to a few banks in Canada."

"First, get your loan approved and then lets' talk further." With these words, he rose up slowly and retired into his room, and I was left with no one's support.

Chapter Nine
Alumina

Other than Pangulal, Kriya Doshi was my near and dear friend. While in college, I used to be Kriya's stand-in boyfriend. She had told her parents that we were seeing each other, and somehow I was in her parents' good books. Every time Kriya had to meet her real boyfriend, Amol Dixit would come to the rescue. Other girls in college also thought we were dating, which practically killed my chances of finding a girlfriend for myself. That was then.

After completing her engineering degree, she had gone to Law school and had become a successful lawyer who specialized in contract Law. We used to spend hours together while in college, working on this assignment or preparing that report. But we had met only once in the past year, because her work kept her very busy. I had been told that she rarely kept in touch with any of her friends these days, so her phone call came as a pleasant surprise.

"Amol, let us go to the Alumni meet," she ordered.

"So nice of you to remember me," I said sarcastically, and continued, "And why do you plan to ruin my Sunday afternoon?"

"Shut up and let's go. I will pick you up at 5 PM. Be ready."

The Maharashtra Institute of Technology in Pune is an institution known both for its academics as well as its founder. In the proverbial rags-to-riches story, a boy from a very poor family went on to establish one of the largest groups of colleges in India. But as alumni, none of it mattered to us. We were here to meet old friends, say our 'Hellos' to the professors, and of course, enjoy the free dinner. Kriya, Pangulal and I had never missed a lunch or dinner while we were in college. We used to believe that since we had paid so much money in fees, it was our right to have every possible meal that was paid for by the college.

The alumni meet was held in a roundish hall which was covered with a dome-shaped roof. The layout offered a mixture of poor acoustics and bad seating. The bulky circular columns blocked the view to the stage, and the dome caused the words to echo. The pigeons who had made the roof their home added to the chaos.

On the stage were three alumni who had gone on to create a mark for themselves after graduating from college. One was a real estate developer who had joined his family business, second was a film-maker. The third had entered the Police force. These alumni came from different backgrounds and had followed three very different career paths. They had graduated in the same year. Twenty years later, they were being recognized as distinguished alumni.

"I am very proud to have such alumina amongst us today. This institution is known for its academic rigor and I personally like to call it a furnace. Here, we refine the students, and the finished product is a strong metal that is out to prove its mettle in front of the world," the Dean of Alumni Relations began to speak.

He was a short man with a high-pitched voice and a bloated ego. He had started his career in the metal shop, and he liked to remind others about his background. Over the next fifteen minutes, he spoke about the achievements of the three alumni. To my amusement, he kept referring to them as alumina. Kriya looked at me inquisitively.

I said to Kriya, "Look, he is referring to us alumni as alumina. That is aluminum oxide. It kind of makes sense. The incoming students are like bauxite, that is, the ore of aluminum. Here in college, they get heated, belched, molten and beaten. Finally, they come out as shiny metal, and are ready to make the world a better place. But after a few years, they begin to get oxidized, and that's why they are called alumina instead of alumni. Too bad he is talking about aluminum and not steel. Otherwise, they would have been called as rusty, or short for rusted steel."

I could hear laughter all around me. My comment had been amplified several times, and everyone in the circular room, including the speaker and the distinguished alumni, had heard me. Nearly two hundred pairs of eyes began staring at me. Kriya was embarrassed and hid her face behind the program for the event. I followed suit.

*

"How is the food?" I asked Kriya as we stepped out into the lawns outside the auditorium. "The food is nothing much to talk about and thanks to you; most of the alumni have chosen to keep their distance from me. I wanted to talk to someone who owns a cement agency, but he looked at me and walked away in a different direction." She said, looking disappointed.

Somewhere between the starters and the main course, I ran into an old professor of mine. When I had last met him five years ago, he was very interested in knowing what I did for a living. Today, he simply ignored me. He had learnt from the grapevine that I was no longer the NRI alumnus that he could brag about to others.

Around the same time, Sanjay, the library assistant, came up to me with tears in his eyes.

*

I could never thank Sanjay enough for all his help during my student days. He would help me in finding the odd books and journals that I needed for my research papers. Once, he had let me into the library at two in the night through the back door because I needed to complete my journal paper.

Sanjay had a worried look on his face when we had met five years ago. I had asked him the reason for his look. "My mother is in the hospital and I need money to pay for her treatment. Her stomach is filled with fluid, and she needs the surgery soon," he had told me.

I had written him a check for fifty thousand Rupees that day, and said, "Once you are in a position to pay this money back, help a student out. If someone is unable to afford their fees, pay it out of this money."

Two years later, I had received an email from him:

"Dear Amol,

My mother has fully recovered now, and she would like to meet you the next time you are in India. I had asked several people for help that day. Some had expressed sympathy, while others had asked me to approach a bank for a loan. But nobody except you had actually given me the money when I needed it.

I have been able to save the fifty thousand Rupees, and have decided to pay the fees for Chandru. He is also in the civil engineering department, just like you used to be. His father is a good friend of mine, and used to work in a foundry before he lost both his hands in an accident. Chandru is a hardworking boy, and he takes his studies seriously. I am sure he will benefit greatly with this support.

Regards, Sanjay"

I could understand why Sanjay had tears in his eyes, for mine had filled up too at the sight of him standing there. We were grateful to each other, for different reasons.

We talked for a bit, and before I left, Sanjay said to me, "Do come and visit our home next week. My mother wants to meet you. My wife and daughter will also be happy to see you."

"Sure, but hey, what happened to that boy?" I asked.

"The boy you helped, Chandru, is now a Captain in the army. He is posted somewhere in Rajasthan."

Kriya had overheard our conversation. As we left the alumni meet, she asked me, "Sanjay was talking about some boy you helped.

What is that about?"

"It's a long story," I replied, not wanting to tell Kriya.

"I want to hear it. Keep talking."

Over the next several minutes, I told her the story.

"I did not know that you still have a heart somewhere within you," Kriya remarked as I finished my narration.

"Sometimes I feel like ripping it out and throwing it away, Kriya. That way I will not feel the pain every time I get screwed."

By then, we had reached my home. As I stepped out of the car, Kriya said to me, "Get over it, you have been down in the dumps before, and have managed to work things out. Good night."

Kriya knew me well. After all, she was not just a good friend, she was also my fellow alumina.

Chapter Ten
Decision Time

Over the next two weeks, I wrote to Bank of Montreal and Royal Bank of Canada about my loan. Almost every other day, I sent an email, made a phone call, or faxed a document or two in support of my loan application.

By the end of February, RBC had approved my loan: Seventy Thousand Dollars at an interest rate of four percent per annum. By now, I was all set to go to the Richard Ivey School of Business in April. The classes were to begin in six weeks' time. Now all I had to do was to buy a one way ticket to Toronto, give my one month's notice at work, pack my bags, and leave. I had also received my new passport in the mail by then.

Armed with this information, I said to Baba, "Baba, I have the loan approved, and look what I have here: A shiny new passport to start a shiny new life in Canada."

Baba put down the newspaper that he was reading, and nodded.

*

The first day of the March had begun as a lazy Sunday. It was the day when I was going to send the loan documents off to the bank. Around 3 PM, Aai entered my room with a cup of coffee. "Are you really leaving next month?" she asked me in an unsteady voice.

"Yes Aai, it is time for me to leave."

"I don't want you to go," Aai's emotional blackmailing had begun. "You came back after so many years, and you hardly spent time with us. All you did was work and work. Now once you go, I do not know when I will get to see you again."

"I know Aai, but staying back is not an option for me. As it is, chances are that I will not have this job beyond April."

But Aai was not the one to give in easily. She said with tears in her eyes, "You can get many more chances to live and work abroad in the future. But I may not get to live with my son again."

"Aai, I agree with you. But let us suppose I decide to stay. Remember, the MBA classes start on April 14th. If I don't leave, there is every possibility that I will be let go from my current job by April 15th. What will happen then? What will you do then? Are you going to find me a job?" I thought that my words had sealed the argument, but I was not prepared for what she said next.

"Did you really mean to spend time with us when you came to India, or did you want to *show* people how much you cared for your parents? If your motive was the latter, then you have failed. And that means I have failed as a mother. This is not how I had brought you up. You have become so self-centered. No, you have become selfish," Aai said as she left the room.

For the rest of the afternoon, I simply sat in my chair, staring at the computer monitor and the pile of forms. The coffee had gone cold several hours ago. Aai's words kept echoing in my head over and over again. "Amol, you have failed."

Was I really a failure?

It was late evening when I stepped out of the house and walked towards Tathavade Udyan, a public park named after a War Hero who used to live in our neighborhood. In the park, young parents were playing with their children, and newly-weds dreaming about their future together.

I went and sat cross-legged on the grass, trying to think things through. Some elderly folk were sitting on a nearby bench, talking, as usual, about their aches and pains. But unlike the discussions at the Hanuman Temple, here I overheard them talk about their emotional pain. I learnt that the children of most of their folks were living abroad or away from Pune, leaving their parents to fend for themselves. In some respects, what they were saying was right. The children needed to be with their parents during times of poor health or when they felt lonely and needed emotional support.

I was particularly struck by what one of them said. He was a balding man and his voice choked as he spoke "I was alone and depressed when my wife died ten years ago. Both my children used to live outside India, and neither of them wanted to return. They had offered to sponsor my visa and green card and they wanted me to live with them. But I told them that it is better to cut off an old tree rather than uprooting it and transplanting it elsewhere. Finally, my son decided to move back for me. That was eight years ago. Then he got married, and now I spend most of my day with my grandchildren. My daughter-in-law works too, but she looks after me as if I were her own father. I am alive simply because I have a family. Had I lived alone, I would have died long ago. You see, every year my family has lived with me has added one year to my life."

His words left a lasting impact on me. *One year of living with his son's family had added one year to that man's life.* If I simply went by that logic, one year would get added each to both Aai and Baba's lives for every year that I spent with them. In a way, that was the best return on investment one could think of. I was about to shrug these thoughts off as being too radical or impractical, or both. But

Lalit and Shashi had also moved back to India in recent past. And Shalu aunty and Ganu Kaka, Lalit's father, were both doing fine.

And why look around? Before my return, both Aai and Baba had to be hospitalized several times a year. The doctors had said that they had never seen Aai and Baba in such good shape in recent times.

Over the next few days, my mind was in turmoil. I was torn between my dreams of living abroad and the present reality I was faced with. Aai and Baba were getting older by the day. In a few years' time, they would become even more dependent on others.

*

I had raised the million dollar question when I met the boys at Shabri on the 14th of March: Should I stay put, or should I go?

The trouble was, that neither Lalit nor Shashi were present that day. Mandar and Nitin had not lived or worked abroad so far, and they were not able to offer the perspective that I wanted.

Earlier that day, I had spoken to Pangulal. He was leaving for Boston next morning. "You can figure it out for yourself." He said. "Go ahead and write down your priorities, you will find your answer."

As I hung up, I thought: "Why didn't I think of it?"

The next day was Sunday, March 15th - the eve of the one year anniversary of my return to India. Today was D-Day. I recalled Pangulal's words and wrote down the goals for my move to India.

The three basic goals for my relocation to Pune were:

a. Live with Aai-Baba and spend quality time with them.

b. Experience what it means to work in India.

c. My income in India should be enough to sustain my family.

I decided to evaluate the above on a scale of 1-5, with 5 being the highest. Next, I started my self- assessment.

a. Live with Aai- Baba and spend quality time with them.

A six-day workweek had made it difficult to spend enough time with Aai and Baba. Our family time was limited to a drive on Saturdays, some social events, or an occasional trip to the grocer's. When Aai and Baba were hospitalized, I was not able to spend much time with them either. Natasha, who was visiting at that time, had insisted that I focus on my work while she looked after them.

Work had dominated my week significantly. Overall, my primary reason for returning to India had not been met.

Total score– 1. Utter Failure

b. Experience what it means to work in India.

I worked for a Fortune 500 company, but their Indian operations were run differently. I was not really used to working for a thirty thousand employee company and all the bureaucracy that came with it. I had deferred my MBA by a year; otherwise I would have graduated by now. But the North American economy wasn't doing very well, so finding a job would have been difficult. Things there were, however, expected to turn for the better by the time I graduated one year later. In contrast, the Indian economy was in a mess and there was little hope of a recovery for the next year or two, or even three or four years from now.

However, I would say that returning to Pune was the best short-term career move I had ever made. It was evident that India was not a favorable destination for my career.

Overall Score– 3. Objective partly achieved.

c. My income in India should be enough to sustain my family.

After the initial hiccups with my salary, and then the fall of the Rupee against the dollar, I was able to survive on what I earned. However, I was not able to save any money. The recent goof-up with the reimbursement for my relocation had also hurt me financially.

Overall Score– 2. Objective barely achieved.

Following this, I added up my score. 1+ 3+ 2 = 6. I had scored 6 out of a possible 15, which was a less than 50 percent. By my own standards, I needed to score a minimum 50 percent in order to pass.

Very quickly, I tore up what I had written. This document was not meant to be seen by anybody else, particularly Aai.

*

That evening, I went to Tathavade Udyan again. The bench that was occupied by the group of old folks last week was empty. As I sat on the bench, I recalled something that I had read in the newspaper earlier in the day. The old man who was talking about his son had passed away two days ago. His family had published his photograph and a touching obituary. I remembered the old man's words.

"Every year that my family has lived with me has added one year to my life..."

By dinner time, I had made up my mind. I woke up in the middle of the night and typed our two emails. The first was to the admissions office at the Richard Ivey School of Business.

"From: Amol Dixit <verdant78@gmail.com> Mon, Mar 16,

2009 at 02:32 A.M.

    To: <richard.parker@ivey.ca>

    RE: May 2010 Cohort

    Dear Richard,

I am writing to inform you that I will not be able to participate in the May 2010 Cohort of the Richard Ivey School of Business. As you may be aware, I had deferred my admission because I had relocated to India. Due to my family situation it will not be possible for me to join the MBA program. I understand the repercussions of my decision and my apologies for informing you so late in the process.

    Regards,

    Amol."

Almost immediately, I wrote the second mail to the Account Manager at the Royal Bank of Canada.

    "From: Amol Dixit <verdant78@gmail.com> Mon, Mar 16, 2009 at 02:36 A.M.

    To: <janesmith@rbc.com>

    FW: Ivey MBA Loan

    Dear Jane,

Thank you for your email. I am certainly grateful for all your efforts for my loan approval. Unfortunately due to some recent developments on the personal front, I will not be able to attend the Ivey MBA program this year. I have informed the Ivey School of Business in this regard and I will not be able to avail the loan.

    Best wishes,

    Amol."

I read both the emails one more time before I hit the send button. In six minutes flat, I had altered the course of my life.

I was letting go of my future in Canada. I had paid a ten thousand Dollar commitment fee that was most likely not going to be refunded. It was money that I had saved after a hard day's work in the freezing cold, managing traffic on busy city streets, and working extra hours during some of the best years of my twenties.

In six minutes flat, I had opted to live in India. When I had the choice of taking either a blue pill or a red pill, I had swallowed a poison pill.

But I had resolved that I would continue to live in India for as long as Aai and Baba were alive, and I was going to stay back no matter the consequences. I was not a failure, and I was determined to prove it to myself more than anybody else.

Now that decision time was over, it was time to face the uncertain future that lay ahead of me.

PART II

Chapter Eleven
My Indian Dream Shattered

In the last week of March, Paresh asked me to meet him in his office. When we met, he handed me an envelope and said, "Congratulations".

I opened the envelope and saw that it contained a letter and a cheque. The letter complimented me for my outstanding work over the past year, and informed me that I had been awarded a bonus of forty thousand Rupees. The letter also went on to say that only half of the amount would be paid in March. The rest would be paid in December, provided I and the company both met our goals. Finance had promptly deducted tax on the entire amount. Effectively, my paycheck for March including the bonus was going to be less than what I took home in other months. I thanked Paresh and left the room.

Five minutes later, Rajesh called me and asked. "*Yaar*, did you meet Paresh? Did you get your bonus?"

"Not yet." I replied. Now that I was going to live in India, I needed to learn the Indian way of life. And it meant that I had to learn to answer judiciously.

"*Yaar*, you will get it soon. By the way, I got two months' salary and will receive an equal amount if I stay on till December. Ganesh and Sachin received similar bonuses. I am sure you will get the same," he said as we ended our conversation.

I thanked him and hung up. I took a deep breath, rather, several deep breaths, because I had just been hit below the belt.

*

"Happy Gudi Padwa," Aai greeted me next morning.

"One year ago we had bought the car. And look where we are

today," I replied with a sigh.

The excitement that we had experienced last year was a distant memory. A lot had changed since then. If it was any consolation, I was not spending my time on the construction site during the hot summer days. However, I was still spending long hours at work writing proposals and developing schedules for upcoming projects.

*

Exactly a month had passed since I had committed a professional *hara kiri*. And just like I had predicted, Paresh called me on April 15th to break the news.

"Amol, you will have to move to our Mumbai office, otherwise it will be difficult for me to justify keeping you in my team."

As I updated Baba that evening, Aai walked into the room. "Aai, didn't I tell you that this was going to happen?" I said to her.

"I never asked you to stay back. It was your choice," she said defensively. Tears coursed down her cheeks, unabated. I had to say something to console her; otherwise her tears could have flooded the city of Pune in no time.

"I am not blaming you, Aai. It was my decision to stay back. I am only telling you that this was bound to happen. So now, instead of cool and pleasant London, Ontario, I will be living in hot and humid Mumbai. And I will be able to meet you and Baba only once a week, so please don't create any more scenes."

But Aai had left for the loo by the time I had finished speaking.

Baba was so upset with the news that he refused to talk to me for a very long time. Finally, he looked at me and said, "You will have to pay rent at two places, plus there will be the added cost of travel between Mumbai and Pune every week. How are you going to manage all that?" Baba had faced a similar situation in his working life on more than one occasion. He knew very well what it could do to one's family life, and more importantly, one's finances.

I had no answer to his question and replied," I don't know."

Two weeks later, it was my birthday. Unlike the previous year, I took the day off. I decided to spend the day with Aai and Baba. In the evening I received a call from Ashok.

"Amol, wishing you a Happy Birthday. I also wanted to tell you that I might be let go. There isn't much work to do and the market condition is bad. Moreover, they think I am too expensive. You and I might have butted heads several times over the past year, but believe me, I was only trying to help you. I know how it feels to stay back in India against one's wishes."

Before I could reply, Ashok continued, "Twenty years ago, I had to change three buses during my two-hour ride each way to my worksite. The days were long, and we worked seven days a week. But I survived. Always remember, it could have been worse for you. Whatever the situation you are in, feel free to call me if you need help."

"Thank you," I said and hung up. It was the end of an era.

By now, I was an ordinary Indian with a limited professional network and only a Master's Degree and work experience in the US to boast of. I was no longer Superman, but a humble Clark Kent. But it was also the time to rise above my prejudices and face the challenges that lay in front of me. My Indian Dream had shattered, and it was time to pick up the pieces.

Chapter Twelve
Gyaani Baba Arrives

I am not sure what prompted me to drive to the tea stall that Pangulal and I used to frequent during our college days. This tea stall is located near a canal along a narrow road that connects Law College Road to Fergusson College Road. The road is sinuous, tree-lined, green and quiet. Some parts of this road are drivable; while others are accessible only by foot. There is nothing spectacular about this tea stall, but its location offers a perfect escape from the chaos and the daily grind of city life.

"*Nandu, ek chai any ke Gold flake Lights,*" I told the tea stall owner. I was visiting this place after many years, and my Marathi still had a trace of *firangi* accent. But he had still recognized me.

"*Baryach diwsanni alat saheb,*" he said in a welcoming tone.

I had barely lit the cigarette when it started to rain. Early May was known to bring an occasional pre-monsoon shower or two in Pune. The tea was barely passable. It was dark, sweet, and laden with ginger, but it was a refreshing change from black coffee.

Nandu asked me, "*Bhaji ghenar ka?*"

It was a rhetorical question. In times of stress, or in times of distress, junk food provides emotional comfort. Moreover, eating *bhajiyas* in the pouring rain was a must-do. In a few minutes, Nandu handed me a plate full of onion, potato and chili *bhajiyas*. I emptied the plate in no time, and asked for another cigarette and a cup of tea.

While he was preparing the tea, I saw that Nandu still carried his old Murphy transistor with him. I asked him to turn it on, and heard a voice that was nearly muted by the static from the transistor.

"The true caliber of a good batsman is tested when the scoreboard has less than 100 runs and half the team is back in the pavilion," the voice said.

I figured that some cricket match was being broadcast on the radio. The voice continued, "The batsmen will now have to tackle each and every ball as it is bowled. This is a test match, a game of grit, determination and patience; and not a T-20 game where quick action is a must and a given."

After a few minutes, I walked back to my car and drove home, only to be greeted by Aai at the door.

"You are all wet," she said, the concern in her voice was evident. "Wait here. Let me get you a towel. Then go to your room and change."

This was so much like my schooldays. Back then, I would receive an earful for getting wet in the rain.

Fifteen minutes later, I had changed and was sitting in the *jhoola* in the balcony. The rains had stopped by now, and the leaves on the trees had a glow on them after the shower they had just received. The rocking motion of the *jhoola* had a hypnotic effect on me.

"Did you like my commentary this afternoon?"

"Huh? Who is this?" I looked around, but could see no one.

"I am Gyaani Baba. You have a tough road ahead, and I have come to help you."

"I am beyond help," I replied.

"You are wrong. Everybody can do with a bit of help here and there. I can give you *gyaan*, lots and lots of *gyaan*. You should take it. It comes for free."

"Everyone I meet seems to think I need advice," I shouted.

"But I can be your friend. I will take you to where you are meant to be. Open your eyes. Look at me."

Gyaani Baba appeared out of nowhere. He did not look like a Sadhu at all. He wore a pair of jeans, a printed shirt, and a bandana on his head. A pair of Kolhapuri chappals adorned his feet. Long locks flowed down his neck, and he had a thick beard. So thick, that even the Wolverine would get a complex. He carried a guitar on his left shoulder.

He started playing a Bee Gees Number out of the blue. "Stayin' Alive…Stayin' Alive…"

"What are you doing?" I asked him.

"As you can see, I am playing a song. And I am telling you that is important to stay alive. Live, and live a lively life. By the way, you can call me GB. Gyaani Baba, or GB. GB, who is playing a Bee Gees song. Appropriate, isn't it?"

"Why are you doing this to me?" I asked. He was beginning to irritate me by now.

"Don't worry, I will go now, but I will stay close to you for as long as I think you need my help. All you have to do is to close your eyes and think of me, and I will appear and give you *gyaan*. I will be your personal ATG machine."

"ATG?" I asked. I had never heard this term before.

"*Anytime Gyaan*," GB replied. "I am an ATG machine that requires no card and no password. There are no transaction fees, and there's no limit on the number of withdrawals every month. Isn't it a sweet deal?"

"Whatever." I said out of frustration.

"As you please. If you feel that returning to India was difficult, then wait and see what happens next, now that you have decided to stay put," Gyaani Baba faded away as quickly as he had appeared.

I sat in the *jhoola* for a very long time, wondering who he was, and why he was willing to give me *gyaan*. I was meant to start packing for Mumbai. Instead, I had Gyaani Baba on my mind.

Chapter Thirteen
Mumbai: Hitting Rock Bottom

I had never been a big fan of Mumbai. Its weather, the crowds, the dirt and the traffic all seemed overwhelming. But I was destined to work in the Maximum City.

"I need a place to stay," I said to my uncle when it was evident that my move to Mumbai was inevitable.

"Let me talk to Dan," he suggested.

Dhananjay was an ex-army man, and one of the friendliest persons I had ever met. "You can call me Dan, and I can offer you this place if you like it," Dan said, as he showed me the house. It was a small, one-room unit with an attached bath and a kitchenette.

"Perfect. I am going to live by myself, and this space is enough for me," I replied.

"I met your parents in Pune yesterday before I decided to show you this place. I wanted to make sure your story checked out. Your mother reminds me of my sister, and that makes you my nephew. You can call me Uncle Dan. And you know what; I will reduce your rent to eight thousand Rupees a month and will also offer you parking spot inside the compound," Dan remarked as I paid the deposit.

The rent was more than what I could afford, but it was a steal compared to what I would have to pay at most places in Mumbai. The house was located in an old, quiet, tree-lined neighborhood in Sion, and was merely a few hundred feet away from the Sion- Chembur road. Which also meant that Aai and Baba's house in Pune was only three hours away.

Dan and I got along very well. He brought his spare TV to my room because the IPL season was in full swing. We would spend the evenings watching cricket, and for the first time I was able to follow one complete game every day. To fend off the oppressing and muggy Mumbai heat, we would have a beer or two.

He asked me one day while we were watching the game, "So how is work?"

"So far, so good. I was never a fan of arriving late to work, and I am happy that Mumbaikars also religiously follow the clock. Even the sales representative from the phone company arrived on the dot at 9.30 AM on a Saturday morning with the SIM card," I replied.

"Very soon, you will learn several fine aspects of living and working in Mumbai," Dan said as he nodded in agreement.

My office was located in Lower Parel, an area that was once home to numerous textile mills. But a majority of them had been torn down to make way for fancy offices or million-dollar homes. KMM's office was housed in one such office building. When I drove to work on the first day, the parking attendant did not allow me to park my car inside the building. I could immediately see why: the parking lot hosted a BMW, a Jaguar, and a Rolls Royce. Nobody would allow a lowly Indica to be parked next to such a pedigree of wheels.

Someone had told me that there was a parking area beneath a flyover. This makeshift parking lot was located half a kilometer from my office and it cost fifty Rupees a day to park my car. It seemed that the parking operations were managed by the local mob and probably offered a daytime pastime to the gangsters.

One tough-looking guy would hand over the parking tokens. He looked like a villain from a 1970's Bollywood movie, replete with long hair, bell-bottom pants and a light green Tee shirt. He had *paan* in his mouth and *kajal* in his eyes. All that was missing in this paraphernalia was a Rampuri knife. The parking token was a used packet of cigarettes that had a number scribbled on it.

I had looked at the stub on the first day with surprise. The goon had warned me not to lose the stub, *"Isko khona mat."*

One day, I did end up losing it, and it took them nearly an hour to find my car. I reached home around 8 PM, and found Dan waiting for me at the door. As we sat watching the IPL game, he asked me, "So, do you plan to drive to Pune every weekend?"

"I am not sure. The six day workweek makes it difficult," I said.

"At least you can go home on Sundays," he continued.

"Yes, but I leave Sion by 6 AM and reach Kothrud by 9 AM, just in time for breakfast. The routine is set once I reach home. I drive Baba around the neighborhood, and then the three of us have lunch. Evenings are meant for socializing. The day ends before I know it. The journey back to Mumbai begins early next morning, and I drive straight to work. The drive on the Mumbai-Pune expressway is an absolute delight during these early weeks of the monsoons. But the petrol bills and the toll receipts have started hurting my wallet. It's time to look for alternatives."

"I agree," Dan nodded as he spoke. I noticed that he nodded his head several times whenever he agreed with someone's remarks.

I soon learnt that buses that plied on the Mumbai-Pune route passed through Sion. The bus journey would double my travel time, but it would cost me nearly one-fifth the cost of driving. I began to take the bus to Pune.

"Why don't you bring your car these days?" Baba asked me one Sunday afternoon over tea.

"Baba, driving proves quite stressful," I said, not wanting to tell him that driving was also very expensive.

"I don't like this, Amol. You come only for a day. Did you choose to stay back in India to spend one Sunday with us? Answer me," Baba said angrily.

He was right. Was this the life that I wanted to lead? Staying back in India was my choice, and in a way, I had chosen my destiny.

"Don't ask him such questions," Aai interrupted, as she filled my cup for a second time.

"Baba, eventually things should turn out okay," I said finally.

"Stop being diplomatic. Admit that you have made a mistake. Thankfully, you have not blamed us for your situation so far," Baba's word had stung me hard.

"I know this situation is proving difficult for all of us. Nothing seems to be going right. But let's give it some time, Baba. We will figure a way out of this," I replied. My words were hardly reassuring.

"But I miss the car rides. Drive your car to Pune next time," Baba said, sounding like a child who was deprived of his favorite toy. What Baba really meant to say was that he was missing our Saturday evening 'Temple Runs'. I was to learn some years later that a popular game would be called by this name.

"So, Amol, what time are you leaving tomorrow? I need to get your breakfast ready," Aai asked me as I began to pack my bags.

"The bus leaves at six AM, so I need to leave the house by 5:30"

I would usually sleep during the bus ride, but I was wide awake on that particular day in early July. As I looked out of the window, I saw a railway line a few hundred meters away from the Mumbai Pune expressway. The expressway was built parallel to the railway line when I was in college. We had visited a site where they were building one of the tunnels. Those days, I was hungry to see and learn about construction in India. Today, I was angry with what I had seen and learnt about construction in India.

The shrill whistle of the locomotive engine broke my chain of thoughts. A train was heading in the direction of Mumbai. The Deccan Queen, the train of choice for the travelers along the Pune-Mumbai route, was cutting through the pouring rain. I looked at the blue and white train and remembered my college days.

I used to love traveling to Mumbai by the Deccan Queen on such rainy mornings. I would stand in the doorway; feel the drops of rain falling on my face, and wave at the children who lived in the villages along the railway tracks. When the train would slow down in the hills or *ghaat*, as it was colloquially called, I would feed the monkeys who would sit on the side of the track. Then, I would walk up to the pantry car and enjoy a steaming hot bread-omelet and *chai*. Finally, to top it all, I would eat the *vada paav*. Life was bliss.

As I was lost in these thought, my phone rang. It was Paresh.

"What time are you reaching the office today? We need to discuss an upcoming project," he asked me.

It was eleven o'clock by the time I finally reached the office.

"I have been waiting for you for nearly an hour," Paresh said as I entered the office. "Anyways, there is a new project coming up, it is for the Maganlal Agarwal General Insurance Company."

Over the next several minutes, Paresh told me everything I wanted to know about the MAGIC project.

"They are going to set up 400 sales offices across India next year. We have been appointed to develop a standard schedule and budget for their construction, and find contractors to execute the job. If we get this right, they have promised us more business. I think you should lead this project."

"Paresh, I have not even heard the names of some of cities and towns where many of these offices are to be located," I said to him as I looked at the project details.

"It is a prestigious project, you know," Paresh said, and added, "Don't worry, a team of project engineers will work with you. You will be getting an A team."

The prestigious project in fact turned out to be a preposterous project. The A team never arrived. Instead, a group of four engineers was assigned to work with me. All of them had been drafted into the MAGIC project much against their wishes.

Raksha was an architect who was fresh out of college and into the third month of her job. Paresh was confident of her abilities, a confidence which was unfortunately misplaced. She had visited a few of the project sites the week before. One day, she emailed me two hundred photographs that she had taken during her visits.

"Raksha, in the future, use some other way to send the photos. And do check the dates on the photographs before you send them," I told her over the phone.

"But…I have no such problems when I send photos to my friends by Gmail," she protested.

"Your emails have clogged my mailbox and I had to spend nearly half the day cleaning it up. I also see that each photo has a date stamp that reads 1st January 2005. Did you set the correct date on the camera?" I asked her sternly.

The next day, I received four emails. The first one was from Raksha. "It was very difficult for me to send these photos and your rude words have hurt me." She had also marked Paresh and Manpreet on that email.

The second mail was from Paresh. "I would like to know what happened."

The third one was from Manpreet. "We expect our managers to be professional and respectful of their subordinates."

His words cracked me up. I wished he himself lived up to what that he had just written. By now I had found out that he was a feared culler. He was an expert in getting rid of older, experienced managers and replacing them with younger managers who obviously cost less. He was a smooth talker, and one to watch out for. He spewed venom like a Black Mamba, and had earned this sobriquet for that reason.

The fourth email was from Mithilesh, who was the project director at MAGIC. He wanted to know why he had not received the report and the photos from the site visits in time.

I called up Paresh to tell him what had gone wrong. "Paresh, I received two hundred photos from her that clogged my mailbox."

"You could have asked her to use some file sharing service."

"I did. She used her Gmail account to send the photos. Very smart thinking on her part, except that she sent them all to my work email. By the way, who is going to write the report?" I asked.

"Amol, we do not have anybody to do that work right now. You will have to manage that yourself. Otherwise I see a risk in this."

Paresh saw a risk in everything that he did. He claimed that he had taken several classes in risk management during his MBA. The irony was that all construction projects by their very nature carry a lot of risk. If he was so risk-averse, then maybe he should have taken up a different job.

Ashok had once told Paresh, "I am the biggest risk to the Village Market project. So don't worry about other risks."

*

As the MAGIC project progressed, so did the list of problems, and Paresh's "find a way out" remarks. But one can only pull rank or ask for favors in an organization up to a limit. Day after day, my team kept delivering sub-standard work, and work began to pile up. At first, Mithilesh told me that he understood. But as the project progressed, he began to get agitated. One day, he called me up and said, "Who hires such geniuses in your company?"

"Why, what's the matter, Mithilesh?"

"There is a photograph which clearly shows that some paint is peeling off from a beam. It has been marked as 'There is a crack in the beam'. You are civil engineer; you know what a crack in the beam means. Are you trying to suggest that the structure is unstable and can collapse? I thought you would have done the quality checks on these reports, Amol."

He was right. I should have checked the work. I was spending half the day in phone calls and the other half in meetings, which left me with hardly any time to do any checking. But I had always taken pride in my work, and if there was a mistake in the report, then it was my fault. And I owed up to the mistakes.

*

By the time the end of July approached, Paresh called me and said, "The invoices need to be sent for the MAGIC and make sure that the reports are complete."

Abhijeet, who sat next to me at work, was also a part of Paresh's team. "I wonder what makes Paresh the way he is," and I went on to tell him how I felt about Paresh.

"You should know his background to understand this character," Abhijeet replied, and went on to tell me Paresh's story.

"Paresh is the son of a textile merchant from Bhopal. He took over the family business when he turned 25. Ten years later, he sold off his business and went to the Indian School of Business for his MBA. At 35, he must have been among the oldest students in his class. But what I hear from fellow alumni, he is a class apart."

As we prepared to leave the office, Abhijeet continued, "Paresh lives by two rules. Rule number one is that if there is a chance to save one Rupee, he will try and save two. Rule number two is that if the client desires, we have to remain open for business even at midnight. His rules have made him popular with the management, and he has built up a team of *his* men. But you and I are among them." By then, we had reached the taxi stand. That closed the discussion for the day.

A couple of weeks later, I found Abhijeet looking really busy with some paperwork. He looked up when I entered the office and said, "Amol, you know, about Paresh...if Manpreet is the Black Mamba, then Paresh is a Mama."

"What do you mean?" I asked him out of curiosity.

"This word has many meanings. You may know that in many languages including Hindi and Marathi, a Mama is an uncle, or mother's brother. Children in India are often taught to affectionately call the moon as Chanda Mama. In Maharashtra, traffic policemen are often called by that name. But Paresh is a Mama in a different context. The Madams who operate the brothels in Mumbai are often referred to as Maushi. To me, Paresh is the male equivalent of a Maushi. He manages the bodies that are available for hire. And like a Maushi, Paresh also lacks balls. And by the way, I am telling you all this freely because today is my last day at work," he said, pointing towards the pile of papers on his desk.

*

"You had an option go back but you chose this life. Why do you complain now? Tell me, my man," GB appeared out of nowhere one afternoon when I was in Pune. It had been nearly three months since he had appeared when I was sitting on the swing.

"GB, I am not complaining about the work. It is the donkey work that I have a problem with. I have worked from 9 in the morning till 1 in the night straight on a Saturday or two when I was at Vojak. It was not because someone had asked me to do that, but because I enjoyed doing the work. The work I do here is out of sheer compulsion."

"That was still donkey work," GB continued, "You asked for it, and you got what you deserved. As your friend Paresh says, go and figure it out for yourself," GB's words echoed as he disappeared.

That evening, Shashi offered his pearls of wisdom at Shabri.

"Your life in the US was a dream that is over. Trying to live that dream here won't do any good. Do not try to change the system here, but don't adopt it either. Learn to adapt," he said as we parted ways.

In a week's time, the really long working hours, day after day, took their toll. I fell ill, and it took me ten days to recover from my illness, but I emerged recharged and rejuvenated.

As I was getting ready to leave for work, GB asked me, "So what happens now?"

"I have decided to stop the four hour meetings. The phone calls will be limited to an hour. And my D-team had to transform into an A-team. I will give them two months to shape up."

"Good luck," he said with a smile.

I soon put my plan into action. The first few days went really well, and I was glad that the situation was turning around. I had also developed a set of work buddies at the office. When I had joined the Mumbai office in May, the people I worked with seemed to be very uptight. They were the proverbial *SULSURE*s- Stiff Upper Lips with a Stick Up their Rear Ends. Soon, I learnt later that they thought exactly the same about me. But one day it all changed.

Quite a few of the younger brokers would step out of the office every now and then while making a phone call. Somewhere in the middle of their conversations, they would light up a cigarette. I had unknowingly picked up this habit from them.

One day, a gang of four saw me light up during one such phone call. From that day onwards, I found myself hanging out more and more with Sam, Seema, Luv and Ankit. We would have lunch together, or visit the nearby Hard Rock Café after work. Sometimes, we would just spend the evenings having a beer or two. I began to look forward to spending time at work, and that had a positive impact on how I managed the MAGIC project.

But this lifestyle had a downside. In a short span of a few weeks, I got a forced upgrade from being stocky to overweight. I began to look and feel that I was forty. Fortunately, I received a wakeup call just in time.

*

"There's a party at a friend's place this Saturday. Would you like to come?" Sam asked me one morning.

I had learnt about Sam from Abhijeet a few days before he had quit. "Sameer Pratap Singh used to live in Singapore before moving to Mumbai. He is the son of a well-known exporter. Sam works in the HNI group," he had told me.

"I did not know such a group existed," I had replied.

"This group caters to the high-net-worth individuals, and till recently used to provide housekeeping and concierge services for their apartments. But now they have changed their focus. Quite a few multinational corporations own apartments in South Mumbai, which are meant to provide accommodation for their executives. These companies have started selling these apartments, and they lease them back from the new owners. The buyers have outsourced the management of these homes to the HNI Group, and the multinational companies save a tidy sum in the process," he had informed me.

"That is an interesting business, I was not aware that such a service even exited," I had said to him.

"But there's more," Abhijeet had continued, "finding buyers for these properties was a challenge. That's where Sam's father came in. He influenced many of his peers to buy some of these apartments.

Each property was worth several million rupees, and the HNI division had made substantial profits at a flat three percent commission. But Sam is a genuinely nice and down-to-earth guy. He often jokes that he was hired because of his father's network."

*

I decided to take up Sam's offer.

On Saturday evening, I took a taxi to Juhu. The party was on the rooftop. A famous Bollywood actress from yesteryears used to stay on the top floor of this twenty- storied building in Juhu. One day, she had overdosed on her drugs and died. It was rumored that her ghost resided in that apartment.

"Check the lighting on the rooftop," the hostess said to me as she opened the door. I was the first person to reach the venue.

"Um... I am Amol, Sam's friend," I said, my face flushing with embarrassment.

She apologized, but did not sound nor look apologetic. "I am so sorry. Please make yourself comfortable. And please excuse me; I have to make a phone call," she gave me a head-to-toe scan as she spoke. I could see that I had failed to impress.

"You are heavyset man with a balding head. Your face may be clean-shaven, but another round of razor might have helped. Your eyes are puffed due to lack of sleep for several days," GB was dressed in khakis and resembled a peon in an office as he spoke these words.

"Why are you dressed like this?" I asked him out of surprise.

"I can ask you the same question, my boy. Look at you. You are wearing a blue cotton shirt, dark blue jeans and brown leather shoes. You wear no brands or labels that make a statement that would make you stand apart in a crowd. Your aftershave and perfume are too bland. It would have helped if you had worn a wrist watch that had a dial larger than your fist, or an iPhone with a diamond studded bezel. You resemble a NNI, a No Net worth Individual. You are a blot on the NRI fraternity," GB's words had stung me, but what he said was true.

A few minutes later, I went to the rooftop and began to admire the view. On the beach below, people were taking a stroll, couples were cuddled up in romantic embraces behind the coconut trees, and children were making sand castles. I had never experienced such calm for the past several months.

As I was lost in these thoughts, the roof lit up and the speakers began to play some strange music. "Must be techno." I said to myself. To my surprise, it was a song from a newly released movie. I had lost touch with what was happening on the film and music scene in India, or anywhere in the world for that matter.

For the next three hours, the guests kept pouring in. I was introduced to the son of a stockbroker, the scion of a real-estate developer, and a wannabe actress. After having a brief conversation with each one of them, I realized that we had nothing in common to discuss. I was a cricket guy, and having filled my quota of watching IPL, I was looking forward to discuss the game. Unfortunately, football was the rage among this crop and Manchester United and Arsenal were not my cup of tea. I had never been to Singapore or Dubai for a weekend jaunt, nor had I ever visited Las Vegas. In other words, the guests thought that I was a bore.

The party was not what I had expected it to be. Even the makeshift bar only served Vodka and Limca. The drink tasted funny, but I could not figure out what was wrong with it. Around 10 PM, I decided to call it quits. I was on the city streets a mere five minutes after saying my goodbyes.

*

I woke up the next morning to find myself sleeping on the sidewalk. It did not make sense to me. Was I not at a party last night? Did I not leave for home? My head was hurting, and I was feeling really weak. My mouth was sandpaper-dry.

"It must have been a rough night," I said to myself and began to raise myself up. There was stack of bricks to my left. I used them for support. That's when my head began to spin and I threw up.

"Ugh!" I said out aloud and looked around me. The street was quiet. Three other persons were sleeping to my right. They were all wrapped up in their shawls. I realized that I had slept next to street bums. I had no idea where I was, or how I got there. My cell phone and wallet were still with me, so was the gold chain that I wore around my neck. I checked my wallet and saw that I had a couple of hundred Rupees with me. It was enough to take me home.

It was nearly 6 AM, and the sky was lighting up. A little later, I saw a taxi approach in my direction. I flagged it, and told the driver, "Sion Circle," that was all I could manage to say before I blacked out.

The braking of the car woke me up. The area around me seemed familiar. I was at Sion circle. After paying the taxi driver, I went home. Today, I had experienced the lowest low of my life. I had slept on the city streets, and eight hours of my life had been erased from memory. For the next several hours, I tried to reconstruct the entire incident. Finally, I gave up and closed my eyes.

"Looks like you have no idea what happened to you," GB's familiar voice said. He was dressed in khaki pants and a white shirt and resembled a traffic policeman.

"*Traffic policeman!*" I said out loud. Then it all came back to me. Unable to find a ride home last night, I had approached a traffic policeman and asked him where I could find a taxi or an auto-rickshaw. I must have passed out right after that. I had vague memory of some persons lifting me and putting me on the sidewalk. A part of me wanted to go back to the spot and ask around to know what had really happened. The traffic cop was the key to the mystery.

"Amol, you are lucky to be okay. But you need to realize that your life is a wreck, and that you have brought it upon yourself. It is time you climbed out of the hole that you have dug for yourself. You need to stay away from spiked drinks. And by the way, I need to remind you that your PMP exam is merely a day away," GB was right. My life had hit rock bottom.

Chapter Fourteen
Déjà vu

The exam was indeed on the next day, and I hadn't even started preparing for it. I showered, had breakfast, and opened my books. Twelve hours later, I was exhausted, and fell asleep as soon as I hit the bed. When I woke up, I was a man transformed. On this day, Amol Dixit was a man on a mission.

As I left for the test center, GB's voice echoed, "Go for it!"

Once my auto-rickshaw reached Andheri, I said to myself, "I have been here before."

By the time I reached my destination, it all came back to me. I was at the Marwah House near Saki Naka in Andheri. I had taken my GRE at this very venue. I could recall each event vividly. It was in December 1997 that I had traveled to Mumbai because Pune did not have a center for GRE those days. I had stayed with Shalu aunty. She used to live in Vile Parle during those days, which was not very far from Andheri.

A tap on my shoulder brought me back to the present. "Do you have an appointment, and may I see your passport please?"

The Parsi lady behind the desk smiled at me. I remembered her from my previous visit. She hadn't changed a bit. In contrast, so many things about me had changed. I took a deep breath, took my passport out of my trusted Northface backpack and handed it to her. The backpack went into the locker shortly after.

Ten minutes later, I sat facing a computer screen. After a few moments of anxiety, I shrugged off any thoughts about the past or my present life, and focused on the task at hand.

"May the Force be with you," GB said, appearing in front of my eyes. He was dressed like Obi Wan Kenobi, and was wearing a red cape and had a flowing white beard. Only the light saber was missing. The easiest thing to keep my focus was to follow the instructions on the computer screen. A few clicks of the mouse later, my test was under way.

For the next five hours, I was scratching my head, yawning, stretching, and murmuring, "I wish I had prepared better."

Finally, the screen in front of me read, "You have completed the test. You can either report the score, or opt not to."

I selected the option that read, "Yes, I want to report my score."

The result was displayed on the computer screen. I had passed the exam and was now a Project Management Professional, just like Rajesh Tickoo.

*

On my way back to Sion, I remembered what had transpired after I had completed my GRE test. I had taken an auto for Vile Parle outside this very building. The driver was a chatty fellow and he spoke in Marathi. Those days, Marathi-speaking auto-rickshaw drivers were a flourishing breed in Mumbai. Today, folks from other parts of India have taken up the mantle of driving the rickshaws.

The drivers' words had registered loud and clear, *"Ithe mula muli roj ka yetat?"*

I told him the reason why so many boys and girls visited Marwah House every day. They all aspired to go abroad to study.

"Mag tumhi pan America la janaar?" he had asked.

"Ho," I had replied.

"Maza mulga pan motha houn America la jail," the driver had told me excitedly.

His school-going son was another one of the millions of Indians who wanted to leave the country for higher learning, better-paying jobs, and a more comfortable lifestyle. I had tipped the auto-driver an extra ten Rupees that day, and told him that I would pray that his son's dreams would come true.

When I had reached Shalu aunty's home, Shashi had opened the door. He was visiting during the Christmas break. "Let's open a bottle of champagne, because I am going to Urbana Champaign," I had told him.

I had not even applied to that school at that time. But such was my passion, my madness, and my resolve. I wondered where it all had disappeared.

*

A bump on the road brought me back to the present. I wanted to go back to 1998, and wanted to go to Pune. Better still, I wanted to buy a one-way ticket to Toronto and never come back. I also began to wonder whether the earlier auto-driver's son had been able to realize his dreams.

"Mumbai ke raaste bahut kharab hai Saheb," the driver had stated the obvious. The monsoons had wrecked the roads.

"Hmm," I said, as I was lost in my own world.

When I reached home s few minutes later, I had a big smile on my face. For the first time since my return to India, *something* had gone right in my life. I closed my eyes and thanked GB.

"Passing today's exam is okay, and it's good that you are getting serious about your life again. But you need to start thinking about the long term, laddie. You cannot live like a clown all your life," GB had a red ball on his nose, which he had probably borrowed from a circus.

He continued, "You are living in Mumbai, while your parents are in Pune. You are able to spend time with them at the most one day every week. You are paying rent in two cities, have two sets of expenses and hardly have any savings left. You work long hours and have no social life other than your Boys' Nights in Pune; or more recently, spending time with your buddies at work."

"My life has indeed become quite monotonous," I concurred.

"That is not all. You are sliding down a spiral. The bottom line is: working in Mumbai is *not* working out for you. You would be better-off flipping burgers in Toronto," GB, and continued, "There's more. Your income is several thousand Rupees short of your expenses and you are forced to dip into the savings that you have back in the US. But your 401 (K) has tanked significantly. Do you realize that you are practically living like a broke teenager?"

I nodded in agreement. There was silence.

GB spoke after what seemed to be a very long time. "Have you thought of getting a MBA in India?"

"I am not sure...." I replied.

"You have resolved to stay put in India for as long as your parents will be around. And it means that you are not going to leave India anytime soon. You were planning to get an MBA anyway, so why not here? You need to get out of construction if you want to continue living in India. It is not for you. Think about it," he suggested.

"I like the idea. It's brilliant," I replied excitedly.

*

Over the next few days, I began to research the business schools in India where I could apply. However, my initial excitement was short-lived. Most of the schools offered two-year MBAs, but I was looking for a one-year MBA program because I could not afford to stay away from the workforce for two years. And that limited my options to two. One was the PGPX program at Indian Institute of Management, Ahmedabad and the other was the Indian School of Business in Hyderabad.

Unfortunately, ISB reminded me of Paresh. But one bad alumnus was not a reason to discount the school altogether. Some of its alumni were doing very well, but a majority of them were hardly thirty years old. This was logical, considering that the incoming class was made up of students who were in their mid-20's. At my age, I would be one of the oldest students in the cohort.

I recalled my experience at the nightclubs in Pune. I was going to pay nearly 2 million Rupees in fees for the MBA, so I had a right to be with the people I could relate to. The profile of the PGPX participants was very similar to mine, so the decision was made.

It was nearly the end of July and the deadline for application was less than two weeks away. I was still working fifteen hours a day, and that left me with very little time to locate my GMAT score sheet and transcripts, write the application essays, and get recommendation letters. But then I noticed something that caused me to smile. The application for PGPX did not require me to submit the essays right away. Over the next few days, I was busy getting the ammunition ready for my application.

"Looks like filling the application will take quite a while. Make sure you leave your office early tomorrow," GB advised.

The next day, I left for home at 6 PM. Two hours later, I set about completing the online application. The form asked for a number of details. It somehow reminded me of my first day at work, when I had to fill out the paperwork given to me by Sudha, the HR lady. And yes, I had to upload the obligatory photograph. But this time around, I was prepared, and had already scanned my photo.

For the next few hours, I filled the application form, and double-checked the details. Finally, at 11:55 PM, I clicked the 'Submit' button. The application for my MBA was on its way. Two years ago, I had done the same when I had applied for my MBA in Canada. Today, it was Déjà vu.

Chapter Fifteen
On the Move Again

Paresh called me a few days after August 15th. "Amol, how is it going? I see that the MAGIC project is shaping up really well. Mithilesh was praising your work. What do you think?" he asked. I knew by now that he didn't really expect an answer.

"By the way, I am in Gurgaon for the past week. It is an exciting place. You should visit it and check it out yourself."

"I am not sure...why?" I was surprised by his question.

"I have Manpreet here with me. I will let him explain."

I heard the Black Mamba's hissing voice take over. "We are nominating you as the Project Head for a new school campus in Mohali near Chandigarh. It's a very high-profile project, and the client is very impressed by your credentials. The work is scheduled to start next month. By the way, how soon can you move to Chandigarh?"

My jaw nearly dropped when he asked me this question.

"Let me talk to Paresh," that was all I could say.

Paresh's spoke almost immediately, "My hands are tied, Amol. The business is slow, and we had to let go of a lot of people. I am trying my best to keep you in my team. The management is against it, and it is getting difficult. Please try to understand."

It was another take-it-or-leave-it ultimatum from Paresh, the second one in less than four months. I knew my time was up with KMM. It was time to start looking at other options.

"Let me go to Chandigarh for a few days, I will let you know then," I finally replied.

"No, you will first to go to our Gurgaon office for a week. I will speak to HR about it." Paresh responded and then he hung up.

I could almost visualize the Black Mamba licking his lips with his long tongue. I could almost hear him say, "Now you will know what it means to earn the wrath of the Black Mamba."

On the other hand, the Mama was happy that I was no longer his headache. I was simply going to get moved a different department in a different city. The Black Mamba would see to it that I was out of Paresh's way for good.

*

The next Monday, I left for Gurgaon. After spending three days with the project team, I returned to Mumbai on Thursday.

"So you want to move further and further away from your parents. And how often will you get to meet them when you are in Chandigarh? Once a month? Not really. Let's say once every quarter. My boy, wouldn't you be better off in Canada than in Chandigarh? As it is half the population of Chandigarh dreams of living in Canada. And here we are, aspiring to do exactly the opposite," GB was least helpful as always.

"What other choice do I have?" I asked him in an irritated voice.

"You know what to do. Bring one change and things will turn around for the better," he said and then disappeared.

I followed GB's advice and resigned the very next day. Aai and Baba were shocked when they heard what I had done. The Boys thought that I had gone mad.

Mandar admonished me for my act. "You should never leave a job unless you have another offer in hand. This is India, my friend. Other employers will not respect you if you tell them that you are out of a job. The demand for jobs is high and supply is limited. And by the way, have you received your salary for this month?"

I learnt next day that HR had promptly put my salary on hold.

"You will get the salary for August along with your full and final settlement," the Back Mamba wrote to me when I asked him about it.

I had just learnt another valuable lesson: in India, one should always quit after receiving the current month's paycheck. If there was a memo floating around to this effect, I had missed it.

In a matter of days, the team for MAGIC was replaced with fresh faces, and Paresh himself took charge. My team was re-assigned to other projects.

I could not help but think how this was such an antithesis of my last days of working at Vojak. Everyone there had wanted to make sure that I would be okay in India. Some had volunteered to help me with my move. Others had offered to sell my stuff for me in case I wasn't able to do so in time.

*

When I reached home that Saturday evening, I found Dan standing at his usual place in the balcony. From his observation post, he would admire the women on the street below, particularly the young lasses who walked in and out of a nearby college.

Dan waved his right hand to attract my attention. "Hey young man, Happy weekend!"

I looked up and simply said, "Hi."

Dan must have sensed from my body language that something was wrong. An hour later, he rang the doorbell. As I opened the door, he pushed a bottle of whiskey in my hand.

"I know you prefer beer. But you need something stronger, because whatever is bothering you needs to come out of your system. I also know you should watch what you are drinking after your sidewalk incident. But that's why I am here," he said with a smile.

Half-way through our drinking session, Dan ordered the food. There was a restaurant nearby that made excellent butter chicken. Other than the fish from Shabri in Pune, the butter chicken was my only link to the world of non-vegetarian food. I recalled how I had begun to eat non-vegetarian food.

*

Till the time I was in graduate school, I had remained a vegetarian. However, my first job in the United States required me to spend almost the entire day in the woods where we were surveying for laying a water supply pipeline. There was a deli a few miles from the project site that also served a decent breakfast, but there was nothing in the menu that I could eat. For the first few weeks, I would order a chicken sandwich, but without the chicken. The store still charged me full price for the bread and a piece of lettuce, with some mayo spread on the two pieces of bread. This was obviously not enough, so I had to order two sandwiches. One day, I decided that I had enough, and ordered a turkey sandwich, this time with the turkey.

*

Dan's words broke into my chain of thoughts. "You look like a child who has lost his puppy. In fact, you look like a lost puppy yourself. So lets' hear your woes," he spoke as he settled his broad frame into the armchair and lit his pipe after dinner. His wife did not allow him to smoke inside their house.

"They asked me to move to Chandigarh, so I quit my job."

"Good," he said calmly. "You may be screwed up, but you are a good man and you are committed to the cause. You didn't want to move further away from your parents, did you?"

I nodded affirmatively.

Dan continued, "Let me tell you a story. I wanted to be with my parents during their last days. But my leave kept getting cancelled for three years in a row. By the time I could get some time off, it was too late. You see, for me, my cause was my country. We all have a price to pay for the causes we are committed to."

"Thanks. I appreciate it," I replied.

"I will pour you a Patiala peg. On the rocks," he said, as he proceeded to pour me a drink. "This is what you need right now."

We talked about our lives for a very long time, and the food had to be warmed up twice. It was a past midnight when we finished the bottle of whiskey.

"Time to head back. But think about what I said. Don't worry about the door, I will close it on my way out. Good night!" said Dan as he left.

I sat in my chair for a very long time. Then I rose and pulled out my diary from my backpack. It was time to revisit the past now that I had refused to be on the move again.

Chapter Sixteen
How it All Began

I turned several pages of my diary until I reached the part I was looking for. The entries read as follows:

Day Zero. February 12, 2008. Pune.

It was the last day of my vacation in India. It was also the day that would change my life forever. I had a job interview lined up, even though I was perfectly happy with my job in Chicago and not really looking for work.

My interview was scheduled for 11 AM, but the interviewer was running late. I waited for him in a dimly lit windowless room. A lanky mean with neatly cropped hair entered the room around noon. He was talking to someone over the phone animatedly.

"Hi, I am Paresh." He finally spoke as he introduced himself.

Before we could talk further, his phone rang again. This time, he asked me to leave the room for a bit. The 'bit' turned out to be a good thirty minutes. I was angry by now. These guys seemed to be so unprofessional, I should have walked away. After all, I had a flight to catch in less than twelve hours' time.

Against my better judgment, I chose to stay. Paresh called me a couple of hours later I had reached home and made me an offer to join his group. It was an offer I should have refused.

Day One. February 13, 2008. Early AM.

At Mumbai airport, on way to Chicago. I had a decision to make- should I accept the offer, or should I let it pass? While mulling over this matter, a thought crossed my mind:

"I have never worked in India before, and getting work

experience in India would be great. The job is in Pune, where my parents live. They have been after my life to come and spend some more time with them. What more could one ask for? As for the MBA program, it can be deferred. I am sure this is doable..."

Day Two. February 14, 2008. Detroit.

Valentine's Day. My flight had to be diverted because of a snowstorm in Chicago. I could only manage to talk to Nandini for a few minutes and did not get a chance to tell her about my decision.

Days Three and Four. February 15 & 16.

Having an extended family nearby helps. My brother-in-law braved the weather, drove for an hour and a half in the snow to pick me up from the airport.

Day Five. February 17, 2008.

Rented a car and drove back to Chicago. By now, I was keen to reach home. Rather, what was to be my home only for the next few weeks. I had made up my mind to move to Pune.

Day Seven. February 19, 2008. Chicago.

Back at work. I told my boss about my decision to relocate to India for a year. He thought that I was crazy.

Day Ten February 22, 2008.

Called up Paresh and asked him about the offer letter. He asked me to call someone called Manpreet in the HR Department.

Day Eleven. February 23, 2008.

Finally managed to talk to Manpreet, who said that the offer would be sent soon.

Day Twelve. February 24, 2008.

I received the offer. It had ten pages of dos and don'ts, but the numbers were not what we had agreed upon.

Day Fourteen. February 26, 2008.

Received the revised offer, which I accepted and sent it back.

Day Sixteen. February 28, 2008.

Gave my two weeks' notice at work.

Day Eighteen. March 1, 2008.

Woke up in the middle of the night, shocked, and wondering, "What have I done?"

Day Twenty. March 3, 2008.

Made a list of things I had to sell, donate, throw, or ship to India. Started listing things on Craigslist, eBay, Sulekha, and their ilk. I needed to find a buyer for my car soon.

Day Twenty Two. March 5, 2008.

I was running a fever. Bicycle, mattress, bookshelf, and TV were sold. There was no buyer for the car yet.

Day Twenty Three. March 6, 2008.

Natasha made a surprise visit. Her flight had arrived late due to a snowstorm, and she had to wait outside my house for over two hours in the freezing cold. My medication had knocked me out cold, and I did not hear the phone or the doorbell ring. Around 3 AM, I had somehow heard the bell, and opened the door. Seeing her, I remarked, "I hate surprises," and went off to sleep again.

Day Twenty Five. March 9, 2008.

Natasha went back to Baltimore. All boxes shipped, car yet to be sold. One week to go before my job starts in Pune.

Day Twenty Seven. March 11, 2008.

Woke up with a terrible hangover. It was a bad idea to get drunk when there was so much work to do.

Day Twenty Nine. March 13, 2008.

Sold the car at CarMax. I did not like the price they offered, but I did not have a choice.

Day Thirty. March 14, 2008. Chicago.

Rohan came to drop me off to the airport. We loaded the bags in his van. I turned around and had one last look at the house where I had spent the most memorable years of my life. As we left, I had tears in my eyes.

Day Thirty. March 14, 2008. Early evening. O'Hare airport.

Boarded the Air India plane to Mumbai with a one-way-ticket back to India.

*

It was six in the morning by the time I had finished reading my diary. By now, it was evident that I had acted in haste my move to India was not well thought out. In my eagerness to live and work in Pune, my move was executed without weighing the pros and cons.

"It could be worse. Remember your mail to that lady in HR about your insurance card? What if Abhay Yadav had happened for real?" The speaker was stroking his beard as he uttered these words.

"Will you please talk in a way that I can understand," I screamed.

"You know, you did a kind thing a few days ago. You saved a kitten from getting run over by a car," GB was clad totally in whites, including the cap, pads and gloves. He held a bat in his right hand.

"Thanks," I said, "but what's with the cricketing gear?"

"You save a kitten, and then I save you. In a way, we all bat for the next person, you see? But remember to think before you act. What if you actually had put her into greater danger, leaving her as you did, on the sidewalk? Did you notice the stray dogs on the road?"

"Yes, there were a few dogs nearby."

"You see my point? You tried to save the kitten from the cars but there were dogs around. You did not think through the situation. By the way, the kitten is safe. A young couple adopted her that evening." After a long pause, he continued, "but you see my point?"

I rose from my chair and took a cold shower. I spent several minutes below the running water, dried myself, and lay down on the bed. And that's when the weirdest dreams began.

I was standing in the balcony watching the rain. All of a sudden, a pigeon flew in and sat on the ledge to seek shelter from the rain. It had only one leg, and one of its wings was also damaged. Because of the damaged wing, it couldn't fly too far. It was unable to hold its weight on a single foot. But the pigeon had survived so far without any help from anybody. After a while, it stopped raining. The pigeon looked at me for a few moments and then flew away. Did it mean to thank me for letting it rest till the rains receded, or was it suggesting, "If I can do it, so can you?"

Next, I was standing in front of Marwah House in Mumbai. I was supposed to take the IELTS exam, the English language test that I had to take as a part of the Canadian Permanent Residency process. A very pretty girl was sitting next to me during the exam. I was distracted by her beauty, and was unable to concentrate on the test. Somehow, I had completed all the four sections, and the score report had arrived a week later. I had scored 9 out of 9. The irony was that I was in Chicago when this had actually happened. How could I have taken the IELTS in Mumbai?

All of a sudden, I was sitting with Phil in Chief O'Neil's Pub in Chicago. Phil and I had stopped to grab a drink before heading home. As usual, we were munching on French fries as we waited for my Guinness and Phil's Jameson.

"So my man, when you visit India the next time, do you plan to get married?" Phil asked me.

"Not sure, because I would prefer to meet someone who is already here in the States."

"So no arranged marriage for you?" Phil sounded surprised.

"I don't believe in it, but have a lot of respect for the system. Arranged marriages have worked for more than five thousand years, that too with a divorce rate that is less than five percent. Something must be right about this system," I commented.

Phil continued his questioning, "So does it come with a try before you buy option?"

"Try before you buy?" I asked.

"You know, a little boom-boom with the girl before D-Day. You need to find out if she's a hottie in bed. Also, if you can fit in fine…"

"No such luck on that front, my friend," I said.

"It's a shame," Phil remarked as he gulped down his fourth drink. "You know, I will come to your wedding, and will wear a sari."

Next, I saw him in a sari. He held a bottle of Jameson in one hand. He asked me, "How do I look?"

How did he look? He was a tall and lanky man with wavy blonde hair and week-long stubble. And he looked hideous in the sari.

*

"Amol, wake up." The loud knocks on the door accompanied these words as I stirred in my bed.

"Amol, are you okay?" I could barely recognize Dan's voice in my dazed state. I walked towards the door unsteadily and opened it to find Dan and his wife Sheila with a worried look on their faces.

Half an hour later, I was on my third cup of coffee when Dan finally spoke. "I had a word with your father a few minutes ago. He told me that he hasn't heard from you for four days. You should have at least called them over the weekend. He was worried about you."

"Moreover, your phone has not been reachable since Friday," Sheila added. She seemed equally concerned.

"My phone is not working and I do not have the money to repair it. In my rush to leave for work on Friday, I had forgotten to put the phone in a Ziploc bag. By the time I reached the office, the rains had soaked both me and my phone. Around lunch, I thought of calling Pune. I always call Aai and Baba once a day to check how they are doing. The phone's screen lit up when I turned it on, blinked a few times and then went dark. The service technician at the mobile phone store had told me that evening that there was nothing he could do about it."

"Is your SIM card working?" Dan asked me. I nodded positively.

"You are lucky," Dan said. He left the room, and returned a few minutes later. "It is all set. I have talked to your parents. And here is a phone that you can use," he said as he handed me an ancient Motorola flip phone. Shortly after, Dan and Sheila left.

I realized I had slept for 48 hours straight. But I now that had revisited how it all began, and it was time to put it behind me.

PART III

Chapter Seventeen
The Job Search

Armed with Dan's historic phone, I began to call companies to enquire if they had any openings. The phone would often give up in the middle of conversations. Half the buttons in the phone did not work, and the battery barely lasted for half an hour. One day, the phone died as I was in the middle of an interview. That very evening, I went to a mobile phone store near Sion Circle.

"I want the cheapest phone in this shop," I told the salesman.

"Sir, we have the Samsung Guru," he replied. Five minutes later, I walked out of the store with a new phone. One year ago, I had bought the most expensive phone that was on sale in this very store.

*

The next day, I was leaving the makeshift parking lot near the office when I received a call. "Amol, this is Surya. I head the Mumbai office of STQ Architects. Why don't you come and meet me tomorrow at 4 PM?"

"I would be glad to, thanks," I said and hung up. Sam accosted me as I reached the office.

"Hey! What happened to your phone?" he asked. I told him how the rain killed it.

"It's a good thing that the SIM card is okay. But you should have called me. I know the distributor for Blackberry in the city, he would have offered you a good discount."

"Thanks, but no thanks," I said with a smile. "It took me nearly three months to get over my Blackberry addiction. I used to be the proverbial crackberry addict, you know," I did not want to tell him that I could not afford to buy a more expensive phone.

"So, how is your job hunt coming along?" Sam asked, changing the subject.

"I have had two interviews so far. The first company offered me much less than what I am making now. Imagine that, their starting salary was even less than what I earned a year-and-a-half ago in Pune. And Mumbai is much more expensive than Pune."

"What happened with the other one?"

"The HR guy from the second company called me yesterday and said that they had a hiring freeze. For the past few days, we had exchanged several emails and spoken over the phone multiple times and he had assured me that I could expect an interview very soon."

"This is very typical. I am sure you know it by now," he said.

"So I have learnt," I replied as we entered the office.

*

STQ's office was located in a dilapidated building in Bandra Kurla Complex, next to the Reserve Bank of India buildings.

Surya was a balding man in his 40's who sported a small moustache. My interview with him went well. We discussed a number of areas, including our experiences on projects, construction methods, and opportunities in the Real Estate scenario in India. Finally, he asked me how much salary I expected.

"Fifteen lakh Rupees plus benefits," I said. A million and a half Rupees was a fair salary in my view.

"Amol, you have shocked me. No, you have insulted me. Five is the most that I will offer you and that too, you will have to convince me why I should hire you," he said and walked out of the meeting.

I sat stunned for a moment, then I rose and left the room. On my way out, GB appeared and said, "Let it go. He doesn't have the balls to tell you that he is a cheap bastard, and that's why he is posturing."

"What happened to the stories of foreign-returned construction managers who had been hired for several millions of Rupees?"

"You answered your own question, my boy. These are stories…outliers, which are picked up by the media. If the employer sends someone to India on an expat package, they will naturally earn the millions that you spoke about. But how many such jobs exist?"

"Life's a bitch," I said out of frustration.

That's when I noticed that GB was dressed in a brightly-colored blue *kedia*. This swirly frock is worn by men during Dandiya, the famous Gujrati dance that is performed during Navaratri. He wore a red *dhoti* and a red *pagdi* and carried a painted stick in each hand.

"You should also practice Dandiya," he remarked as I stared at his avatar.

"Why?"

"You need to check your emails more often," he said, as he faded away.

*

GB was cryptic as always, but his words made sense when I read that IIM Ahmedabad had shortlisted me for an interview. The way things had unfolded over the past month, I had completely forgotten about my application. As the next step, I had to submit four essays by September 20th, and the interview was to be held on the 25th in Ahmedabad. I only had two weeks to write the essays and barely a handful of days to prepare for the interview.

The essay questions asked the usual information such as what did I expect from the MBA program, what were my strengths and weaknesses, and a situation where I was able to demonstrate my leadership qualities.

I thought the questions were straightforward, but answering them in three hundred words each was going to be a difficult task. Two years ago, I had written similar essays when I had applied for my MBA. But back then, I knew where I wanted to be in life. Today, I wasn't so sure.

"You know what you want to do, so stop worrying," GB's voice echoed in my ears.

I wrote several versions of the essays over the next week, but was simply not happy with the outcome. I began to take a taxi to work to give me an extra hour and a half every day to refine them further. Fortunately, work at KMM had come to almost a standstill. The long hours that I used to spend on the MAGIC project seemed like a distant memory. All the others, except Sam, had stopped talking to me, and Paresh and I communicated only over emails.

"You look lost these days," Sam commented as we stepped out for lunch. I told him the reason.

"Cool. Let me know if you need any help. And good luck," he said.

*

During one such day, I received a call from an unknown number. I had thought that it was another telemarketer; they had made my life miserable. But something within me told me to go ahead and answer the phone. The caller spoke in a refined fashion, unlike the telemarketers who spoke in some alien language that remotely resembled a mixture of Hindi and English.

"Amol, this is Raghuram from DCSD. I heard that you are leaving KMM and are looking. Why don't you come and meet me tomorrow evening? I would like to talk to you."

"Sure, thanks for calling Mr. Raghuram. I can be there by five-thirty. Will that work for you?" I asked.

"Lets' make it 6 PM," he replied.

DCSD was the biggest competitor of KMM, and I was surprised to hear from them in the first place. I hardly had any time to prepare for the interview when Paresh emailed me the next morning.

"Can you go for a site visit? A developer would like to build a new office building at Nariman Point in place of an existing one, and they want our opinion on this project," his email read.

After I had looked at the building and its adjacent sites, I told the developer, "It will be a nightmare. The project will take at least three years to get the approvals. Till then, you will be left with this dying building."

The developer was not pleased to hear it, and neither was Paresh. "We can lose out on the deal," he wrote to me.

"I told what was in the client's best interest. If he wants a baby to be delivered pre-term, he is welcome to do so. But he should be ready to spend time and resources for meditation sessions to cope with the headaches and the stress that will follow," I wrote back.

It was 5 PM by the time I was back in the office. Fifteen minutes later, I packed my stuff and headed downstairs. There is a small window of opportunity between 5 PM and 5.15 PM, when one can find plenty of vacant taxis along Tulsi Pipe Road in Lower Parel. In a matter of minutes, the chances of finding a cab become exponentially smaller. That is because most of the offices empty out by 5-30 and the folks in these offices head for home or their preferred watering holes.

Fortunately, I found a cab in less than ten minutes. It was a Maruti Omni van which had a Sardarjee behind the wheel. I had to chase away two other suitors for this taxi, one of them was a smartly-dressed woman. Taxi drivers prefer to ferry *Chicas*, especially the good-looking ones, so I had a slim chance. But that day I got lucky, and stepped into the cab. The taxi was clean from inside, and incense sticks had spread a pleasant aroma. A photograph of Guru Nanak adorned the dashboard.

"A pleasant environment leads to pleasant thoughts," GB said, as I sat in the taxi. I was about to call Raghuram and inform him that I might be running late when my phone rang.

"Hey, Raghu here. I am stuck in the traffic. I am sorry; you will have to wait a little. Let's say 6.30 PM?"

"Amol, is that okay?" Raghuram asked again a few seconds later.

"That should be fine, I am on my way," I replied.

"Okay, see you then!"

By 6 PM, the taxi had snaked its way beyond Mahim to the road that leads to the Bandra-Kurla Complex. The six lane road was crowded, and rush hour was evident everywhere. It took me another fifteen minutes to locate the office, walk through the security, and sign in the visitors' register at the DCSD reception desk. As I sat waiting for Raghuram, a realization dawned upon me: I had forgotten to bring my resume along for a job interview. As I was lost in my thoughts, Raghuram called me in.

*

Raghuram S. Iyengar was a six-foot, three-inch tall giant of a person who sported a very thick handlebar moustache. His English lacked the typical South Indian accent. Instead, he sounded more like he was from the North. I wondered why, but this was not the time or the place to ask this question.

"Hi, I am Raghu. Sorry for the delay," Raghu said, as he extended his hand for a handshake.

"Good evening, I am Amol," I said as we shook hands.

We entered a small meeting room which had walls made of frosted glass. This room reminded me of the small meeting room at the Village Market project office which was my office for the first three months of my stint with KMM. As we settled down, Raghu asked if I would like to have tea or coffee.

"Water would be fine, thank you," I replied.

"Had we met outside, we could have ordered a beer," Raghu said with a smile. "So, do you have your resume with you?" he asked me once the office boy had cleared the table.

"I am embarrassed to admit that I am not carrying one with me, but would be happy to send it across later today."

But to Raghuram, it was no big deal. "That's okay. Most of the resumes I have seen are bloated and full of lies. I am not saying yours would be like that. Anyhow, I would prefer to talk to you first. You are already working with our competition, so either you must be good, or they didn't do their homework correctly," with these words, he burst into a loud laugh. I smiled at his remark.

Half-an-hour later, Raghu asked me how soon I could join him, and how much salary I expected. "We are not as good a paymaster as KMM, but I will try something in your case. By the way, one last question: why are you leaving them?"

I told him the reason.

"Ah, family first!" he said as we rose. The meeting was over.

Raghu wrote to me the next day and said that he would like me to join his group, and added that an offer letter was to follow shortly. Over the next two weeks, I had interviewed with four other companies, but DCSD remained my first choice. In the middle of September, I received their offer. The pay was indeed less than what I earned at KMM, but Raghuram had assured me that I could leave for Pune every other Friday. I would be able to spend every other weekend with Aai and Baba rather than my day-long jamboree every Sunday, and that alone was worth the pay cut.

Having a job in hand also meant that I could keep looking for a better opportunity if the need ever arose.

*

Somewhere in the middle of my work and the job interviews, I had managed to finish my application essays and send them to Pangulal for his comments.

"You, Sir, have started writing rubbish," he responded in his email. "I am afraid you have a lot of work to do. Considering that the deadline is two days away, my recommendation is that you should really apply yourself, or let it pass."

Pangulal was hardly a polite speaker, and his emails were even more acidic. But he told me the truth, and that is the reason why I valued his opinion. I literally poured my heart out the next time.

"Much better. One or two minor edits and you will be good to go. All the best," Pangulal wrote the next day. I submitted my essays a full twenty four hours before the deadline.

GB seemed pleased that night as he walked in singing, "It's been a hard day's night..." given GB's track record so far, this song was a quite a change of taste.

"You sound different today," I said to him.

"I am happy that you have sent off your essays. Now, there's the interview, and then...well, then you will see. No point in discussing that just yet," he said, just as he disappeared.

Things seemed to be moving for me in the right direction. But most importantly, the job search had ended.

Chapter Eighteen
Winds of Change

September 25th arrived even before I knew it. My early morning flight from Mumbai brought me to Ahmedabad around eight A.M. I was wearing a woolen suit, which wasn't the best choice of attire for the dry and sunny Ahmedabad weather. I was left wondering what had prompted me to wear it in the first place.

As the auto-rickshaw cruised along the nearly empty road from the airport to Vastrapur, I could see that the buildings along the tree-laden street were old yet impressive. There was a military installation to my left, followed by the Sardar Patel Museum a few minutes later to my right. Soon, we reached an underpass and the areas of old money gave way to the areas of new wealth. We had crossed Shahibag.

"I am beginning to like this city. It seems small and manageable," I said out loud. The auto-driver stared at me through the rear view mirror and then continued looking ahead.

"It's not bad for a city of nearly four million people," GB added his expert comments. "But compared to Mumbai, almost every other city in India would appear small and manageable."

We soon approached one of the many bridges across the Sabarmati River that connect the old city to the newer areas of Ahmedabad. On the other side of the bridge was the National Institute of Design. I could see several food joints that sold *fafdas, khamandhoklas* and *theplas*. I remembered the Gujju entourage on the Air India light from Chicago and smiled. Along the way, the view had changed and one could see working-class neighborhood on both sides of the road, which was soon replaced by the commercial district.

"The city has character," I said to myself.

Around 9 AM, we were at the main gate of a large campus. I could see structures made of red bricks on the other side of the gate. This did not make sense, because I was expecting to see gray concrete buildings.

"Nava campus, next signal?" The auto driver's Hindi had a very strong Gujju flavor; it was a flavor I was beginning to like.

The new campus was on the other side of a very busy road. As we were waiting for the traffic light to turn green, I noticed that the green and yellow auto-rickshaw had posters of Bollywood actors on either side of the passenger's seating area. I recognized the male actor as Salman Khan. The girl I could not, though I remembered seeing her in some movie called, 'Singh is King'. The traffic light turned green and we soon reached the main entrance of the new campus. I got down, paid the driver, and looked at the sign that proudly read: 'Indian Institute of Management, Ahmedabad' in English, and *'Bhartiya Prabandh Sansthan'* in Hindi.

"This is it," I said to myself, as I entered through the gate and walked up to the security desk.

"Yes Sir, PGPX interview?" The guard asked with a smile.

I nodded and signed my name in the visitors register.

"Please go straight and look for the signs that say 'PGPX interviews'," he said before I left. I walked for about two hundred meters and reached an open area that had lotus ponds to my right. A paved path led to two buildings. The building to my right said, 'International Management Development Center', while the one straight ahead bore no name or sign. There was a ramp to my left that led to the first level of this unmarked building.

I walked straight ahead and reached an open corridor of sorts, and noticed a black metallic stand that had a piece of white paper stuck to it. The A4 sheet read, 'PGPX interviews', below which was an arrow that led me down a corridor. About twenty steps later, I saw the same sign, but this time the arrow pointing towards a room. This room was the waiting area for the interview candidates, where I could see eight or nine persons besides myself. Someone had left their jacket and had probably gone off to the loo.

I walked up to a group and introduced myself. "Hi, I am Amol."

"Hey! I am Siddharth. You can call me Sid," said a balding guy who was wearing a black suit. "This is Gurpreet, and to my left here is Puja" he said as he introduced me to the others.

"Hello all! Looks like you arrived bright and early," I remarked.

"We arrived last night. In fact, all of us met at Pune airport yesterday. Puja and I know each other from before, and we met Sid at the airport. We flew in together," Gurpreet remarked.

"We are the Group 'P'- 'P' for Pune," Puja added.

Group 'P'. The name registered right away. I also wondered if I could still call myself a Punekar.

"So where did you come from?" Sid asked me, as he stared at my suit. He must have thought that I was crazy to wear a woolen suit.

"I came from Mumbai this morning, though I am originally from Pune as well."

"More power to Group 'P'!" Puja exclaimed.

Half-an-hour later, a short man who wore rimless glasses entered the room. He carried a list in his hands.

"I have the schedule for the interviews with me. There are three panels of two professors, and each interview will last half an hour."

I scanned the list and saw my name at the very bottom. I was scheduled to be interviewed by 5 PM. I wondered why the email they had sent me said that I was supposed to arrive by 10 AM.

"Ha! I am first day, first show. Amol, looks like you are first day, last show," Gurpreet said excitedly after scanning the list.

*

September 25th was the first of the several days of interviews that would be conducted over the next four weeks to select the PGPX class of 2011. In the coming days, similar scenes such as the ones I was experiencing today would be witnessed in Bangalore, London and Newark in the United States, and finally two more days again in Ahmedabad. Out of nearly one thousand applicants, around three hundred had been invited for the interviews, and offers of admission would be made to nearly a third of those who were interviewed. The room had sixteen people by now, which meant that about five or six of those present in the room would be selected for next year's cohort. Time would tell whether I would be one of them.

As the interviews began, my anxiety level began to rise.

"I think I blew it," one of the interviewees said as he entered the room, bade his goodbyes, and left.

By the time it was noon, others commented about their interviews that ranged from "It was okay!" to "I am done for."

By 1 PM, Puja had also left. By then, Krisha and Salman had

joined us for lunch, so also had Arjun. Over lunch I learnt that most of the applicants were from the software sector. I heard names like Infosys, Wipro, and Cognizant several times as they spoke.

"Guys, if these companies are doing so well, then why do so many of the IT folks want to get a MBA?" My question was met with a smile. "Am I the only outlier here?" I asked again.

"Arjun is a bureaucrat; he works with the Ministry of Urban Development in Delhi," Salman replied.

"New Delhi," Arjun corrected.

"Yes, New Delhi," Salman repeated after Arjun.

I had always thought that both cities were part of the National Capital Region, but obviously I was missing something. By now, the heat and the anxious wait weren't making things any easy for me. I had taken off my jacket and tie. The air-conditioning in the room wasn't helping much, and beads of sweat began to form on my forehead. There was a break for half-an-hour at 3 PM. I stepped outside the room and joined Arjun for a smoke.

Arjun, who had just completed his interview, asked me, "In about five minutes, they will show us around the campus. Are you interested?" By now, Salman and Sid had also left. Krisha was next to be interviewed.

"I can see the housing, but will have to pass on the tour of the campus. I need to stay indoors. It is hot outside," I said. My clothes weren't helping the matters either.

"No issues," said Arjun as we left the waiting area. By now, I had stopped wondering what the term 'no issues' meant.

A few of the current students showed us around the housing complex for married students, followed by the dorms. The latter were meant for those who were either unmarried or did not want to bring their families along.

By 4 PM, I was on my fourth cup of coffee when my phone rang.

"Amol, where are you? We have been looking for you," Paresh asked me.

"I am in Ahmedabad today Paresh, and will be back in the office tomorrow. Will talk then." There was nothing more left to discuss with him as far as I was concerned.

At 5 PM, I was asked to wait outside a room, which bore a sign that read, 'Syndicate Room 8'. This was the interview room. I waited outside this door for the next several minutes for the door to open. The support staff who had been updating us on the interviews throughout the day had left by now. There were a few stray dogs left for company in the corridor. I closed my eyes and took a deep breath.

"You know, there is a song by Enigma that goes like this - 'Turn off the lights, take a deep breath, and relax'. I couldn't agree more. Meditation is good for you," GB said in an effort to calm me down.

He was sitting in a meditative pose on a tiger skin, and was clad in orange from head to toe. He resembled a Sadhu.

"You have wondered several times why do I keep appearing every now and then. But do not worry about it right now. By the way, I saw a Marathi play today, it is called *Ughadle Swargache Dar*. You know, it means 'the doors to Heaven have opened'. So, all you have to do is to knock on Heaven's door...all the best!"

Just then, the door to the interview room opened and I was

called in.

"Good evening," I said to the two interviewers who were sitting on the other side of a long table.

The interview room seemed quite bare. The walls were covered with fabric of some sorts, most likely to improve the acoustics. There were seven chairs around a squarish table and a small steel Amirah in one corner of the room. A blackboard was mounted on one of its walls, and a pair of air-conditioners was installed on the same wall above the blackboard. There was a set of double doors behind the two interviewers.

The duo was a study in contrast. One was tall and lanky, while the other was a thick-set man who resembled a wrestler. They looked like Tweedle-Dee and Tweedle-Dum. No, they looked more like 'Jai' and 'Veeru' from the movie Sholay.

Neither of them introduced themselves, so their monikers stuck. They did not even acknowledge my presence in the room for the first few minutes. Jai was sifting through a folder; he was probably reading my dossier. Veeru appeared to be reading a newspaper and had put his feet up on a chair.

"Mr. Dixit, why are you here today?" Jai asked as he finally made eye contact.

"You may call me Amol, Sir. I am here for the PGPX…" before I could complete my reply, Jai interrupted me and said,

"I prefer to call you Mr. Dixit, and I know what people say about the PGPX program. So Mr. Dixit, why are you really here?"

I felt as if I was Neo from the Matrix, and was being interviewed by Agent Smith in a windowless interrogation room. I wondered if they would glue my mouth and insert a bug into me.

"I am here because I want to get a MBA. This program is the right fit for my background," I replied, and realized that it was perhaps the worst answer I had ever given in my life.

"You really think so?" Jai asked me again.

"Yes," I was much more assertive this time around.

"I disagree. Anyway, sit down."

"Thank you," I said as I sat on a chair.

Jai continued his questioning, "So what do you do for a living?"

"I am a project manager for construction projects."

"So why do you leave a sector that is doing so well, and invest so much money to get a MBA degree? And why do you want to leave construction?" He had probably read my essays.

"It will help my career growth. Plus, I can..."

"Okay, besides real estate, what are the other markets that you keep track of?" Jai interrupted me in the middle of my reply.

"I follow the stock market and gold."

"Why are you interested in commodities?"

"There seems to be a relationship between real estate, gold and stocks. If one goes up or down, it affects the other two."

"Interesting. So do you invest in the stock market?"

"I used to, but not anymore," I replied candidly.

"Why not? The Sensex is hovering close to its highest levels in

2009. It is a good time to invest, right? And both gold and real-estate prices are rising," Jai had summarized the market conditions well.

"I don't invest because I do not have any money to invest."

"What do you think about the rising gold prices?"

"I think gold has had its day," I replied and could feel that Jai was not impressed with my responses.

"Do you know what a Black Swan is?" he asked me all of a sudden. I had not heard that term before.

"No Sir, I don't," I replied.

"Why do you think real estate is so expensive in India?"

"Can I take a couple of minutes to answer this one?" I asked but continued to talk without waiting for his response. "The cost of land, materials and high dependence on manual labor are the major causes."

"So you want machines to replace the workers? You must be aware that the construction sector is the second largest employer in India after agriculture?"

"I am aware of that, and I am not suggesting that we should replace skilled workers with machines. But unless one is building a Taj Mahal, I see no need to employ thousands of workers to construct a high rise building for example. It is, after all, a vertical box," I replied confidently.

"Have you ever built a Taj Mahal in your life, Mr. Dixit?"

"No I have not, nor do I wish to, unless I was the Emperor."

"Why is that?"

"Because I love my hands," I replied spontaneously, alluding to the legend that Shah Jahan had ordered to cut off the hands of the workers who had built the Taj Mahal, so that they could not build another building that could rival the monument.

"Good. I love my hands too," Jai said with a smile, and continued, "So tell me, are there any other factors that affect the real estate prices in India?"

"Black money," then I thought that I had stated the obvious.

"What could be a solution to India's black money problem?"

"If I knew, I wouldn't be interviewing here right now."

My reply cracked him up. He turned and looked at Veeru, who seemed disinterested in our conversation. Then, he spent some more time shuffling some pages and asked Veeru, "Do you have any questions for him?"

"No," Veeru replied, as he put his feet on the ground and stretched his arms. Then, he yawned loudly and said, "It has been a long day. You can go now."

"Thank you." With those words, I rose, nodded, and left.

In ten minutes flat, I had experienced the worst interview of my life. I walked back to the waiting room and loosened my tie.

"Knocking on heaven's door, my foot," I said to myself, "I have been grilled over charcoal and then skinned alive. It was hell."

"Oh, don't worry. I think they were just messing around with you. They have made up their mind. Either they have decided to offer you admission even before the interview, or they have given you the boot," he said with a smile. I could have strangled GB right then.

The journey back to Mumbai was by one of the several trains that run between Ahmedabad and Mumbai every day. Coach S7 of Aravali Express was my bedroom for that night; it was a bedroom that I shared with seventy other chatting or snoring passengers.

*

"Paresh has sent an AWOL notice about you to the management," Sam told me when I reached office the next day.

I called Manpreet right away. "Manpreet, if I had absconded, I would not have answered Paresh's phone. I was in Ahmedabad yesterday, and my last day at work is only two days away. So there is no need for me to stop coming to work."

"Ok," the Black Mamba replied as he hung up.

I saw two notes on my desk by the time I walked back. One was from Riya, Paresh's assistant. Her note said, "Paresh wants to talk to you." The other note was from the IT department. They wanted the laptop back that day itself.

"Let me note down the contact details of the folks from finance, HR and payroll, in case I need to follow up with them regarding my full and final settlement," I said to the IT manager.

"Ok, but I need the laptop back today," he replied curtly.

At 1 PM, I called Paresh. "Amol, can you stay on longer, for maybe two weeks? There are some challenges in finding your replacement," he said, probably he thought that I would readily agree.

"I would have loved to help, Paresh, but I have just handed over my laptop to IT. They have signed off on the exit checklist," I replied.

It was also the last time I ever spoke to him. The same day, my eighteen-month stint with KMM ended. These eighteen months had taught me lessons for life. There was no point in holding any grudges against KMM. Instead, I wanted to thank them: after all, it was their job offer that had brought me to India.

Just the way all good things come to an end; all bad times also do eventually come to an end. I was confident that my bad times had ended because the winds of change were beginning to blow.

Chapter Nineteen
Pit Stop

"Why do you want to stay home for an entire month and start your job in November?" Shashi and Lalit were surprised when I told them about my future plans. We Boys were meeting after a long time.

"I need a break to lick my wounds. In hindsight, I should have spent the first month after returning to India with Aai and Baba. Reaching Pune on a Sunday and starting work on a Monday was a mistake. I had not even factored in jetlag, let alone getting used to life in India. But that is history," I informed them.

Shashi remarked, "I still don't understand what you are trying to do. You are starting a new job, and then you will go for MBA in less than six months."

"It's a long story. But hey, the new job is a necessity. As far as MBA is concerned, it needs the blessings of the admissions committee at IIM Ahmedabad."

"How do you find living with Aai and Baba again?" Lalit asked, as he tried to change the topic.

"It is no cakewalk. Aai and I argue a great deal, and Baba and I often fight a lot. I argue with Aai because she wants me to get married, and also because she forces me to eat every now and then. Mothers who express love for their children by forcing them to eat are a caring but dangerous lot. Unfortunately, Aai belongs to that clan. Baba and I get into fighting mode because I force him to go for a walk in the morning, but he wants a ride in the car before the walk. And finally, Aai and Baba argue simply because they are married. No other reason is required. We are one small, happy family," I paused to take a breath.

"And how is their health?" Lalit continued his questioning.

"I took them to the doctor's yesterday. Aai's kidneys are still in a poor shape, but it is a big improvement compared to last year. Baba's blood sugar levels are also under control. There are the occasional spikes, and we need to watch out for them," as I spoke these words, I recalled what the old man in Tathavade Udyan had said. In a comfortingly silly way, his logic was right on the money.

*

Without a doubt, my spending time with Aai and Baba had caused a marked improvement in their health. However, during this time, the pressure on me to get shackled increased. One incident sealed my fate - it began with watching a movie.

"Let us go and watch a film in the theater," Baba declared one morning. "It is better than butting our heads all day, as you like to say. Plus, it would pacify your Aai."

I bought the tickets for the afternoon show of 'What's Your Rashee' that was running in a nearby theater.

"I can almost see your life's story being played on the big screen," Aai said during the break as I bought popcorn for her and tea for Baba.

She was right, there were indeed a few similarities. The protagonist in the movie lived in Chicago, where he worked and enjoyed his life as a single man. One fine day, he was asked by his family to come to India, because they wanted him to get married for their own selfish reasons. The rest of the story revolved around how he kept meeting eligible bachelorettes and how he finally got hitched.

I liked the movie, and so did Baba. But the movie had a different effect altogether on Aai. She was now hell-bent upon getting me married. I protested and looked at Baba for support, but he chose to keep quiet.

That evening, GB gave his gyaan session. He was draped in a yellow-colored cloth that had 'Aum' written all over it in orange.

"Yes, it is time for you to leave behind your wayward life. That can be arranged, you know. I have a long list of lost causes like you. I often help some of them, just the way I help you. Quite a few of them are single girls, eligible, and good looking..."

"No thanks. GB, I am not interested," I protested.

"You worry too much about the past and the future and forget to enjoy the present," he remarked, and asked me all of a sudden, "by the way, what's your favorite Hindi movie song?"

"Huh?" I was confused by his question. If GB's remarks were difficult to understand, his questions could be even more confusing.

"There is a 65% probability that it would be a romantic duet. In general, solo songs are less popular than duets," he replied.

"Whose research is this?"

"Mine. But the important point is that the road you are traveling on needs a bicycle, and a life partner will form the other wheel of this bicycle. Otherwise, you will end up like a clown from a circus who rides a cycle that has only one wheel," GB remarked.

"I disagree with you," the anger in my tone was evident.

"That is your choice. But sleep over it. By the way, men in your family have been very active proponents of marriage. I don't need to tell you that."

GB was right. Some of my ancestors going back three or four generations had married multiple times. But people had a much shorter lifespan back then, and in those days, it was a common phenomenon. Then there was a family friend who so strongly believed in the institution of marriage that he had been married twice, and both his marriages were concurrent.

That night, I had a dream. All of my friends and family had turned into Borgs of sorts, and they were preaching, "You should get married. Resistance is futile."

I woke up the next day and gave in. It was one less battle to fight.

*

And so it was settled: I was going to spend the rest of October finding a life partner. Aai was relieved and excited at the same time.

For the next several weeks, I met a different girl every day. And almost every day, I met a different girl in a different coffee shop. And almost every day, my meeting with a different girl in a different coffee shop ended in disaster. But these disasters were the culmination of a long process that began with Aai's phone call to Shalu aunty.

Shalu aunty was an ace networker, and once she learnt that I was 'in the market', she called everyone within her network to spread the word. Not surprisingly, her network probably had more members than Facebook could boast of.

She also became my tutor. She showed me what to look for in the proposals for marriage, and trained me to ask the right kind of questions. She also taught me new terms like BHP, which meant Bio Data, Horoscope and Photograph. I had only known that BHP meant Brake Horsepower, a term used in the automobile industry. Shalu aunty also made me look up on the Internet on how to read a horoscope. She believed that the traditional way of searching brides resulted in marriages that lasted. The data supported her claim. The downside was that arranged marriages often were not the fastest way to find a bride.

"While the Internet could be a handy tool for learning, the online match-making websites stood no chance before word of mouth." Shalu aunty told me one day. Little did she know that when Shashi and I were in the US, we would spend several hours looking up profiles of eligible bachelorettes, or EB's, on sites like Shaadi.com and Bharatmatrimony.com. We used to find the experience quite amusing and entertaining.

In the Dixit household, there was a debate on where to look for the EB's. Aai was a firm believer in marriage bureaus, while Baba wanted to place ads in the newspapers. I wanted to go the online way.

*

"Should I try one of the matrimonial websites?" I asked Shashi.

He replied calmly, "I am not sure you will like what I am going to tell you. Using the matrimonial websites involves several steps. First of all, you have to register and create a profile. Then, you have to upload your photograph and horoscope. Next, you pay the membership fees. Paid members have a greater chance of success, or so these sites claim. The last step is to go to an office known as a 'contact center' and get your details verified. These contact centers are mostly run as franchisees. This step is also recommended. They also advertise that verifying your profile can *really* improve the chances of success."

"This seems like an unbelievably cumbersome and a ridiculous process to me. I have no idea how my data would get used," I remarked.

"Then you should just go for word of mouth. Since we have a large family, we have many mouths that can spread the words far and fast. But what's your preference, Kobra or Debra?" Shashi had asked the million Dollar question, and rightfully so.

*

The Dixits and their extended family are Maharashtrian Brahmins, and most of the people we know also belong to the same clan. By a process of self-selection, I thought that the first group of EB's would come from this pool. But it was not as easy as it seemed.

There are three main types of Maharashtrian Brahmins: Konkanastha, Karhade or Deshashtha. The Konkanasthas hail from the coastal areas of Maharashtra, a region also known as Konkan. Colloquially, they are often referred to as Kobras. They are typically fair skinned, and their eyes are grey or green, also known as *'ghari'* color. A Konkanastha girl is therefore commonly described as *ghari-gori*; that is, a fair-skinned girl who has *ghari* eyes. The Konkanasthas are known to be thrifty, though some might go to the extent of calling them stingy. They are also known to be neat freaks. Mumbai and Pune have a significant number of Kobras.

The Karhades form the smallest of the three groups. They originally hail from Karad region of Maharashtra, an area which lies South of Pune. They are known to be a disciplined lot when it comes to eating habits and their lifestyle.

The Deshashthas, or Debras, hail from the rest of Maharashtra. The word 'Desh' typically refers to the regions east of the Sahyadris, which is the mountain range that separates the Konkan coast from the rest of the state. Whether someone hails from cities as far apart as Nasik in the north, Nagpur in the east, or Kolhapur in the south, they are still referred to as Debras. They have a darker skin, and are known to be foodies. And much to the consternation of the Kobras and the Karhades, they are extremely clumsy and often do not know the meaning of the term spic-and-span.

For obvious reasons, Kobras prefer to marry other Kobras, and Debras prefer to marry other Debras. To add to my woes, our family name added to the confusion.

Dixit is a common family name among the Kobras. As a result, the Debras thought that we were Kobras, and said no to my proposal. When the Kobras learnt that we were Debras, they sent their regrets as well.

Dixit also happens to be a common family name among Gujaratis, Tamils, and in the Hindi speaking states of Madhya Pradesh and Uttarakhand. There were many folks who thought that we belonged to one of these groups. Aai had a tough time explaining them the geographical and linguistic origins of our family.

To me, caste, religion, profession, horoscope, Kobra or Debra did not matter. In fact, I preferred women with no bras.

*

As time progressed, I realized that my biggest challenge was to identify the kind of woman I was looking for. Marketers call this profile as a target customer or an ideal customer. Several years ago, Hindustan Lever had popularized a character called Lalitaji who was shown to be a street smart, practical woman who could haggle with the shopkeeper or a vendor to get the right product at the price that she wanted. At the end of the commercial, she would recommend a particular detergent because it was a product that she believed in. Lalitajis of the world were the target customers for that brand of detergent. Similarly, I had to define my Lalitaji in order to find her.

But before thinking about what kind of a life partner I preferred, it was important to describe myself first. This turned out to be more challenging than I had imagined.

In my schooldays, we had several writing assignments in our English classes. The topics could be as varied as:

Describe in less than 200 words an accident that you witnessed. Or,

Write a letter to the editor of a local newspaper and highlight how the water crisis in your city will impact its citizens.

I used to enjoy writing such essays and letters in school. That learning came in handy as I as began to write down my profile. An hour later, I came up with the following note:

"Seeking alliance for a Marathi Brahmin groom, 32, 5'7", US returned, now living in Mumbai and working in a reputed US based real-estate consulting firm. Good natured, loves the outdoors, and belongs to a cultured family. Seeking a well-qualified, professional woman as his life partner."

This was probably one of the lamest matrimonial ads that would have ever been written. Aai shook her head in disapproval when she read it.

We both knew that we had a long road ahead of us. Changing my status from 'single' to 'married' on social networking sites was not going to be an easy task.

*

Vadhu, or the bride, meets *Var*, or the groom, in a *mela*. Simply put, the boy and the girl meet at a fair, fall in love, and ultimately have a fairy-tale wedding. This promise, if printed on an attractive handbill, is sure to excite the parents who want to get their sons and daughters married. More so, if it is targeted towards the NRIs.

One such handbill that caught Aai's attention had arrived with the local newspaper. Some marriage bureau had organized a NRI *Vadhu-Var mela* near our house.

"Amol, let us go to this event on Sunday. I am sure you will find someone to your liking," Aai said to me one morning.

"Aai, I am not interested. It sounds like a scam. Worse still, it sounds like a cattle fair— something like the Pushkar Mela in Rajasthan, where people buy and sell camels. Of course, it would be interesting to you," I replied sarcastically.

"Don't be so rude. Let's go there. I am sure it will be a good experience," she persisted.

I did not see any point in wasting my time trying to reason with her. Moreover, the word camel reminded me of a conversation I had with Phil nearly three years ago.

*

Phil and I had just left the office in Chicago and were walking towards the parking lot, when he had asked me, "So my man, are you getting any action at all these days?"

"None, nothing after my break up with Maria two months ago."

"That is shameful, you are a sex camel," he had remarked.

"A sex camel?"

"Yes, a camel can go on without water for weeks. I see you doing the same when it comes to sex."

*

Recalling Phil's words caused me to smile. I nodded to Aai, letting her know that I would go with her.

On that fateful Sunday, Aai and I left bright and early to reach Shailesh Hall in Karvenagar for the *Vadhu Var* meet. I dropped her off at the entrance of the venue. By the time I returned after parking my car, Aai had entered into an argument with a group of ladies who were clad in bright green saris.

"My son is a NRI, but he is living in India now. What do you mean he is not eligible to participate?" Aai asked them angrily.

"Madam, this event is only for those who are living abroad at present. Your son might have lived in the United States, but now he is not living there. So as per our rules, he is not eligible," one of the women replied. She was the leader of the pack, the Alpha female.

"But he is a Green Card holder," Aai was still not able to understand the difference between a US Green Card and a Canadian Permanent Residency card. For her, they were all the same.

"Madam, we are sorry," the women spoke in a chorus.

Aai was quiet as we drove back home. She was concerned that I would be furious over this incident. I was actually quite amused by the turn of events, even though my Sunday morning was wasted.

"Aai, I see a big flaw in their NRI-only logic. Had I been on H1B or any other work visa, the green brigade would have let us in. But what if my visa was to expire in a month's time? Or, what if I was a NRI today, but I were to return to India next year and never go back?

Better still, what if I were to book a ticket to Toronto and fly out this very evening? Would I become eligible to participate in this Pushkar fest?" Aai chose not to respond. My attempt to cheer her had failed.

As we reached home, I told her again, "Let it be, Aai. There are other fish to fry."

Baba was sitting at his usual position in the living room when we entered the house. He was surprised to see us return early, and looked at me inquisitively.

"Pachka," I said to him as I took off my shoes. Pachka was a term used in the Dixit household that meant a 'flop show'. Baba was mighty pleased to learn what had transpired. Learning that Aai's efforts had gone in vain caused him to break into a laugh.

*

But Aai was never the one to give up. It was one quality of hers that I admired and respected, but her perseverance was also something to be fearful of. She believed that there was more than one way to skin a cat, and she would come up with ideas that most people would not even dream of. Management professionals refer to it as *Out of the Box Thinking*. True to her nature, Aai had already decided what to do next. She called up Lata V as soon as we entered the house, who responded positively. Her enthusiasm pleased Aai to no end.

"Mohini, yes...my sister and her sister-in-law, both of them got married through Mohini.... So did our neighbor's son," she told Aai.

*

A marriage bureau is a clearinghouse of sorts for men and women who want to get married. Rather, it is an exchange like the Chicago Mercantile Exchange, where commodities are bought and sold. You see, a man or a woman of marriageable age is a commodity with a fixed expiry date. But the marriage bureaus had rescued countless such commodities and caused many happily ever after moments for aspiring brides and grooms. That was before the Internet had challenged them in recent years and created a billion Dollar market of matrimonial websites. But with over 500 million people under the age of 30, India's demographic dividend had ensured that marriage bureaus like Mohini were still thriving.

*

"What is this Mohini business?" I asked Baba that afternoon.

Baba replied, "Mohini is the go-to marriage bureau in Pune. It is a tried and tested institution right from the time my cousins were in the market for marriage nearly half a century ago. Our family holds Mohini in very high regard. In those days, the bureau used to publish a monthly magazine. I hear that today they have a website also. The highlight of this magazine is its matrimony section. The Diwali edition of Mohini is something to look forward to. It has over 200 pages, and more than half of these pages are occupied by profiles of eligible *Vadhus* and *Vars* wanting to get married. There is something for everyone in the Diwali edition. The profiles are organized by caste, religion, and geography. Then they are also classified by professions for those specifically looking for say a doctor, or a lawyer. There are special sections devoted to the differently-abled and the divorcees. And finally, there is a section for those who were over forty."

As Baba continued talking, GB commented, "In less than a decade's time, you can get listed in the last category if you don't get married soon," and added, "though isn't it a scary thought?"

*

Mohini means casting a spell, and a charming spell at that. Lata

V was under the influence of such a spell when she led me to Mohini's office. It was five in the evening as we climbed the rickety wooden stairs of a century-old building which was situated a few meters away from Tilak Road. The narrow stairway was dark because the lone light bulb at the landing had been turned off.

We approached a woman as we reached the office and Lata V spoke to her, "We want to register my brother-in-law's profile," she told a young woman who was sitting behind the reception desk.

The woman was pretty. No, she was beautiful. I wondered if she was available. But as it happens in most cases, this good looking woman was taken. Her license was visible around her neck. She was wearing the Mangalsutra, which is a string of small black beads woven in golden thread, which were the hallmark of married women in India. Many people in Maharashtra call a Mangalsutra wearing woman as a "license wali".

I smiled at her to hide my disappointment, and she smiled back as she handed me an envelope. "She must not be from Pune," I thought to myself. Women from Pune were SULSUREs too, and they rarely smiled.

"This is the application form, please complete it and put the required documents in the envelope. All the best," she told us.

The form ran into six pages. The first page required us to fill in the mundane details: name, address, date of birth, education and details of driving license. The second page asked a series of questions that I had only seen on immigration forms.

Do you have a passport? If yes, provide the passport number and its date of expiry. Have you traveled or lived abroad? If yes, name the places you have visited. Do you have a visa? If yes, of which country? What is the type of visa and what is its validity?

The third page asked all sorts of information about the applicant's parents: their age, occupation, whether they had any health ailments, where they lived, and so on. The fourth page asked for similar details about the siblings. There was space on the next page to attach the applicant's photograph and horoscope.

The last page had a very interesting section called, 'Any other information'. The only other information that they had not asked was how big my member was or what was its girth, or in case of women, how well-endowed they were.

I could visualize a website where one could filter the profiles based on the size of one's member. There were options to filter profiles by age, height, location and profession, so why not include this option as well? Similarly, a guy could filter women's profiles based on the size of their breasts.

I would have said, "I scored straight A's while I was in school. But in this case, I prefer someone with a C cup."

"Amol, we should fill the form at home and submit it later," Lata V's words broke my chain of thoughts.

"Vahini, they are asking for too much personal information. If data thieves lay their hands on this form, they could hijack my profile and do with it whatever they please: apply for a job, sign up for credit cards, even get married by pretending to be me," I replied.

"Look, you must fill all the details. If not, you can go. That is our policy. We get over one hundred registrations every day, and nobody has objected to providing the details we ask for," a balding man who sat in the manager's chair said in a stern voice. His glasses nearly slipped from the bridge of his nose as he spoke.

I stared back at him. "Thanks, we will leave now, but please turn on the light in the staircase. If one of us trips and falls, I will sue you. That is my policy," I snapped back at him and left.

In the process, I failed to notice that Lata V had put the form and the envelope in her purse. The very next day, she went with Aai back to the marriage bureau. Without my knowledge, I was enrolled as member number MM332490 with Mohini Marriage Bureau.

*

Shalu aunty's outreach efforts and Mohini began to yield results. In a matter of days, my parents' phone started ringing, and the ringing never stopped for the next several weeks. October 2009 became the most exciting period that my parents had experienced in recent years. Some of the callers chose to follow up with letters, while others opted for the electronic option.

I spoke to Lalit over the phone one evening. "Almost every girl is described as being fair-skinned. That cannot be possible. Have these people ever stepped out on the streets and looked around? People should be proud of the amount of melanin they carry in their skin, and not be ashamed of it," I remarked.

"There seems to be an overwhelming preference for fair-skinned persons in our family," he replied. I guessed that he must have undergone a similar ordeal, and chose not to probe him further.

Shalu aunty had tutored me the following during my Bride Searching 101 classes:

"There are four categories of skin color that can be used to describe a woman: *gori, nimgori, gahu varna, and savli. Gori* means fair, *nimgori* means fair but not white-skinned. *Gahu varna* implies that she has a complexion like a grain of wheat, or light brown. And *savli* means that she is dark-skinned. And always read the descriptions with a grain of salt. Usually, *gori* means she is actually *nimgori*, *nimgori* means she is *gahu varna*, and so on."

This was an eye opener for me. I wondered how I would describe myself. Not that it mattered. I was proud of my skin, whatever color it was. And it was my duty to save it from getting bracketed into one of these categories.

I brought up this subject over dinner, and said "Aai, I don't agree with all of this. A small minority of women in India falls in the *gori* category. Almost every parent tries to promote their daughter as being a gori. Our country has been ruled by fair-skinned people for more than a thousand years, starting with the invaders from the North-West. Somehow the thought has been ingrained in our mindset that fair means better," I could see that Aai was not amused, and Baba was nodding his head in disapproval.

"That is still the case." He spoke as he rose, effectively ending the conversation.

*

The series of interviews with my prospective spouses began almost immediately. After meeting a few of them, I realized that those working in the IT sector were not my cup of tea. Others were too uptight, too committed to their careers, or simply thought of a husband as an add-on to their lifestyle. Some of them were so arrogant that they did not show up at the agreed upon time and place.

But Aai was the consummate salesperson, and she always had a list of EB's with her. Unfortunately, most EB's on the list were not my types. As if GB was not enough, the EB's were causing me to lose sleep.

The experienced folks, Shashi, Lalit and Mandar, had told me that it was futile to ask too many questions when I met someone, because the women were often tutored to say things that people wanted to hear. In other words, most of the answers they gave were not to be believed. I had to learn to read between the lines.

"When someone says that she loves cooking, she actually means that she loves to eat in restaurants. Similarly, when she tells you that she is a family person, she actually means that only the persons from her family would be welcome after marriage. And loving outdoors means to love shopping, so be careful," Mandar warned me.

But most of all, it was the kind of questions that people asked me took me by surprise.

"Would your parents continue to live with you after you are married? Our daughter is independent, and though she respects family values, she is not comfortable with the idea of living with her in-laws. Can you live separately, or can you come and live with us instead, after marriage?"

And then there was the classic.

"Our daughter's passport is ready. She aspires to go abroad and study further. She also has an international driving permit."

Such comments would crack me up. By writing 'aspires to go abroad and study further', were the girl's parents implying that their daughter's husband should pay the fees? Or better still, did she plan to work part time as a cab driver abroad? While I respected the latter, I did not appreciate free riders. After all, I had gone to grad school in the United States by my own efforts and merit.

There were the opportunists who thought of me as a loaded NRI, and then there were those who thought I was a loser because I had moved back to India. The parents of NRI girls balked at the prospect of their daughter living with her in-laws in India.

Someone once wrote to Baba, 'Let us think about it; we will get back to you.' They never contacted us again.

As Diwali season came around the corner, Aai's list of prospects was reduced to a mere six EB's that I was yet to meet. But before that, there was one more hurdle that was yet to be crossed.

*

"So what's happening with your MBA?" Nitin asked me one evening when he had stopped by on his way back home.

"D-Day is October 31st, three more days to go," I replied.

"Do you know the exact date?"

"Right now, it is just speculation. From yesterday, discussions on the Pagalguy forums are abuzz with rumors that the results would be announced on the 31st of October. Have you heard about Pagalguy?" I asked Nitin, who replied in the negative.

"Pagalguy.com is the oasis for the MBA aspirant. The discussion boards there have become very lively over the past week. Users are writing about how anxious they are. There are also many level-headed folks and a couple of alumni of the program who help the forum members keep their tempos high and tempers low," I informed Nitin.

"Sounds interesting. Good luck with it," Nitin said as he left.

*

October 31st began like any other day had begun for me over the past month. But at 5 PM, it all changed. That's when I logged on to Pagalguy.com and learnt that the offers of admission were being sent out by IIM Ahmedabad. The members of the forum were sharing their joys and disappointments.

User Anitaa11 had written: "My journey ends here. Will try again next year. All the best to others."

Tango213 was elated, "Ahmedabad, here I come…"

MitraKol was disappointed and had written, "Waitlisted. The uncertainty continues. Congratulations to those who made it."

The most recent post was from Bobba_Feet, whose words caught my attention, "I cannot log on to the results page. The server seems overloaded. Cannot wait to know the outcome…"

I was surprised and shocked to see these messages. The results had turned into a multiple choice exam of sorts, with four options: (a) In, (b) Out, (c) Waitlisted, and (d) cannot log in/don't know.

My immediate answer was (d), but I hoped to make it to (a).

My evening was screwed even before I knew it. For the next hour, I kept hitting the refresh button on the two browser windows that were open on my laptop. One was the page on Pagalguy forums; the other was the results page on the IIM Ahmedabad site. The trouble was, the server for the latter site was indeed overloaded, and I was simply unable to sign in.

That very day, I had promised Aai and Baba that I would take them to a new Chinese restaurant that had opened on Senapati Bapat Road. Aai and Baba were ready and were waiting for me to follow suit. We were supposed to reach the restaurant by 7 PM, so we had to be on our way by 6-30. Looking at how excited Aai and Baba were, I knew that the sooner we left, the better it would be for us. In a sheer act of desperation, I called Pangulal.

"*Kya hai?*" he sounded irritated. It was early morning in Boston.

"I need help. Have to leave for dinner. The results are out. Can you check mine?" I asked him, hoping that he would agree.

"Can't. I am still in the bed," he replied.

"How soon *can* you do that?" I asked him again.

"8 PM your time at the earliest. Send me the details and let me see what I can do," he hung up the phone before I could speak further.

In my haste, I only emailed him the link to the IIM Ahmedabad website, and forgot to send the login ID and password.

While sitting in the restaurant, I kept checking the time. The nearly seventeen year old Timex was the most special watch for me, because Baba had gifted it to me on my sixteenth birthday. Over the years, I only had to replace its battery every few years. I had worn it on every special occasion. When my wristwatch showed that it was nearly 8:15 PM, I began to wonder why Pangulal hadn't called me yet. Fifteen minutes later, I couldn't take it anymore and walked out of the restaurant when my phone rang.

"You did not send me the login and password," he said angrily.

"I sent it to you already," I reacted out of frustration.

"As they say in Russian, Nyet. Check again," he persisted.

"Ok, here it is," I replied. It was not the time to argue." My ID is AmolD31. Password is DixiA4478. That is upper case D and A."

"Ok, hold on," he said, and continued, "Server slow *hai*." A minute later, he added, "Your password is incorrect."

"What did you type?"

"DixiA4478. D and A in upper case," he parroted my words.

"Sorry. Password is DixitA4478."

"Ok. Try to give the right information next time around. "Wait... now... too bad..." Pangulal's words weren't too comforting.

"What happened?" I asked anxiously.

"My condolences. Check your mail. Bye."

That was typical of Pangulal. He could have very easily told me the outcome over the phone, but he wanted me to undergo my agony for a little while longer. I tried to log on to my email account on my phone. The two inch screen had a font so small that one almost needed a magnifying glass, and the slow data connection did not help either. In the soft yellow light of the lamps that lit up the foyer of the restaurant, I was finally able to log on to my account.

Several minutes later, I read Pangulal's email, which said, "You made it. Congratulations. Let's talk tomorrow."

"Bastard," I said out loud.

*

My month-long break had ended on a positive note. Two days later, I was going to start working with DCSD. The last lap of my race was about to begin, and the pit stop had helped me prepare for it.

Chapter Twenty
Mumbai Gone Right

I had not informed Aai and Baba about my application to IIM Ahmedabad, and they had only learnt about it the previous night. As usual, Aai tried to talk me out of my decision.

"What is the need for going back to student life at this stage in your life, that too, by taking a loan? By now, you should be enjoying your married life. Who will marry you when you are 35 years old?"

"Aai, I am 32 today, and nobody wants to marry me even at this age," I said, and continued, "Moreover, if I stay in my current profession, I will only have about 20 years' worth of career left. Look at how KMM treated Ashok. Ganesh is facing a similar problem. A MBA is what I really need for my career growth. And who knows, the MBA may even extend my career by a few years."

My logic was beyond Aai's ability to comprehend, but Baba understood it very well. He had worked in the same company for thirty five years of his life. Then one day, he was informed that he was no longer needed. They had offered him a generous severance, but the incident had left him heartbroken and bitter. That was nearly twelve years ago. Baba never took up any work again.

"You do what you feel is the right thing to do. Go and get that MBA, you have my support," he told me, overriding Aai's objections.

"Where is the money going to come from? Tell me Amol," the self-appointed attorney of the world was making sound arguments.

I tried to pacify her concerns by commenting, "Aai, I have some savings to pay the first installment. The rest, we will have to borrow."

"Amol, exactly ten years ago, we faced a similar situation. You had listened to me back then. But now you seem to have made up your mind. I would be happier seeing you married and starting a family. But my happiness does not matter," Aai's emotional blackmailing had begun, but it was not going to work this time.

*

That weekend, the Boys met at our usual hangout. Once we had settled down into our usual routine, Lalit asked me, "Amol, what's your CPS ratio now?"

"CPS?" Nitin sounded surprised. He was also in the matrimony market, and he had also not met any success so far.

"Amol, tell him," Lalit said to me.

"CPS is cost per screw. If you are dating someone in the US, you typically get to score on the third date. If the first three dates cost you, say 500 Dollars, then your CPS ratio is 500. It is quite high initially, but it gets better if you are in a relationship," I told Nitin.

"I get it," Nitin exclaimed, "the lower the CPS ratio, the better."

"Exactly," said Lalit. "So Amol, what's your CPS now?"

"It doesn't matter," Shashi replied on my behalf.

"No, I have the numbers. I have met ten of them only once and three others only twice. No third dates yet," I told the gang.

"And how much have you spent so far?" Nitin asked.

"About eight thousand Rupees," I replied.

"But you could get a third date soon," Nitin seemed optimistic.

"Wrong!" Shashi interrupted, "this is India…first there is

marriage, then lovemaking, and finally love. That, too, if you are lucky. Anyway, *second wala hua to third one does not matter.*"

Shashi's had summed it all up. My CPS in India was going to stay very high. It was cheaper to order another Old Monk and get high.

*

The next day, I traveled to Mumbai by bus. It was time to start living frugally for several reasons. First of all, I had hardly any savings left. Second, I had to get used to student life. Third, I would not get paid till the end of the month. And finally, I had maxed out my credit cards and was tight on cash.

I also had to pay the first installment for the MBA fees in less than ten days' time, which amounted to nearly half a million Rupees. I had to sell a part of my 401- (k), even though its value was much less than what I had invested. I knew that it was time to take some drastic steps in order to bring down my expenses. It also meant that I had to look for cheaper accommodation in Mumbai.

Mandar had suggested that I should go and check out a few places near Matunga Railway Station. One such place was Sharda Bhawan Lodging. I was not impressed by what they offered, but the rent was much lower than what I was paying Dan, so this was where I was going to stay for the time being. I had just left the lodge when I heard a familiar voice.

"Hey, you! What are you doing here?" Dan asked me.

We were both surprised to see each other in Matunga. "I came here for lunch at the Udupi restaurant up there," he said, pointing to a building that was right next to the railway station. I merely nodded.

"Speak up, young man," he smiled as he spoke. "By the way,

when did you come back to Mumbai? How is your new job?"

When he looked at me again, he exclaimed, "No, no way! You were looking for a place to stay here, weren't you? I saw you step out of the lodge. Why, what's wrong with my house?"

I remained silent. Dan continued his questioning, "You don't like our house? You don't like our company?"

"I do like you guys, Dan, and I love the apartment. But…"

"Yes, speak up…" he insisted.

"I cannot afford the rent. My new job would pay me much less."

"Bullshit. Have you eaten yet? Come, let's grab a bite," with those words, he literally dragged me across the street and brought me to a narrow staircase that led up to Rama Nayak's Udupi Restaurant. In spite of my somber mood, I noticed that the food was served on a banana leaf, and the menu consisted of *chutneys, buttermilk, dahi, papad, rice, rotis, dal* and *sabji*. It was a meal enough for two people, or even three.

After the lunch, we went to a paan shop downstairs and Dan bought us cigarettes. Gold Flake Lights for me, and a Wills for himself.

"So here's what you and I are going to do, and that's an order. You will stay with us for as long as it takes. Don't worry about the rent. Pay me whenever you can. We don't plan on renting it out anymore because we have had too many jokers as tenants in the past. You are a joker too, but a likeable one," he said with a smile.

I probably didn't deserve Dan's kindness, but I took up his offer.

*

In less than a week's time at my new job, I sensed that working with DCSD was a hundred and eighty degrees apart compared to working with KMM in some ways, and similar to KMM in others. The people here were warm and friendly, and the work was enjoyable. However, I did not get a laptop for nearly a month, and it took over two weeks to get my email account set up.

"This is nothing," Raghuram said to me one day, "it took them one year to set up my email account. Till then, I was using Hotmail."

Raghuram had worked for several years in South-east Asia and Australia. As a former NRI himself, he could relate to my situation. He was well entrenched in the organization, and had several years of experience in the business. He was not afraid to say no to even the toughest customers if he felt that it was the right thing to do. For this reason, he was held in very high regard. He also believed that work was important, but it should not come at the cost of family or other important matters in life. He would frown if someone stayed in the office after 6:30 PM, and he led by example.

He had once told one of the assistant managers, "Go home. It's nearly 6:15 PM. You had the whole day to get the job done. If you are still here, then you must have slacked off during the day. Come in tomorrow early and finish off whatever you are doing."

Raghuram was a great boss to have around. Had I had worked with someone like him instead of Paresh, my time in KMM would have been much easier.

GB disagreed with me, "It is good that you had to deal with someone like Paresh. You have learnt to appreciate a good boss because of him. More importantly, you will try not to become like him. And, by the way, Paresh's heart is in the right place, it's just that his priorities are screwed up. He values money more than people. He will learn with time what comes first. But don't worry about these matters. You will understand them when you take up a job in a different industry after your MBA. As an outsider, you will be under the microscope all the time. Raghuram can take certain liberties with the system which Paresh cannot. Other than their personalities, this is what sets them apart."

*

"Amol, how do you find the work?" Raghuram asked me one day.

"Yes, it is familiar turf, so that helps. But I would rather spend more time with the customers," I replied.

"Let us see what we can do about that. I don't think you should spend time on construction sites," he suggested.

Gone were the days when I would spend months at a project site that had no roads, electricity, or toilets. If I had to work in an environment like that again, I would be better off in the US. At least I would make more money there.

*

During daytime, getting an auto-rickshaw ride to Bandra-Kurla Complex from Sion was a cakewalk. But in the evening, neither the taxis nor the auto rickshaw drivers would want to go to Sion because it was too short a distance for them. Moreover, traffic is really bad in the evenings and the cabbies do not want to get stuck in it.

There were two ways to reach Sion from where I worked. One road went past the Sion railway station towards Kurla. It was the shorter route, but very few cabs would go that way. In contrast, the road going through Dharavi was an absolute nightmare. The trip would sometimes take nearly an hour for a three kilometer ride. Just like the auto rickshaw drivers from Pune, the taxi drivers in Mumbai would routinely refuse to take me to Sion.

It was the middle of the work week, and three taxis in a row had refused to take me home. The buses were overcrowded, and there was hardly any room to enter them. All of a sudden, a thought crossed my mind, "What if I walked home today?"

It was a spontaneous decision, one that GB would not have approved of. As luck would have it, the skies had opened up that evening. Rains in Mumbai at this time of the year were an anomaly. I could almost visualize GB making an entry, singing, 'November Rain'. The situation caused me to smile. I was walking on the streets of Mumbai in the pouring rain in the month of November. It was a combination of circumstances that otherwise had a low probability of occurring together.

The rains made the walk bearable. The stench that one had to bear while walking on the sidewalks was gone, and the exhaust from the vehicles did not rise up to irritate my nose. Walking allowed me time to think about what was happening with my life.

It was nearly ten in the night by the time I reached home. The rains and the crowded streets had slowed down my pace. I was soaking wet, and there was no food in the house. I took a warm shower and went to bed.

The next morning, I woke up feeling refreshed, as if the rain had washed off the anger and the frustrations that had built within me. For the first time in nearly 18 months, I was beginning to enjoy living in India.

*

The very next day, I went to the bank and made a demand draft for four hundred and fifty thousand Rupees in the name of Indian Institute of Management, Ahmedabad. Then, I went to the post office to mail it. I paused before handing over the envelope containing the draft to the woman behind the counter.

"Go for it. But make sure you have at least thirty-five thousand Rupees set aside," GB's remark surprised me.

"Why?" I asked.

"If you are not able to get the loan to pay the rest of the fees, this money can buy you a one-way ticket to Canada. But I hope you will not have to do that," he disappeared, singing Pink Floyd's 'Another Brick in the Wall'.

There was no question of me going to Toronto. Things were looking up for me. This was Mumbai gone right.

Chapter Twenty One
No Wedding, Only Funerals

"This weekend, you should meet at least two of the shortlisted profiles," Aai told me as she woke me up.

It was a Saturday morning, and I had arrived the night before. Having spent the night on an uncomfortable bed, it had taken me a while to realize where I was. Before I could respond, the phone rang. Aai went to answer it. It was a call from a parent who was anxious to get his daughter married, one of the many calls we had received so far.

"Yes, that's him. Yes, he used to live in the US and works in Mumbai now. No, he does not have any plans of going back." Aai had narrated this story many times recently. All of a sudden, I heard her say, "Hello? Hello?" It occurred to me that the caller had hung up.

"Aai, just forget them," I said to her.

But Aai far from done. That afternoon, she showed me a list of prospects that I was supposed to meet over the next two weeks. It was an interesting mix of profiles.

Varsha, 29, Mumbai, Advertising Specialist

Grishma, 30, Pune, Consultant

Sharda, 28, Mumbai, Doctor

Hema, 29, Mumbai, Chartered Accountant

Vasanti, 28, Bangalore, Banker

Shira, 27, Pune, Biologist

While looking at the list, I said to Aai, "Shira? What kind of name is this? I thought only the Bengalis named their daughters after desserts. I used to know a girl whose name was Mishti. She was a Bengali. By the way, Shira's profile seems familiar, and so does her face. Let me look at her photograph again," I said to Aai.

"Oh! She was born in the winter season, or Shishir Rutu as we call it. That's how she gets her name. She has just returned from the US after completing her PhD," Aai said as I saw the photograph again.

That's when I realized why Shira seemed so familiar. Nearly two years ago, I had flown from Chicago to meet her. Shira was then a PhD student at Johns Hopkins University. Natasha, who knew her, had played the role of a matchmaker. I had borrowed Natasha's car and driven through the pouring rain to Baltimore. I was seated by the window of a Starbucks at a mall, and could see the parking lot getting hammered by the downpour. I had waited for Shira for nearly two hours, but she had never arrived. The next day, she had sent me an email saying that she was not keen on getting married. Her reply was as cold as the cold temperatures that prevail in Shishir Rutu.

"Aai, I do not wish to meet Shira."

"But why?" Aai asked. I told her the reason.

"Okay, but what about the remaining five?"

"Sure, I can meet them Aai. Let's start with Varsha. Interestingly enough, the remaining five also bear the names of five Rutus or seasons." I smiled, wondering whether this was a coincidence.

*

Varsha was copywriter in an advertising agency. Much against my wishes, we met at the Barista on Law College Road on a Sunday morning. In the past one month, I had had contributed more than enough money to India's struggling coffee industry, and wasn't really keen on spending any more time or money all over again.

Varsha had chosen to sit outdoors. Even at nine in the morning, it was hot and humid, and I was uncomfortable.

"So why did you return to India?" Varsha asked me as she lit a cigarette. "Coming back for parents' sake is bullshit."

"Why do you think this is BS?" I asked her back.

"Look, I have friends who have lived abroad for a number of years. None of them have packed their bags and moved back to India. Who wants to leave a comfortable life and return to this hell-hole, unless they are forced out? So tell me Amol, what's your true story?"

I was beginning to lose it by now, but I remembered my promise to Aai that I would spend at least an hour with each of the five women.

"Look Varsha, it was my decision to return to Pune, and it was my choice to stay back. My parents are old and they have not been keeping well. Who else will look after them if I don't?"

She spoke as she blew the smoke in the air, "Look here Mr. NRI, or shall I say former NRI? I repeat. What you just told me is utter BS. NRIs take care of their parents in India by sending money, hiring domestic helps, and calling them once a week. If they feel too guilty, they spend a week or two every year with their parents. It's a trip they want to avoid, because it exhausts their vacation time, and more importantly, their savings. The more desperate ones invite their parents to live with them for a few months, and show them places like Niagara Falls or Buckingham Palace or whatever. I haven't heard of a single person who has returned for their parents."

With these words, she stubbed out her cigarette. Then, in one swift move, she picked up her purse and rose to leave. By now, other patrons had turned their heads in our direction and were beginning to whisper in hushed tones.

The Varsha season is known to be hot and humid, and is also known to bring the heavy monsoon rains. True to the characteristics of this season, Varsha had poured out her thoughts in a deluge of words, but she was not done yet. Before leaving, she asked me, "And by the way, if your parents are so much dependent on you, and if you care for them so much, why did you go to America in the first place?"

Her last words kept echoing in my head as I paid for an uneaten Tiramisu and a half-finished coffee. I asked for the food to be packed, and gave it to the street urchins who were asking for food.

I saw a familiar sign across the street which read, 'Dilip Oak's Academy'. This was a well-known academy which helped students to apply to graduate schools in the USA. As I read the name one more time, my thoughts travelled back in time.

*

"Amol, you should apply to Universities in the US. It will be good for your career," Natasha had called me one morning. It was nearly Diwali time in 1997, and she had just started her PhD program in the United States. "Take the GRE and the TOEFL. I will help you out with the rest of the process," she had told me.

A couple of days later, I was sitting in the *jhoola* in the verandah of the house. Aai had come up to me with a cup of coffee in her hand. "Natasha called again this morning. She wants you to go to the USA. I also think you should go there," Aai had added.

"But Aai, I want to get a MBA here in India," I had replied.

"Amol, your father is retired now, and we cannot afford to pay for your education beyond your bachelor's degree. For MBA, you will have to take a loan. On the other hand, if a US University offers you a scholarship, your education will be free. It's your choice," she had left with those words.

Study for free, or take a loan to learn. Aai's logic was on the money, so to speak. And it was practical advice, too. Working in India as a civil engineer was not really a viable option. Construction companies paid peanuts to civil engineers. In return, one had to work long hours in the heat, and dust for six or even seven days a week.

The long working hours or the harsh work environment did not bother me. I had a problem with the extremely low pay and lack of respect for the work that civil engineers did. A local contractor, Mittal Yamuna, had offered to hire some of my classmates for a salary of three thousand Rupees a month. Computer science or electronics companies paid three times as much. In the caste system of engineering, we civil engineers were the proverbial untouchables.

I had stayed up the whole night thinking: should I go for an MBA in India, or a Masters in the US? Nothing else occupied my mind, not even Pacman or Porn.

"I will apply for my Master's Degree in the US," I had declared over breakfast the next morning.

"What? What about the MBA classes that you are taking for the CAT exam? We just paid the fees for them," the anger in Baba's voice was evident.

"Baba, I will continue taking those classes. I will prepare for the CAT, but take the GRE," my reply had taken him by surprise.

"Are you behind all this?" Baba had asked Aai, and said, "Of course, you are!"

"No Baba, it is my decision. Aai only told me the facts."

*

Why did I go to America in the first place? Because I wanted better career opportunities. I had gone to America because my dream school had offered me a fellowship for my graduate studies. Ten years ago, I had left my parents for the United States because it was the best option at that point in time.

*

I returned home around noon. Aai had made *sabudana khichadi,* a favorite dish in the Dixit household. Baba was sitting at his usual position next to the door that opened into a balcony. He was sitting in a red swivel chair and was reading the newspaper. Aai brought three platefuls of *khichadi and dahi*. We sat around the table when Aai asked me, "So..."

"Aai," I interrupted her, "I am not what she is looking for, and she is not what I am looking for."

"How can you decide in one meeting?" Aai shot back.

"For heaven's sake, please stop it," I protested.

"Varsha came highly recommended. I was told that she is a very well-mannered girl."

"Aai, she is very opinionated, she smokes, swears, and is only interested in living abroad," I said in exasperation.

"Sounds very much like you," Baba said, as he put the newspaper away and looked at the food with interest. As he ate the *khichadi,* he said, "It is tasty."

'Tasty' in Baba's definition meant that the *khichadi* contained lots of ghee and peanuts. In other words, it was packed with enough calories that would put a Big Mac with extra cheese to shame.

In the afternoon, Aai approached me with her list again. Of the remaining four, I liked Hema's profile and agreed to meet her next.

*

That evening, my 'Shabri at nine,' SMS to the gang had resulted in three replies in less than five minutes' time: two yes's and one negative. The quorum was complete and the Boys' Night was on.

"Why do you go every weekend to that place? You should stay home. Have dinner with us," Aai said to me as I was getting ready to leave.

"Aai, it is my only social activity in Pune. It is my only escape from this life," I said angrily.

"I don't want you to go. Anyway, you need to stop all this since you will be getting married soon. Learn to spend some time home, get domesticated," she tried to reason with me.

"You mean castrated?" I shot back almost immediately.

"What?"

I thought it was wise to tone down. "Never mind. Let me go today, and I will stay home next weekend. You have my word."

"Okay, take care," she said as I stepped out of the house, and went on to tell me something that I couldn't quite hear clearly.

"How did it go with the Ad agency girl?" Nitin asked me as we met. He had offered to drive us to Shabri.

"Bad," I said with a sigh.

"*Arey*, I am in the same situation. Shit happens. Who is next?"

"She's a banker, and I liked her photograph. Not that I consider photographs to be a basis for selection," I replied.

"Good thing, because I found that many of the photos are doctored. One girl's parents had sent a black and white photo of their daughter. But in real life, she looked like the X-ray version of her own photo. In fact, had her parents sent a negative of her photograph, the effect would have been the same," Nitin said with a smile.

"That is really funny," I said to him.

Nitin continued, "There is more. On one hand, some of the photographs ca be best termed as *Horrorscopes*, they are that scary. On the other hand, there have been photos that give the girl's assets more credit than they deserve. And once, I got a photo that only had the girl's headshot. She had a pretty face, but had the body of a pachyderm."

"This is nothing," I said to Nitin, "I experienced the ultimate case of conning. The girl's parents had sent the photograph of their younger daughter, who was much prettier than her older sibling. They had used the younger daughter's photo as bait to catch unsuspecting families. And of course, Aai had fallen prey. I told Aai that I was willing to consider the proposal only if it was a buy one, get one free offer, that is, I get to marry both the sisters," I said with a grin.

Once we reached Shabri, the discussion turned to how often married men have sex with their wives. As the discussion started picking up, Shashi ordered the *Surmai*. He had taken it upon himself to convert us into fans of this fish.

When the *Surmai* arrived, Shashi's face lit up. "You only need to figure out if she has enough in her to meet your quota of two thousand," he said while admiring the fish.

"Quota of two thousand?" Nitin sounded surprised.

"The number of times a married couple has sex with each other. That is the magic number, if we go by Lalit's theory," Shashi said.

"Lalit, please explain," Nitin pleaded.

"There was a time when I was reading this book called *Garbhasamhita*. It tells you when a man and woman should and should not have sex if they want a child who is smart, well behaved, etc. This book also mentions that there are a handful of such days in one year when a man and a woman should have sex if they are planning to have a baby," he replied as he savored the *Surmai*.

"Lalit, a man's objective is to maximize the number of intercourses that he can have every year. What you are telling me is exactly the opposite," I sounded frustrated. By now, my dry spell had run into years and not just months. I was a starving sex camel by now.

"Let him finish, Amol," Shashi interrupted.

Lalit spoke again, "That got me thinking: do people in other cultures also have similar beliefs? That's when I came across an interesting survey. It said that on an average, a married couple in India has sex two times a week. That would make it 100 times a year. Now that's a lot, trust me. But this number also varies with age. In their twenties, a couple may have sex three to four times a week. So if a man gets married when he is 25 years old, he is likely to have around one thousand intercourses by the time he is 30. In his 30's, with kids and all, the number goes down to maximum twice a week. That's one thousand more encounters by the age of 40."

At this point, Lalit paused, took a sip from his glass of Old Monk, and continued, "After 40, every single one is a bonus. And just like the bonus you get at work, this one is also a hit or a miss. So that's your quota of two thousand. And that's a very, very ambitious," he said with a sigh.

Nitin looked morose, and said, "Nobody I know has ever analyzed this subject using such prolific logic. I am nearing my mid-30's, and if Lalit's theory is right, I will be forced to survive on mere bonuses in a few years' time." I realized that my situation was no different.

It was past midnight when Nitin dropped me home. He had just left when I recalled what Aai's was trying to tell me. I had forgotten to take the keys to the house. My first thought was to ring the doorbell, but that would have woken up Baba. I tried calling Aai on her cell phone, but she did not answer. In a sheer act of desperation, I rang the doorbell. Not once, not twice, but three times. Each time, the door remained closed.

"Can I stay at your place tonight? I've been locked out," I said to Nitin over the phone.

"You are what? Anyway, you are welcome to come over, but I am taking a dump right now. If you start walking, it will take you about ten minutes to reach my place," he replied.

Half-an-hour later, I reached Nitin's house. "You took your time getting here," he remarked as he opened the door.

"It's is dark and I kind of got lost. Hey, where's your couch?"

"I forgot to tell you. I sold it last week," Nitin replied.

"So where am I going to sleep?"

"I have the bathtub, or you can sleep on the floor," he suggested.

The next morning, I woke up with a sprained neck and a stiff back. The bathtub was not a comfortable place to sleep, and it made my bus ride to Mumbai even more uncomfortable. As the bus reached the expressway, I wrote to Hema and suggested that we should meet on Saturday over lunch.

"Ok, lets' meet at High Street Phoenix at 1 PM," she wrote back.

*

High Street Phoenix is an upmarket mall in Lower Parel, and is a part of large redevelopment project, under which old factories were torn down to make multi-million dollar homes and fancy offices. I agreed to meet Hema there because it was a few minutes' walk from KMM's office.

We met at a small Italian restaurant and were seated at a quiet, secluded corner. The setting reminded me of the restaurant in Chicago where Nandini and I had once met over dinner. However, I learnt in a little while that the food in Chicago was twice as tasty and half as expensive. But I was not meeting Hema to enjoy a meal.

I was quite taken by her. She had large brown eyes, long hair, and had good assets.

"A CA with good assets!" I thought to myself.

"Hey," Hema said to me, "why are you smiling?"

"You ordered Penne. That's my favorite," I lied.

"Ok. So our mothers spoke yesterday. I understand that you will be going for your MBA next year," she ignored my small talk and set the tone for our meeting.

I made a mental note to talk to Aai more often. It would have been beneficial to know what she had discussed with Hema's mother. Not that I had anything to hide, but mothers are known to say things about their sons that can sometimes get the sons into trouble.

"Amol, I am talking to you," Hema's words brought me back to the present.

"Sorry, I was trying to think," I replied.

"Trying to think?"

"Never mind. Yes, I will be going to IIM Ahmedabad for a year, starting April," I asserted.

"Great. So will you be taking a sabbatical from work?"

"No, I will quit my job in March."

"So who will pay for the expenses while you will be studying?"

"I have some savings to pull me through," I told her candidly.

"And what about the fees?"

"I have paid the first installment from my savings. For the rest, I will have to get a loan. And I think that the questions are getting too personal. I don't mind giving you the details, but let's get to know each other first." It was time for me to take charge of the conversation.

"Amol, your mother also told my mom that you gave up your MBA plans in Canada, and now you are going to IIM Ahmedabad."

"That is correct. The school in Canada had offered me a fellowship, and I had even paid my commitment fees to them. But I decided to stay back."

"And you let go of the money?" Hema was astounded.

"Yes," I replied.

"And now you are taking a loan because you are broke?"

"I don't like to discuss my financial situation in the first meeting itself."

I felt that our conversation was heading down a slippery path.

"Look Amol, if you take a student loan, it will take you three to four years to pay it off. That is assuming that you will get a job right after your MBA, and we will talk about that later. Let us also assume that there will not be any emergencies like any hospitalizations during this period." Hema paused to catch a breath.

"Correct" I replied.

"In other words, you will have to depend on your spouse's income till then." Her assumption was misplaced, even though it was based on facts that might have led her to make this assumption in the first place.

"Not quite." I replied, not sure where she was going with this.

"So where do you plan to work after your MBA?"

"Most likely in India," I replied, and wondered whether I really wanted to work in India, having experiencing one shock after another.

"Good, because I have no plans of leaving India. And what happens to your Canadian Residency if you do not go back?"

"It will lapse if I do not go back in time, or they may cancel it."

"It must have cost you some money to get a PR card. I have also heard it's not easy to get one," Hema's questioning continued.

I had guessed her next question and pre-empted it with my

answer. "Yes, and it cost me Eight thousand Dollars to be precise."

"Do you know that you have let a lot of money go waste?"

"That's one way of looking at it. However, my take is that I got to spend time with my parents and now the doctors are of the opinion that their health has improved. I would say that's money well spent. In fact, the medical bills could have cost me much more than the money I lost." If Hema's questions were pointed and direct, I thought my replies were based on facts and to the point.

I was impressed with Hema so far. She was not only sharp as a razor blade, but also was good with numbers, clear in her thoughts, and not afraid to ask tough questions. Had this been a job interview, I would have hired her right away. But that was not the case, and it was time to end our meeting soon.

"I do not agree with your thoughts...but let us assume you know what you are doing," she continued, "so tell me Amol, what would you like to do after your MBA?"

Hema's question broke my chain of thoughts again. This was turning out to be a rather one-sided discussion. She was asking me about my past, present and future, but in return, she was hardly telling me anything about herself. I looked again at Hema. She had a piercing gaze, and she was looking into my eyes. This was another plus in my book, but I had concluded by now that this was the first and the last time I would be meeting her.

I took a deep breath and replied, "I would like to get into real estate finance. I have worked in construction, so it seems like a logical choice. Some of my friends in the US have done so recently."

"You mean raising debt, entering into joint development

agreements, and the likes? Sounds interesting, I am guessing you have done all of this before" her gaze pierced me some more.

I had no idea what she had just said, and replied, "No, I haven't."

"Look Amol, I liked your profile, and also enjoyed talking to you. While I may not agree with what you have done so far, I think you are an honest guy," her words were a hint as to what was coming next.

"But with your MBA plans...I am not sure if I want to make a commitment just yet. If you get into real estate finance, let's talk again. Don't get me wrong, but I don't want to be a party to my husband's financial woes." With those words, she left the restaurant.

Even before I was able to ask her a single question, our meeting had ended. I had hoped that Hema's nature would be as pleasant as the season after which she was named, but that was not to be. The CA with good assets had given me the boot because she thought that I was a liability.

Hema's parting words reminded me of what Nandini had said to me in Goa, "... *if you are back in Canada, let us see if we can start our relationship all over again. Till then, let us cool it off.*"

"Let her go, you will find someone who will accept you for what you are, and the way you are. Let us see what the next one has to say," GB was wearing a maroon gown and he resembled a monk.

*

Grishma's mother had first approached us with the proposal a couple of days after I had started working with DCSD. Her email was simple and straightforward.

"Dear Mr. and Mrs. Dixit,

I am writing regarding my daughter, Grishma. I am looking

for a suitable alliance for her, and I thought it would be good if we can talk over the phone this week.

Regards,

Charulata Phatak."

Aai was impressed. "She seems like a good lady."

"Aai, I am not looking to marry the mother," I said in an effort to prevent her from saying anything further.

"*Arey,* one can get an idea about the girl by knowing her parents." If what Aai had told me was valid, then I was sure that the opposite must also be true: the girl's family could judge me by looking at Aai and Baba. I made a mental note of it. In particular, I had to remind Aai and Baba not to talk too much about my decision to stay back and my MBA plans. Not because I had anything to hide, but the conversations would almost always turn into tales of NRI children leaving their parents to fend for themselves. The topic may have been relevant, but the setting was not.

Grishma could be described in one word: Hot. She was as hot as the simmering temperatures one experiences in summertime.

Grishma and her mother visited our home in the middle of November. Something seemed odd about the duo, but I could not figure it out. As usual, Aai had to do all the running around in the kitchen. She prepared the tea and served it with biscuits and *chaklis.* And as usual, I got up to help Aai, even though I had been warned by her not to do so. I knew that she would give me an earful afterwards.

The mother and daughter duo did not even bother to ask if they could help, not even as a courtesy. They were comfortably settled on the sofa, and they remained seated for nearly two hours.

"She is a nice girl," Aai said once they had left, "but I did not like your coming into the kitchen and help me in serving them. It gives a bad impression in front of the girl's family. And after marriage, she will expect you to do all the household work."

"Whatever," I shot back.

Aai's concern did not make any sense. When I was a teenager, my parents took pride in telling everyone that they had made no distinction between their son and daughter while raising us. If Natasha was expected to set the dinner table, I was required to clean up. If she did the laundry, it was my job to fold the clothes and get them ironed. I had hated doing these tasks, but these skills had helped me survive in the United States. As a single guy, I already knew cooking; and other household chores were a second habit. That would have made me a prized possession as a husband, or a domestic help, or both. But in India, it was still considered unmanly to do these tasks.

Aai was so keen that I make a macho impression that she had forgotten her own teachings. Well, it was just too bad. Grishma and her mother were not worth any charade.

The next day, I was rather surprised to receive a SMS from Grishma around noon. It was a one-liner with no pleasantries, and it simply read, "Can we meet this afternoon for coffee?"

My reply was equally bland. "Okay. Let us meet around 4 PM at the Barista on Law College Road."

That venue had proven to be unlucky for me so far, but it was close to where I lived. More importantly, I could find parking. The coffee shop where we were going to meet was located in an area that was once green and quiet. It is a nice neighborhood even today by any standards, though the maze of concrete buildings and the traffic on the road had damaged, if not destroyed, its beauty.

In contrast, going to the Barista on Fergusson College Road was a disaster. The road was half dug-up at any given time of the year, and the store manager had a habit of turning off the air-conditioning in order to save costs. My experience in that store was never pleasant.

I left my house at three-thirty and parked my car in one of the by lanes of Law College Road. This lane goes up a hill and is shaded with trees. There are houses on one side of the lane and a boundary wall on the other. On the other side of the boundary wall is the Film and Television Institute of India.

*

As I entered the coffee shop, the hostess looked at me and smiled. She was on duty when I had met Varsha a week ago. I chose to sit in a corner. It was a cozy place, with seating for two, and an adjacent glass window provided just the perfect amount of lighting.

Grishma arrived at 4:15 PM. "Hi," she said, "my meditation session lasted longer than I thought."

"Great. So you practice meditation?"

"Yes, among other things. In fact, that is why I wanted to meet you. I have seen your horoscope, and I noticed that you have taken some steps recently that will bring big changes to your life."

"You can find that out from my horoscope?"

"Yes, and that's not all. My mother and I are psychics, and experts in *Vastu Shastra*, or the science of building construction. Both of us felt that your house is not a good place to live. But that is a different matter. Let us talk about you first," she said as she sat in the chair opposite to mine.

"What do you want to know about me?" I asked her. By now, I was tired of one way conversations in which I was quizzed left, right and center. However, I decided to play along because Grishma had been struck off my list the day before, so there was nothing to lose.

"You have done something that will bring a lot of changes and uncertainty into your life. Is that true?"

"Well, I started my new job recently, and will be going to business school in April."

"Yes, that's the one, Amol," she said, giving me a strange look. "I do not like the idea of too many changes in my life. So, I am going to have to say no to you. Hope that's okay."

"It's cool, thanks for telling me," I began to rise from my chair.

But Grishma waved her hand at me and said, "Wait. I may not be interested in you, but we can spend some time together. Can you eat *thele wala* food?"

"Sure, street food is okay with me," I said, and wondered why I had answered her in the affirmative.

"Great. There is a great *pani-puri* stall not too far from here. Do you mind if we go and eat there?"

I was about to refuse, but GB advised, "You have a chance to get introduced to a new joint. If the place is really good, then you can take your fiancé there. Chicks dig junk food, particularly *pani-puri*. You will score some brownie points with her. Go try out the street food."

Ten minutes later, I had parked my car near the *thele wala*. Grishma was right. The food *was* very tasty. But why on earth had I agreed to come to this place?

Grishma began her monologue while we were eating. "By the way, I am seeing someone these days. He is a smart, independent guy and has a steady job. We have a movie date in an hour's time."

I simply nodded in response and began to wonder why I was spending my time and money on her.

Almost immediately, GB's voice echoed in my ears, "Look at the rate at which she is eating. You would have gone broke paying for all the food that she would eat, and then the medical bills that would eventually follow. Hundred Rupees is a small price to pay for learning this about her. Treat it as alimony for a marriage that never happened."

It was nearly 6 PM by the time I reached home.

"How did it go?" Aai asked after I had showered and changed.

"Negative," I replied.

After the first ten 'negatives', Aai had learnt by now not to ask me too many questions. But then, I surprised her by saying, "Grishma is a psychic, and so is her mother."

"Really? Did she tell you that?"

"Yes," I replied with a smile.

"She is a smart girl. A physicist and a psychic," Aai said.

"Grishma is not a physicist, Aai. She is a tax consultant or something."

But Aai was adamant as ever. "No, it is written in her profile. Wait a minute; I will show you."

There is a phrase in Hindi called *'Mere murge ki ek hi taang'*. It is based on a story in which a stubborn person keeps insisting that his rooster has only one leg, even though both the legs of that bird are perfectly okay. Aai had a habit of insisting that her point was always right, and Baba would make fun of her by quoting this phrase every now and then.

Aai brought Grishma's profile and we both read it together. The first few lines had the usual details like her education and family background, but the second paragraph proved my point.

'I am learning to read horoscopes and I am a psychic.'

"Look Aai, here it is. Read what she has written. It is time we got you new glasses..." I said to Aai, who conveniently ignored my remark.

That night, the Boys, all five of us, met after a long time. They listened attentively as I narrated the Grishma episode to them.

Mandar spoke first, "Good for you that she said no. Look, had you been married to her, she would have said, 'Your horoscope says you will not get an erection, so no sex for you tonight'."

Lalit added, "Or better still, 'I will marry you but will have sex with another guy'. Something like the *pani- puri*. You paid for her food, while the other guy got to feel her up at the movies."

Not to be left alone, Nitin added to the comments that I had to face that night. "She would have turned you into a monkey. She is a Psychic who reads horoscopes. Who knows, she may have been a *tantric* too,"

"Women want a man who can stand up for himself. And then they turn the man's life into a stand-up comedy act," Mandar added, stroking his chin reflectively.

"Ignore them, Amol," Shashi said, and continued, "this is nothing compared to our man Mandar here."

Mandar gulped down his drink, took a deep breath, and spoke:

"There was this girl I met in a bookstore. We dated a few times. I had really liked her. *Lekin...*"

"What happened?" Nitin was equally intrigued.

"One day, she took me to meet her father. He offered me a drink, and then led me to his office. He was a psychiatrist, and he made me undergo a series of tests," Mandar looked pensive as he spoke.

"You agreed to all this?" I asked, surprised.

"Look, Lord Ram had to pick up a very heavy bow and Arjun had to show his archery skills in order to win the hearts of the women they wished to marry. I think Mandar had it quite easy," Lalit remarked.

Mandar ignored our comments and continued, "As each test progressed, her father's reaction changed from surprise, to shock, and finally one of disgust. Nearly an hour later, he finally said, 'My daughter should not marry somebody who changes his decisions every now and then, and definitely not someone who would like to have anal sex. The tests show that you fantasize it. Let me tell you it is not only a taboo in India, but is also illegal.' It was embarrassing," Mandar confessed.

"He actually said that to you?" Nitin couldn't control his laughter as he asked this question.

Lalit said something that evoked our curiosity even more. "Our man Shashi had a fantasy during his bachelor days. He wanted to screw at least one girl from each continent. His conquests included a

Polish, Vietnamese, Egyptian, US and Mexican woman. He was turning into a one night stand champion," he said while observing the looks on our face.

"Leila was Algerian, not Egyptian," Shashi corrected him.

But Lalit was unperturbed. *"Southern Hemisphere baki tha, lekin uski gaadi equator par aa kar ruk gayee."*

We all had a good laugh at Shashi's expense.

"Yeah, right! Had I not been married, I would have met my goal," Shashi's words nearly died in the cacophony.

At this point, Lalit signaled to the waiter, who arrived at our table. It had become our tradition of sorts to ask the waiter to get the bill, and bring a bottle of Old Monk along with it.

The waiter soon arrived with the bill and our final order of drinks. Nitin shook his head and said, "Many people have skeletons in their closets, but you guys have an entire graveyard."

*

I wrote down on the results of my search for the elusive bride upon returning home that night. Over the past several weeks, we had received over 30 proposals, and I had met 24 of them. Almost all of them lived in either Pune or Mumbai. Out of these, I had been rejected by 20, whereas I had said no to the rest. The remaining six had either not followed up, or had decided that I was not worth pursuing.

The pipeline for the coming days looked very weak. "Things are not looking good," I said to myself before going to bed.

That night, I dreamt that I was back in Chicago, and was meeting countless women through dating sites. I was able to score with many of them, and my CPS ratio was fantastic. And then all of a sudden, I saw an old man who was shouting, "No anal sex, it is illegal."

My dream had resulted in the right kind of reaction between my legs. I thought to myself, "there was no traction on the ladies' front, which meant that I was not getting any action, so what was the use of this reaction?"

The next day, I met two more jewels from the list. The meeting with Sharda happened over coffee, and I met Vasanti over dinner

*

Sharda was a doctor. She had recently completed her MD and was working at Sion hospital. Even though we both lived in the same neighborhood in Mumbai, we ended up meeting in Pune.

She seemed like the female version of Gyaani Baba, but with a much better dressing sense. More importantly, she did not have a beard. As we got talking, she told me that she was also handling the marriage proposals for her sister, her younger brother, and a cousin. In short, she was running her own mini-marriage bureau.

"Ask her if she plans on making all the four weddings happen on the same day; she can get a good discount!" GB commented.

As Sharda and I got talking, she opened up to me. "Amol, I come from a middle-class family, and I do not earn much as a doctor because I work at a government hospital. I want to marry a very rich man. You see, I have dreams. I want to travel abroad, go shopping, and drive around Mumbai in a BMW."

I was tempted to tell her that brains alone would not help her in achieving those dreams. The necessary and often the sufficient condition to impress a rich man was that the woman should possess beauty, stunning beauty. Somehow, she was not quite up to the mark on that front. I thought that it was better to let nature take its own course and chose to keep quiet. Moreover, I had no right to comment on how others looked when I was myself so out of shape.

One never knew, she might just be one of the lucky ones and find Mr. Moneybags who would fulfill her dreams. Sharda was a gold-digger but at least she was honest to admit it. And her goal in life was clear, just like the clear skies that are a characteristic of Sharad Rutu.

*

That evening, Aai, Baba and I met Vasanti Deshmukh and her family over dinner. Malacca Spice in Koregaon Park has a good ambience, and the food is palatable. We had agreed to meet the Deshmukhs at 7 PM. By now, I was tired of reaching on time and waiting for others to show up, and decided not to ask Aai and Baba to hurry. As a result, they took a long time to get ready, and we left at quarter to seven. We reached the venue an hour late. The Deshmukhs were relieved to see us. They were based in Bangalore. Mr. Deshmukh was an executive with an automobile company and his wife was a principal in a school.

"We are a small, closely knit family. We believe in honesty, and have no secrets between us. Honesty is valued in our house," Vasanti's mother told Aai.

I learnt that Vasanti had recently been transferred to Pune. Even though she worked in her bank's IT department, her profile noted that she was a banker. This seemed odd to me, very odd.

Vasanti and I soon moved to a different table so that we could talk. Vasanti had a pleasant smile, and she seemed to have very high energy. Compared to the cold and dry nature of the women I had met so far, Vasanti's nature seemed to do justice to her name; after all,

Vasant Rutu means spring season.

Before I could even look at the menu, Vasanti said to me, "Amol, I am getting an opportunity to travel to the UK for work. Because of this marriage business, I have been saying no to such chances so far. But the job market is tight, and I have no choice but to say yes to my manager. Therefore, I will not be able to go further with our proposal. And please, do not tell this reason to my mother. She would throw a fit if learnt what I told you just now."

I wondered whether her disclosure fell in the honesty category, or the in errors & omissions section of the Deshmukhs' Charter of Family Values. The claim made by Vasanti's mother of not keeping any secrets within the family seemed like a farce.

"Sure, no problem," I said after a pause, and continued, "You can tell them that I wasn't interested."

"That would be great, thanks. But reason shall I give to them?"

"You can tell them that I am planning to move to Toronto next year, and that I expect my wife to shovel two feet of snow without complaining," I replied nonchalantly.

"You really mean it? I mean moving Toronto?" she asked.

"Yes and the shoveling of snow part also," I remarked.

Over the next two hours, I told the Deshmukhs all the things that they wanted to hear, and avoided any discussion on my career plans in India. I could see that they were impressed.

*

That night, Baba and I were looking at some of his emails, we received a message from the Deshmukhs:

"Dear Mr. Dixit,

We very much liked meeting you and our daughter has liked your son. We would like to proceed further in this matter.

Vishwas Deshmukh."

After Baba had gone to sleep, I replied to that message:

"Dear Mr. Deshmukh,

Thank you for your mail and the kind invitation to dinner. We liked meeting you also however, when we matched the horoscopes of our son and your daughter, we found that only 12 out of the 36 *guns* are matching. Therefore we will not be able to proceed further. Please accept our apologies. We wish your daughter all the best.

Sincerely,

Dixits."

When I hit the send button for the email, I had mixed emotions. First, I was elated. It was the kind of rush one gets when they score a strike on the very first ball while bowling. But almost immediately, I was angry. The Deshmukhs lived in a world of lies and deceit, and yet they preached honesty and claimed that they believed in nurturing family values. I also felt guilty because I had written the mail pretending to be Baba, and not sought his permission before doing so. And I had deceitfully used horoscopes as a reason to reject Vasanti. In a way, I had insulted my newfound knowledge.

The next morning, when I told Aai and Baba about my email to the Deshmukhs, Aai came to Vasanti's defense right away. "*Arey*, for a woman it is a very difficult decision; whether to choose career or family life. But you should have told us before writing to them."

"Aai, my bus leaves in half-an-hour and I need to leave. By the way, that's the end of your list for this marriage business," I declared.

Just as I was about to leave, Baba said, "Amol, we should receive an email from a family who lives Vadodara. The girl's father had called me yesterday. He had seen your profile in Mohini and asked me to send your photograph. When you reach Mumbai, send your details."

"Ok Baba," I said, "but this is the absolute last."

That morning, as the Metro Link bus left Paud Road and was on its way to the expressway, it got stuck in a traffic jam. A truck and a car had met with an accident a little ahead of Chandni Chowk. While we were waiting for the bus to start moving again, I looked around. A young woman who was seated across the aisle was reading a book. Its cover read, "Many Lives, Many Masters." Curious, I enquired about the book.

She asked me, "Have you heard about Dr. Brian Weiss?"

I replied in the negative. She went on to tell me about soulmates, rebirth, and how two souls are related to each other across births. "You may not believe any of this, but it is true. When I met my husband, I felt that I had known him forever. When you will find your soulmate, you will feel the same."

"Thanks," I said as she went back to hear reading. As I closed my eyes, GB gave his two cents, "Don't worry; it will all change once you meet your soulmate."

I knew that six weeks is a very short a time to find the right person you want to spend the rest of your life with. It was no surprise that my vain attempts to find a bride had resulted in no wedding, only funerals.

Chapter Twenty Two
The Benefactor

Lalit, Shashi and I were discussing expectations life at our usual hangout one evening. I had just started working with DCDS. Before we parted ways, Shashi said to me, "You find it difficult to accept what is going around you. For me, my family and my kids matter the most right now. I don't care if my career has hit a plateau, this is just a phase. Except for Delaware, I have never worried about my future. You, on the other hand, always want to keep reinventing the wheel."

"Amen to that," Lalit added.

On my way back home, Shashi's words echoed in my head: *"Except for Delaware..."*

On a cold, snowy day in February 2004, Shashi and I were driving down Interstate 95 from Connecticut to Delaware to meet a friend. Shashi looked worried. His application for a Green Card had been stuck for the past few years and nobody knew how long the process would take. In the meantime, Shalu aunty was by herself in Pune. Shashi wanted her to stay with him. He had recently been offered a job in Austin, Texas, and he was thinking of moving there. He also wanted to buy a house and also get married. I had thought that he was crazy because he had wanted it all.

"As you can see, I have five problems," Shashi had told me.

"Looks like you only have one question that you need to answer," I had replied once he had finished narrating his tale of woes.

"Why only one? And what is the question?"

"Tell me, what is your biggest worry right now?"

"My mother. She is nearing seventy and she lives alone in Pune. Her visa application keeps getting rejected. It is strange, considering that she has visited me four times already."

That's when I had asked him, "So why don't you move to India? As an IT man, you are in the right industry at the right time."

"What about my Green Card?"

"You can't have it all, right?'

Shashi had sat quietly for a while, and had said, "And there is no need to buy a house if I am not going to live here."

"Exactly," I was glad that Shashi was beginning to see my point.

"And moving to India means a new job, which can happen with or without my current company. As for marriage, without a Green Card, the women here are not interested. Once I get it, the women back in India will not be interested. I can always drop the Green Card application, go back to India, get a new job, and get married. And I already own a house in Pune. It's deal!" Shashi had said excitedly.

It was the first and the only time that Shashi had opened up to me and asked for my advice. A year after our conversation, he had moved back to India. Six months later, he was married.

*

That weekend, Aai once again came up with a list of reasons as to why I should focus on getting married. I wondered why she had always objected to my preference for a management degree.

"Where will you get the rest of the money from Amol," she kept asking me that morning.

"It does not matter right now, Aai. I have already paid the commitment fees, and will figure out about the rest of the money. Of course I will apply for a loan, and this time around I have no plans of letting my efforts go waste," I asserted.

While we were engaged in this heated discussion, the doorbell rang. Joshi kaka was at the door. Madhukar Joshi was like family. He was also my childhood friend, it was something he liked to tell others with pride.

I was five years old when I had asked him, "Are you my friend?"

"Yes," he had replied with a smile. He was fifty years old then.

Joshi Kaka lived in Karvenagar with his wife and grandchild, and he used to stop by at our house often to meet Baba. Even though he was nearly eighty, he liked to walk everywhere he went. It must have taken him nearly an hour to reach our house, and his face indicated that he was exhausted.

Sensing the tension in the air, he asked, "I am sorry. Did I come at a wrong time?"

"Joshi Saheb, you are always welcome here." Baba told him.

"*Namaskar* Kaka," I said with a smile.

Aai went to the kitchen to make tea. Joshi Kaka hailed from Vidarbha in central India, just like we did. In Vidarbha, it is mandatory to offer tea to a guest irrespective of the time of the day. And that included lunchtime, as was the case now.

"So what's new, my young friend?" Joshi Kaka asked me.

"Kaka, I have received an offer for MBA from IIM Ahmedabad."

"So that explains all the ruckus I could hear outside. Congratulations! You must be excited," he remarked.

"Absolutely! The program starts around mid- April. I am looking forward to it, but…"

"Amol should be getting married and not studying. That too, when he does not have the money to pay the fees," Aai interrupted.

Baba stopped her from speaking further. "I also think that he should go there. Most of the fees will be paid by taking a loan, but we are worried about the next installment," he added.

"How much money are we talking about?" Joshi Kaka asked me.

"Five lakh Rupees," I replied. At fifty Rupees per dollar, Five hundred thousand Rupees amounted to ten thousand Dollars. It was the exact amount I had let go of last year. I quickly shrugged off any thoughts of regret.

"I will give you the money," Joshi Kaka said calmly as he finished his tea. "Come to my house tomorrow, I will write you a cheque. Your Kaku would also be pleased to hear what you told me. Had I known that you needed the money, I would have brought my cheque book with me."

"Kaka, I don't know when I would be able to repay," I told him.

"Don't worry about it right now. We will talk about it tomorrow," he said as he left.

The next day, I went to Joshi Kaka's home. The cheque was ready, and Kaka wished me luck as he handed it to me. There was no contract, no agreement that I was required to sign.

"Kaka, should I give you a receipt or something?" I asked.

"Shut up and deposit the cheque. Nobody before you had asked me if I was their friend. I will always remember that. Your parents have raised you well, and I know you will not let me down. And you can pay Vibhu if we are not around," Joshi Kaka remarked.

Kaka had lost his daughter and son-in-law in a car accident three years ago. Vaibhav, who was affectionately called Vibhu, was the sole survivor. He had lived with his grandparents ever since.

That night, GB appeared in a jolly mood. He was singing an old ABBA song: "Money, Money, Money... it's so funny..."

"What's with the song?" I asked him.

"You should be happy. You got rewarded for your good deed today. Someone has rightly said: Whatever you give to others comes back to you a thousand fold," GB said as he put the guitar away.

"What good deed?"

"Remember money you gave to Santosh, the library assistant? Your act had been repaid. Now don't start thinking that you had given him a gift, whereas this is a loan. It's your good deed that has come back to help you. The money is just a medium to make it happen," he remarked.

If what GB had said was true, then life was a zero sum game of good deeds. I was once a benefactor and today, another benefactor had come to my aid.

Chapter Twenty Three
Goofball

I had just about had it with the entire business of getting married when Baba called me early in the morning one day.

"Amol, why have you not sent your profile and photo to the girl from Vadodara? Her father called me again this morning. I had to apologize to him. This is not good. Send that mail right now," he was upset, and rightfully so. I had no choice but to comply.

Two days later, I saw a message which read, "Dear Mr. Diskit, we have not received your son's details. Kindly send the same at the earliest."

I was aggravated. It was not my problem if they had not received my mail. I was also irritated that they had mis-spelt our family name. Diskit is a town in Ladakh and is known for a Buddhist Monastery, while our family name was spelt Dixit. Didn't they know the difference? It seemed like a hurriedly written mail by a man who was eager to get his daughter married. I simply forwarded the previous email and asked for her phone number. I wanted to talk because I was tired of emails. A phone call from me would end this charade once and for all.

To my surprise, I received a reply the next day, and along with it, a phone number. The email said that I could talk to her the following Tuesday. Was it that small town girls were more approachable and their parents more open minded?

I promptly called up Baba. "We have received their mail."

Half-an-hour later, Baba called me back. "I just spoke to her father and confirmed that we have received their mail. I like her profile and photograph. Call her next week as they have mentioned."

*

The second Tuesday of November 2009 began as any other day of my life back then. Work had ended by 6 PM, and I was home an hour later. Today, I was supposed to call the girl from Vadodara.

Around 9 PM, I sent her a SMS and asked "Can we talk at 10?"

In the days gone by, I would have called her right away. 10 PM was rather late in the night to call an unknown person. SMS or a text message was not my preferred method of reaching out to someone, but in India, people live and die by SMS, and when in Rome…

I received a message from an unknown number a few minutes later. "Hi, this is Mala. I am sending this message from a different number. 10 PM is okay with me."

"Who was Mala? I had texted Manjiri," I said to myself. Unable to figure out who the sender was, I wrote back, "Who is this?"

"You just sent me a message asking if we could talk at 10 PM," came the reply.

"Very funny," I wrote again.

A minute later, my phone rang. "Hi, this is Mala. I called you to clear the confusion. I am sorry, the message was sent from my other number. Talk to you at ten."

It was I who should have apologized. Her name was not Manjiri, it was Mala. Aai in her usual style had confidently told me the wrong name. But I was no different, and did not correct her name in my phone's address book. I realized this when I called her at 10 P M.

"Hi, this is Amol…"

Two-and-a-half-hours later, I hung up the phone. I had a smile on my face as I went to bed. That night, I slept soundly for the first time in weeks. I slept like a baby for the next several days as we followed this routine every night. Soon, I had used up all of my free talk time minutes and my telephone bill had run into five figures.

Things were on cruise control when Mala asked me towards the end of November: "So, when do we meet?"

*

Her question was a googly, and it was so well-bowled that Shane Warne would have been impressed.

"Maybe next week? We are trying to bid for a project in Vadodara. The Wah Re Wah Electrical Company is expanding their factory. I am sure you must have heard of them," I replied.

"Didn't they just get acquired last week? Are you coming in relation to that?"

My jaw dropped when I heard Mala's words. If the company had indeed been acquired, then the expansion of the factory could be put on hold, which meant that I would not get to travel to Vadodara. Not that I was looking forward to meeting Mala.

GB appeared that night and said, "You, my boy, are an idiot. You have chased skirt, and gone after dead-end relationships, but now you are dragging your feet when you are likely to meet someone who has potential. What is wrong with you?"

The next day, I told Raghuram about the acquisition. Somehow, both of us had missed the story.

"If they are getting acquired, then how can we bid on the project?" Raghuram's words echoed my thoughts. He picked up the phone and called up Murugan, Wah Re Wah's project manager.

"I can assure that there is no such hold on the project," Murugan told Raghuram. Half an hour later, he wrote back:

"Dear Mr. Raghuram,

Due to some recent developments, we are extremely sorry to inform you that the factory expansion project has been put on hold. We regret the inconvenience and we will get back to you as soon as possible. Thank you for your interest in our project."

*

"So, the Vadodara trip is cancelled?" Mala asked me that night.

"I guess so," I replied.

"Can't you come just to meet me? We have been talking for quite some time now. We should meet." She insisted.

I had a rule that the guy should always travel to meet the girl. But by now I was tired of spending time, money and efforts on meeting women. Mala sounded like a nice person, but it did not mean that things would work if I were to travel all the way to meet her.

As far as I was concerned, this was going to be another dead-ender. I would travel to meet her, she would ask me about my life in the US and life in India, her parents would learn about my business school plans, and that would be the end of the story.

"Don't even think about saying no to her just yet. You two most certainly need to meet. If you do not want to go to Vadodara, ask her if she can travel to Mumbai," GB advised me.

I ignored hi "Listen Mala, I am not sure about travelling to Vadodara. I am kind of tied up at work..."

"Never mind I asked," Mala said as she hung up the phone.

"Too bad, she sounded like a nice girl," GB remarked.

"She sounded too pushy," I replied angrily.

I received an email from Mala the next day. It was a long message, and I grabbed cup of coffee before settling down to read it.

"Dear Amol,

I have enjoyed our chats and or long phone conversations. I think you are a witty, sensitive, frank person, so different from the others I have met so far."

I knew what was going to follow, and was about to hit the delete button. Mala would have written a long list of reasons why thing would not work out between us. I had heard most of them by now.

"Finish reading the message, and then delete it if you want to," GB ordered, and I continued to read.

"I would like to meet you before I decide about investing more time in us. I am sure you have a valid reason for not wanting to travel, but it does not help the situation. So here is what I am going to do. I will come to Mumbai on December 12th. You are welcome to meet me. If not, I have other plans."

It was crystal clear what the next step was going to be. Mala's mail was a threat and an ultimatum rolled into one. As I finished the coffee, I remembered that I was going to stay back in Mumbai on December 12th because Ashok had invited me to his daughter's wedding. The timing could not have been more convenient.

"Yes, there are reasons why I cannot travel. I will be in Mumbai on the 12th and am looking forward to our meeting," I wrote back.

"Okay then, I will call you on the evening of the 11th to decide the place and time," she replied.

*

In the first week of December, I had to visit Nagpur for my nephew Ramesh's wedding. Aai had cried a great deal when I had called her a day before my trip to Nagpur.

"Ramesh will have a child in a year or two and you will become a grandfather even before you get married. Your grandchildren will be older than your own kids. What's the point of you going to student life again, Amol?"

Almost every other person who was present at the wedding asked me when I was getting married. Out of frustration, I declared that my marriage would be finalized by end of the year. Soon, the barrage of questions began. "How? Where? With whom? "

"You have set a deadline for the biggest decision of your life. But there is a necessary and sufficient condition for this to happen. Where's the girl?" GB asked me.

"I just said that to fend off the crowd," I replied. "By New Year's Day, they would all have forgotten what I had said."

"Be careful of what you wish for, my boy. Hari Aum…"

The Hippie was finally getting Indianized, and I was glad that he was around to help a goofball like me in the process.

Chapter Twenty Four
Soulmate

The Kentucky Fried Chicken outlet on Linking Road in Bandra may or may not be a popular landmark, but it marked a landmark moment in my life. I was supposed to meet Mala near the KFC at 11 AM. I reached there before time, and phone rang a few minutes later.

"It will take me another half an hour. I'm sorry," Mala told me.

"Sure, no problem," I replied. At least she had cared to tell me that she was going to be late. Others had neither informed that they were running late, nor had they apologized for keeping me waiting.

I looked around the area to find a place where we could sit and talk. That's when I noticed a sign on a building across the street, which read "Mumbai Street Café". I had read somewhere that the place had received good reviews.

"How is Mumbai Street Café?" I asked Abhijeet. We had kept in touch and occasionally used to share our woes over a drink or two.

"Haven't been there, but see if it's open during daytime. Some joints in that area operate mainly in the night," he advised.

I asked the staff at the café if they were open for business, and they replied in the affirmative. Ten minutes later, I was back on the by lane that went up to Linking Road.

Almost immediately, my phone rang. It was Abhijeet again. "There is a Chinese restaurant a little farther down the street...."

Right then, my phone beeped. Mala was trying to reach me.

"Listen, I've got to go. That's her on the other line," I said to Abhijeet, and proceeded to accept Mala's call.

"I have reached. Where are you?"

I looked in the direction of KFC. A woman wearing a red kurta was talking over the phone. She had shoulder length hair, and her back was turned towards me.

'I hope that's her,' I prayed.

"I don't see you," Mala said, "I am standing next to the KFC."

GB appeared before my eyes. He was dressed in a tuxedo and was singing, "Lady in Red..." I ignored him. This was not the time to entertain GB's antics.

"I am right behind you," I spoke into the phone excitedly.

She turned around, and said, "Hi, I am Mala,"

"Hi, I am Damol... I mean...Amol Dixit," with those words, I broke into a grin.

"Is there someplace we can sit and talk?"

We proceeded to the Mumbai Street Café. As we sat in a cozy corner in the restaurant, Mala said,

"I've been meaning to ask...you have this grin on your face ever since we met. Is this your normal look, or is this the Trishul effect?"

"No, this is not my normal look. It's my happy look. And by the way, what is the Trishul effect?"

"In the movie Trishul, there is a scene in the film in which Shashi Kapoor meets Hema Malini for the first time. He has the same grin on his face, and then...anyways, it's not relevant."

"So you like movies?" I tried to change the subject and hoped that it would drive her attention away from the silly look on my face.

"Yes, my friends call me the Wikipedia for Hindi movies."

"Interesting. So what kind of movies do you like?"

"I watch romance, sometimes the classics. DDLJ is one of my favorites. I am not much of a Hollywood fan. In fact, I haven't seen too many movies from other parts of the world, but would like to someday, starting with Casablanca."

"A romantic movie lover! Wonder if she is a hopeless romantic," GB said with a smile. I wished he would disappear for the rest of the afternoon. Better still, maybe he could drown in the Arabian Sea and never be found again.

"So what else do you like?" I asked her.

Mala took a deep breath as the hostess came up to our table.

"Good afternoon, Ma'am and Sir. Welcome to Mumbai Street Café. Is this your first time here?"

"Yes," Mala and I replied in unison.

"We can offer you coffee and some light snacks or pizza at this time of the day. Will that be okay?"

I looked at Mala, who nodded. "That should be fine. Can you get two coffees please?" I told the hostess, who smiled and left.

"So where were we?" I asked. "Oh yes, your areas of interest. By the way, how was your journey to Mumbai?"

"I thought you would never ask," she smiled as she spoke. I could feel the bite in her words. If looks could kill, I would have been dead by now. If I were a cat, I would have used up my nine lives.

"The trip was okay. I leave tomorrow evening, and I like to follow what's happening around us. Current affairs, politics…"

"Ah! So what are your thoughts about a separate Telangana state?" I asked, trying to keep her engaged.

Over the next three hours, we had discussed the pros and cons of dividing every state in India. In the process, we had overlooked that the café had not served our coffees or the pizza that we had ordered. We learnt later that both their espresso machine and the oven had gone kaput. The hostess offered us fresh lime soda instead.

As we finished the drink, Mala asked me, "Do you think your spouse should live with you on the campus in Ahmedabad?"

I closed my eyes before replying. GB appeared in front of me again. He was on the rooftop of the Sears Towers and was flying a kite.

"Ladki dheel de rahi hai," he said to me and winked. Then, he let loose the string that held the kite, and the kite soared up in the sky.

"Amol, I asked you a question," Mala said to me again.

"Yes, I would prefer that. I think it is important for a husband and wife to live together in the first year of marriage. They have housing on campus for married students," I had just hit the ball for a six. In baseball, it is called hitting a homerun.

"Em? I think so too. By the way, I am hungry. Can we go somewhere else where we can at least eat what we have ordered?"

"I think there is a Chinese place down the street," I replied, and made a mental note to thank Abhijeet.

"You just said something. What does that mean?" I asked as we rose.

"Oh, Em? It means 'Is that so?' in Gujarati," she replied.

"Mala who says Em. You should call her M," GB remarked.

Over some delicious noodles, dim sums, and loads of jasmine tea, we both discussed our experiences while searching for a life partner. M told me that I was her prospect number 46, and was thrilled to learn that she was number 31 in my list. Our conversation had just supported the theory that women are choosier compared to men when it comes to selecting a spouse.

"By the way, you are a rebound for me," Mala said with a smile as we finished the main course.

"Huh?" I asked.

"I am asleyambers14 from Shaadi.com. I had rejected you."

*

My cousin Tushar Dada had volunteered to create an account for me on that website. Aai had provided my details to him behind my back, just like the way she had done in case of Mohini Marriage Bureau. He was already looking for grooms for his 23 year old daughter, and for him, scanning the matrimonial websites had become an addiction of sorts. Much against my wishes, he had approached several prospects over the past few months on my behalf.

"I know what to do, leave it to me," he had told Aai.

Tushar Dada was a Vice President in a cement company. He used to check the profiles of eligible women in his office during lunch break. It was fine as long as he was looking for grooms for his daughter. But when he started the bride-hunt for me, the staff in his office was amused. Sheetal, his daughter, worked in the same office. When she learnt what her father was up to, she was aghast.

"Baba, what are you doing?" she had asked as she had barged into his office one day. A young intern walking into the VP's office was considered sacrilege in that old-fashioned company, but Sheetal was not a believer in rules or etiquettes.

"I was just checking some profiles for Amol," he had replied.

"Can you at least turn the computer monitor away from the door? Everybody can see what you are up to," Sheetal suggested.

"Oh. I didn't realize that," Tushar Dada had replied.

I figured it was he who had probably contacted Mala.

*

"Let me also tell you that I am also a rebound for you, for you had rejected me. I am Jeevansathi.com as well. My handle there is Vat_Patriki," Mala added.

"It is good that we both have rejected each other already," I replied. My face will still plastered with a smile.

"What's with the smile?" M asked me.

"Vat_Patriki. Never heard of anybody using such a name."

"Vata is Banyan tree in Sanskrit. And Vata Patra, means the leaf of a Banyan Tree. Vadodara city gets its name from a grove of Vata trees that used to grow in this area several hundred years ago. And I am but a small part of this city, so in a way, I am a mere leaf in the cluster of trees. That's why I am Vat_Patriki."

"Very interesting. I didn't know this about Vadodara, except that it used to be called Baroda during the Brit times. At least they retained the gender, unlike Victoria Terminus in Mumbai."

She ignored my remark, and asked, "Is somebody else logging on as you and contacting the prospects?"

I told her about Aai and Tushar Dada and my experience with Mohini Marriage Bureau.

"That is hilarious. I have a confession to make. I am the one sending emails to your father posing as my Baba. And fathers, mothers, friends, and sisters of other guys as well," Mala lowered her tone as she spoke.

It was my turn to tell the truth," I too have a confession to make. I was the one sending emails from my father's email account."

"No wonder the emails were so cut and dry," she said with a smile. "My Baba thought that your father sounded very warm polite over the phone, but the emails were kind of rude."

"You had asked me to send my photo and profile three times."

"I didn't receive them the first two times. Honestly."

I narrated the Diskit incident to her and we both had a good laugh. A few minutes later, she spoke,

"As far as I am concerned, I am still waiting to find my soulmate. You must think I am crazy of sorts, a dreamer, like Madhuri Dixit in the movie *Dil To Pagal Hai*."

"Someone, somewhere is made for you," I said, recalling the tagline from the movie that was released a decade ago.

"Exactly," she added.

"And soulmates? Isn't that Brian Weiss Stuff?" I asked, recalling my recent discussion with the woman on the bus journey.

"You know him? Have you read his Many Lives, Many Masters?"

"My neighbor gave it to me to read," I lied.

"How did you find it?" she asked me enthusiastically.

I was in a spot. Just then, her phone rang.

"Yes, we are still there. Yes, okay," Mala said as she hung up, and told me, "That was Kavita, my best friend. She wanted to know if she could join us here."

"Sure, why not?" I wondered how Kavita knew our location. Then I recalled that Mala had excused herself to use the ladies' room a few minutes ago. She had probably texted Kavita then.

"Impress the chaperone, and your job will be done," GB advised.

Kavita turned out to be a bubbly and energetic, and we had a long chat on a variety of subjects. My efforts to woo the chaperone had worked. Heeding to GB's advice was a good thing sometimes.

*

The auto-rickshaw ride back to Sion was a breeze. The road leading from Dharavi to Sion Chembur Highway is a boundary of sorts. Auto-rickshaws cannot go beyond this road into Sion and the areas further south. They can only head east towards Chembur, or back towards Dharavi or Kurla. By the time I reached Sion station, I was grinning again for no reason. I paid off the driver and crossed the road, and walked past Café Vrindavan to head back to my apartment.

There is a Hanuman Temple situated in the middle of the sidewalk across from the café. I approached the temple to pray to

Hanumanji. I had lived in this neighborhood for nearly six months, but had never visited this temple. As I recalled my visits to the Hanuman Temple on Paud Road, all of a sudden, several bells in the temple started ringing.

"Ghantee baj gayee," GB said, and added, "You must thank Hanumanji; because you have his blessings."

It is said that a man must visit a Hanuman Temple before he gets married. There, he has to seek approval from the 'boss' to leave the world of bachelors and enter the world of married men. The ringing bells were a positive sign and an indication that I had the go-head.

*

Earlier that week, Dan had asked me, "How is your mission coming along?"

I had replied, "My suicide mission is not going well," and had told him about Mala and the woman in the bus and the book she was reading. He had liked the idea of soulmates.

As I walked back towards my pad in Jain Society, Dan saw me enter the building. He came down a few minutes later, and rang the doorbell. "So, how did it go?" He asked as I opened door.

"It went okay," I replied, and updated him on my meeting with Mala. My debrief included her googly that I had hit for a six, meeting her friend at the restaurant, the Mumbai Street Café fiasco, and finally, the bells at the Hanuman temple.

"I like it. This calls for a celebration, and I like that you call her M." Dan said as he brought a couple of bottles of beer from the fridge. "So, what's your take?" he handed me a bottle as he sat down.

"You know Dan, when I met Mala for the first time; I spent over an hour trying to figure out why she looked so familiar. It felt as if I have known her for a long, long time. There was no awkwardness; in fact there was a certain level of comfort talking to her. Of all the things, we spoke about dividing the states in India, starting with Telangana. All along, I was thinking, 'Am I really talking to her, or am I hallucinating?' I recall having this silly grin on my face, and boy, I so wanted to marry her right then."

"Bravo, bravo," said Dan. But once we finished our beers, he had a grim look.

"What's the matter?" I asked him.

He asked me back, "So what happens next?"

"I don't know? We will talk to our parents I guess…"

"Nonsense. I will tell you what happens next. You ask her out for dinner this evening. That's what you are going to do."

"But Dan, Ashok's daughter is getting married today. He has invited me for the reception."

"Screw that. If this works out, you can apologize to Ashok, and invite him, his daughter, her husband and even their dog for your own wedding. But for now, ask her out for dinner."

"Wha…at?" I said out loud.

"I said you should ask her out for dinner, that's what."

I complied with Dan's orders and sent Mala a text message. "Hey, I was wondering if we could meet for dinner tonight."

Her reply came a few minutes later, "Yes."

When we met over dinner, M reluctantly asked me a question.

In response, I wrote down nine numbers on a piece of paper.

"This is my social security number," I said to her, "you can run a background check on Zabasearch or a similar site. I would be happy to send my credit report if you want, but it would be one year old."

"I am sorry we have to do this, but Chandan, Kavita's husband, insisted on it. He thinks your story may be true, but he would like to check a few things. Hope you are okay with this," Mala sounded apologetic and worried at the same time.

"That's absolutely fine. I am impressed. No, I am really happy that you have friends who care about you. Give Chandan and Kavita my regards," I said to her with a smile. "By the way, if you discover that I have a son or a daughter somewhere, do let me know," and I went on to tell her about the insurance policy that KMM had sent me.

"That is ridiculously funny. By the way, I meant to ask, do you share this information with every girl that you meet?"

"I have told the truth every time, but giving my social security number? You are the first," as I spoke, M began to blush.

GB appeared just before we left the restaurant. He was dressed as a priest and was ringing the bell in a temple. "The bells are ringing, it is time," he announced.

That night, I sent a message to Dan. "I found my Soulmate."

Chapter Twenty Five
How Time Flies

The excitement of the New Year had passed, and February had marched its way in. By now, I was beginning to look forward to going to work and the smile was back on my face. My evenings were no longer restricted to watching TV or reading a book while drinking beer. Instead, my evenings were now meant for phone calls with M. The weekend trips to Pune were all about the wedding preparations.

It was a full house at Shabri when the Boys met on the first Saturday of the month. Before leaving home, I thought to myself, "So much has changed since we Boys met for the first time."

Lalit had turned forty last month. "My life actually begins now," he had told us on his big Four-Oh.

Mandar had taken up a new job in Mumbai and was planning to move his family sometime in April.

Nitin had finally found a steady girlfriend, and he planned to propose to her later in the year.

Shashi had a second child, a baby boy this time.

As for me, life was never going to be the same again.

I complained to the gang, "I hate telling the same story over and over again to anybody and everybody I meet. Yes, I am getting married. Yes, M is going to live with me in Ahmedabad. No, I am not going to work for an entire year. Yes, I am crazy to make so many changes to my life simultaneously."

"That's the way you have been all your life," Shashi remarked as we waited for the Surmai to arrive. "You are never satisfied with what you've got. You always want to do something different." He probably had borrowed a line or two from GB's book.

"Shashi, you plan everything. Hell, you probably even planned when and where you were going to be born," I shot back.

"Drop it, you two," Lalit said. After a brief pause, he asked me, "Amol, have you decided where you will be going for your honeymoon? Act on it fast, and make it your number one priority. Otherwise, you will get to hear about it for the rest of your life."

"Is a honeymoon really that important?" Nitin asked.

"Don't worry. You will understand when the time is right. In fact, you should start working out, too. It will improve your stamina," Lalit remarked with a grin.

"I don't get it," Nitin replied. The rest of us ignored him.

"It's okay. We didn't know about it at some point in our own lives either," Mandar told Nitin after some time. Then, he turned toward me and asked, "Have you bought her a sari yet?"

"I think she wants a Paithani sari. Her friend Kavita had insisted that I buy her one, but I have no idea what that means," I replied.

"Get used to terms like Kantha, Phulkari, Kanjeevaram, Banarsi and Paithani. The first two are designs on clothing, while the last three are types of silk saris. The sooner you know what they are, the better it will be for you. As for Paithani, these are saris which are made at Paithan near Aurangabad or someplace like that. Look for the peacock on the sari," Shashi advised me.

"They make something other than beer in Aurangabad?" Lalit

winked as he spoke these words.

The Boys were discussing saris over drinks. It was a shame, a big shame. We knew that this conversation had to end. It was 10 PM, and we had finished the Old Monk, the peanuts and the fish. Nobody was in the mood to stay on any longer. It was time to close the meeting.

"Let me pay. I am not sure when I will be able to pay next," I said as the waiter approached with the bill and our last round of drinks.

Two years ago, I used to call a bill a check, and currency notes were bills. Today, a check had become a bill, and the bills had become currency notes, and a checkbook had become a cheque book. But these were only a few of the multiple changes that had happened.

The five of us stood outside Shabri when Shashi pulled out the last four cigarettes that were left in the pack- one each for Lalit, Mandar, Shashi and I.

"Time to let this go, right?" I asked, pointing to the cigarette.

"Yes. And all the conversations we ever had here never happened," Shashi ordered.

"Too late, I have told my girlfriend about this place," Nitin said.

"Then we will have to kill you," Mandar said, and gave him what he considered to be his dangerous look. We all had a good laugh. Somehow, we also knew that this would be our last meeting at Shabri.

*

Ten minutes later, Nitin dropped me home. This time, I had taken the keys with me, and did not have to sleep in a bathtub.

That night, I received an email from Sharda, the doctor who was a self-admitted gold digger. It read as follows:

"Dear Amol,

How are you doing? I am writing because I have heard great things about the MBA program you will be joining. I wanted things between us to start afresh.

Sharda."

What had caused her change of heart? Was she unable to meet a guy who was rich enough to meet her demands? Not that it mattered to me anymore. I deleted her email.

*

For the first time in my life I spent Valentine's Day with my beloved. One year ago, I was hardly in a position to think about love. Two years ago, I was stuck in a snowstorm in Detroit and could only manage a short conversation with Nandini.

As I lay on the bed, admiring M and thinking how beautiful she looked, I began to think how the past few months had really changed my life for the better. And I had GB to thank for that. He had shown me the way to turn things around. I had always thought that he was a smartass, but everything he had said to me had begun to make sense.

"You are in good hands now," GB said as he appeared.

"I know, and thanks for everything," I said to him.

"You are welcome. By the way, let me tell you a secret. I am your voice of reason that you had chosen to ignore for so long. In a way, I am a figment of your imagination."

"I don't get it." I replied.

GB continued, "It takes balls to do what you have done. You put up with a lot of crap, and yet you did not give up. A lot of people would have simply quit and gone back. You chose to stay put. You also needed a bit of help because you had lost your way. You were in trouble, my boy, and that is why I chose to enter your life in this form. You may think that I am a smartass, but remember, that's also the way you have been all your life."

"I was beginning to think I was schizophrenic and all that was happening around me was a dream. Too many changes have occurred in the past two years. It's too much to handle," I said to him.

"Remember, your present situation is a function of your past actions. You cannot change the past, but whenever you bring a change the present, things will start moving for you. Changes are a part and parcel of life, and your life is about to change again forever. But try to enjoy the journey this time around."

"Thanks, GB. So will I ever see you again?"

"Maybe yes, but maybe not. Who knows? You are in good hands now, remember that," with those words, he faded away.

*

"Amol, wake up," M's words brought me back from my dream.

"I come all the way to Mumbai to meet you, and instead of spending time with me, you doze off. By the way, you were murmuring in your sleep. Did you dream about something?"

"I dreamt about a friend. I will tell you about him some day."

"You once told me about your rule that the guy should always go to meet the girl. Then how come I have to travel to Mumbai every time we have to meet?" M was right. This boy never went to meet his girl.

"M, I am not sure why you agreed to marry me. You know my life, now our lives, are going to be chaotic. You had mentioned the first time we met that you come from a family of bankers, and you all like to play it safe. And yet, barely two months after we met, you are here with me, ready to take the biggest risk of your life."

"It's okay. I have a feeling that it will all work out in the end, but only if you buy the clothes for our wedding in time. My parents have asked you several times, and they are giving me a hard time over it."

Traditionally, the bride's family buys the clothes that the groom wears on wedding day. But I was still trying to figure out what to wear.

"I don't know what I am going to wear. But hey, I brought you something that you might like," I handed her a packet as I spoke.

As M opened the packet, a note fell out of it. It read as follows.

Hooked or Booked?

I think it happened by hook or crook;
When I looked for the right one, in every cranny and nook.
Read self-help guides and many a book;
And for how much ever time it took;
I continued to look.
Chased away evils, and the occasional spook...
And one fine day, my whole world shook.
Because, to end my solitary path,
I had crossed the last brook.

M blushed as she read the first poem I had written in years.

"Happy Valentine's Day," I said to her.

As she carefully removed the brown paper cover, she nearly screamed in excitement. "It's a Paithani sari! Thank you, thank you, and thank you. How did you know that this is exactly what I wanted?"

"Thank you Baba," I said to myself.

*

Aai had asked me as she was preparing coffee in the kitchen, "What are you planning to buy for Valentine's Day?" February 14th was merely a week away.

"Aai, I think she wants a Paithani sari," I replied.

Baba was in his room when he heard my words, and he came to the kitchen almost panting. He had managed to walk without his walking stick, a sign that our morning walks had done him good.

"I am coming with you," he ordered.

"No Baba, I will manage by myself."

"Nothing doing. I want to come with you, I insist."

That evening, Aai, Baba and I went to Laxmi Road. For the traditional Puneri shopper, Laxmi Road is heaven. At any given time of the year, this place is crowded, and driving through the narrow streets is a nightmare. But this area is home to several stores that sell the choicest saris.

Somebody in the family had recommended a store called Peshwai. It is located on a street parallel to Laxmi Road, and is only a few meters from Vijay Theater where Pangulal and I had watched several movies in our college days. More often than not, we had skipped classes to do so. As I drove past the theater, I recalled some of their names. 'Independence Day',' Twister', 'Congo'…

"I can tell you the material of the cloth, and where it was made just by touching it. And I can also tell you how much the shopkeeper would have paid. It is often several hundred Rupees lower than the price he sells it for. In many cases, the difference is several thousand,"

Baba told me while I was driving.

Baba had difficulty in climbing the flight of stairs that led to the shop, but he persisted. After a very long time, he was going to have an opportunity to see, feel and discuss his favorite topic, textiles. Aai preferred to sit downstairs for a while and she joined us later.

That day, I saw that Baba had not lost his touch. He knew exactly what he was looking for. He had looked at several of the saris the salesman showed him, but had picked only four or five from the lot to feel their material.

"I like the green one," Aai said a short while later.

Baba shook his head and told the salesman, "Don't sell me nylon. I need a silk sari."

"No Kaka, this is silk," the young lad insisted. Baba had never known what voice modulation meant, and he often spoke above a decibel level of 80. "This is nonsense," he said to the salesman.

A balding man who was sitting behind a counter on the far side of the store heard Baba's words. He came up to us and said, "Namaskar, I am Damle. Let me show you what you want."

Mr. Damle said to the young salesman, "*Raju, atun maal aan.*"

Raju went into a small store room of sorts and brought a bundle of saris with him. Mr. Damle himself showed them and spoke about the tones of the color and the quality of the fabric.

Baba's face lit upon seeing the new lot. "Show me the pink and the yellow sari," and he went on to select the pink one. Aai nodded in agreement. Baba continued, "This is good quality silk. The color will not wear out on this one. But Damle Saheb, ten thousand Rupees is not the right price. It should be seven thousand Rupees at the most. You should have paid close to six for it, but I am willing to add another thousand. After all, you also have a business to run."

"No Sir, it cost us much more than that," Mr. Damle responded. "Which distributor did you buy them from?" Baba asked him.

"No, we buy directly from the weavers," Mr. Damle replied. He pulled out a handkerchief to wipe the sweat off his brow as he spoke.

"Okay, seven and a half, but nothing more," with those words, Baba turned to me and said, "Otherwise, lets' go somewhere else."

"Give me a minute please," Mr. Damle said, and he went speak to someone on the phone. He returned after a few minutes, and asked, "Saheb, what is the occasion? Is it for your daughter?"

"We are buying the sari for our daughter-in-law," Aai had a gleam in her eyes as she spoke.

"We would not sell this sari for this price normally, because we will not make much profit on it. But we cannot let go of a customer like you. May I ask how you know so much about our business?" Mr. Damle asked Baba.

"I was in the business for nearly thirty five years," Baba said with a sense of pride, and then he suddenly became quiet.

On our way back home, I said to Baba, "I am not sure if I would have been able to handle this by myself. You really stole the show."

"You have forgotten what your father used to be," Aai told me.

*

"You are lost in your thoughts again," M continued, "By the way, Natasha wrote to me yesterday and told me that there is a surprise in store for us."

I recalled that Natasha had called me earlier in the day.

"You know I hate surprises. Remember what happened two years ago in Chicago," I had told her over the phone.

"I do remember, and I don't care. You will find out soon what the surprise is," she had replied.

*

My idea of a wedding was go to the Marriage Registrar's office with witnesses, complete the wedding formalities, and host a reception for near and dear ones. In any case, registering a marriage was required by Law. But M had insisted that we do things her way, which meant that our marriage ceremony turned out to be the big fat Indian wedding that I had always dreaded. It was loud, chaotic and expensive, and I was both tired and irritated because of this.

Pangulal's parents attended our wedding reception. When his father gifted us ten thousand Rupees, M looked at me inquisitively. "It's a long story..." I told her, and thought to myself, "A deal is a deal."

We were married on March 16th, 2010, exactly two years after I had arrived by the AI 126 flight, and exactly one year after I had decided to stay back in India. March 16th had brought major changes in my life for three years in a row.

I wondered whether it was a coincidence, and realized how time flies.

Chapter Twenty Six
Off to America

"Have you checked with the airlines? Is the flight on time?" Baba asked me for the third time.

"Yes," I replied, as I finished packing the last of the bags.

"I hope the taxi arrives on time," he said again.

"We are all set, Baba. The taxi should be here in half-an-hour," I was in no mood to speak any further. Two years ago, I had traveled to the airport by myself. This time around, Aai, Baba, Natasha and M were going to be my fellow passengers in the taxi.

There was a thin veil of anxiety in the air as we left for Mumbai. Five hours later, we were at the airport, the same place from where my back to India adventure had started. Once the bags were loaded on to the trolleys, I pulled out a small packet and handed it to Baba.

"Happy Birthday, Baba," I wished him. He was going to need the money. Aai said with tear filled eyes that she would miss us. On that occasion, M learnt that I was a cry baby. But I was a mama's boy, and was proud of it.

*

An hour later, Aai, Baba and Natasha had checked in. The trio was off to America, where Aai and Baba would spend the next six months. Natasha and I had been after their lives to visit the United States since 2005, but they had used some pretext or the other to avoid the trip. Today, five years of our persuasion had finally paid off. Rather, Natasha's surprise had paid off.

Next week, the senior citizens would visit Niagara Falls and Las Vegas, while the newlyweds would visit the Sai Baba Temple in Shirdi. It should have been the other way round, but life is full of ironies and there was no use ruined over what was not to be.

*

My move to India began on a disastrous note. Everything that could have gone wrong, did go wrong. I had acted in haste and moved to India without thinking through, and that was the main reason for my suffering. I learnt the hard way that moving back to India does require a lot of planning. It is certainly not a decision that can be made on a sixteen-hour flight. Life in India comes with its own share of challenges, and one needs to be prepared to face them. It's as simple as that. Never again would I act before thinking, or so I hoped.

Two years ago, when I had left Chicago, I was single, had a job, money in the bank, and a planned future ahead of me. Today, I was married, unemployed, broke, and going back to student life.

Two years ago, when I had left Mumbai airport and was on my way to Pune, I was a proud NRI- a Non Resident Indian. Giving up my NRI status was a difficult decision. For the past two years, I had complained, groaned, moaned, and even got stoned. I had often wondered why I had not gone back to Canada, but could not find the answer till today.

Today, as M and I left Mumbai airport for Pune, I realized that I am still a proud NRI: Now, Returned to India.

Epilogue
Four Weeks to Go... Again!

Day Zero— Vadodara, March 16, 2010
   M and I get married.

Day Eight— Mumbai, March 24, 2010
   Aai and Baba fly off to the United States, accompanied by Natasha. Without her, their trip was not likely to happen.

Day Nine— March 25, 2010
   We leave for Cherrapunjee for our honeymoon.

Days Ten to Thirteen— March 26-30, 2010
   We explore what the area has to offer: waterfalls, forest trails, and the unforgettable living root bridges, the pleasant mornings, and golf ball-sized hail.

Day Fifteen— March 31, 2010
   Back to Pune. The taxi from Mumbai was again a blue and silver Indica, but this time without the Sardarjee driver or any accidents.

Day Sixteen— April Fools' Day
   We feel like fools because we had left behind the pleasant 22 degree Celsius temperature weather that we enjoyed in Cherrapunjee.

Day Seventeen— April 2, 2010
   We get scalded in the dry, 40 degree Celsius heat. If M was upset with me, she did not show it. I feel that my wife is a woman with infinite patience, but would learn soon that I was mistaken.

Day Twenty— April 5, 2010

The car is completely loaded with our worldly goods, leaving little room for both of us. We leave at 3 PM and reach a friend's house in Surat six hours later. I doze off on the sofa soon after dinner.

Day Twenty One— April 6, 2010

At last, I have a day of rest in Vadodara, and spend nearly the entire day in an air-conditioned room to beat the heat.

The highlight of the day was that we got married, again. I had always wanted to elope and have a registered wedding. One part of my dream was fulfilled; eloping would have to wait another life.

Day Twenty Two— April 7, 2010

We arrive at the IIM campus by 4:30 PM. An hour later, I get the keys for what will be our home for the next year. It is a Thursday night, and the classes begin on Monday. The AC is not working, we have to get the groceries, and there's laundry to do.

Days Twenty Three to Twenty Seven— April 8-12, 2010

Things finally fall in place, but M is exhausted from the madness.

Day Twenty Seven— April 12, 2010 midnight

The AC is on full blast in the bedroom, and M is fast asleep. She goes back to work from tomorrow. I am lying wide awake next to her, because sleep is hard to come by. Maybe it is the anxiety, or just excitement of starting student life. I look at M and think, "I can't wait to get started. And now, I have found a life partner too!"

There was a period of silence before I heard a familiar voice.

"Don't worry, it will all work out. What could be worse than what you went through in the last two years?" The speaker was dressed in a cap and gown and resembled a graduating student.

Day Twenty Eight— April 13, 2010, 00:01 AM.

The Learning Curve begins.
Upcoming Books in the Amol Dixit Series

The Learning Curve

Amol and M begin their married life on the campus of the Indian Institute of Management, Ahmedabad. With each passing day, Amol realizes that his real learning does not take place in the classrooms, but at home, where he learns what it means to be a husband. As the summer gives way to the monsoons and the receding monsoons welcome the winter, Amol's learning curve continues. Soon, he has to decide what he will do next as his life as a business school student comes to an end.

Urban, Sophisticated

Amol joins an upmarket retail store chain in Gurgaon, where he starts his new job as a merchandiser for the kids' section. For two quarters in a row, Amol's forecasts go horribly wrong: girls' clothes are completely sold out in the cities, whereas the stores in smaller towns run out of clothing for boys. Amol has one last chance to get things right. One day, he makes a discovery that not only provides the solution to his problem, but also changes his life forever. Around the same time, M announces that their first child is on its way. While Amol is working really hard to prove himself at work, he and M wonder: are they Urban, Sophisticated?

About Amar Vyas

Amar Vyas is the pen name adopted by the author Amar Deshpande, who dabbled in the construction sector in the United States for several years before he returned to India in 2008. Two years into his Indian adventure, he hung up his construction boots (and hard hat), and went to the Indian Institute of Management, Ahmedabad for his MBA.

A self-described nomad, Amar has lived in fifteen cities over the past twenty years, including the two years he spent as a graduate student at the University of Illinois at Urbana Champaign. Most recently, he has moved with his family to Bengaluru. When he is not at work or working on his next novel, Amar likes exploring offbeat places, learning Gujarati from his wife, and spending time with his dog, Buddy.

You can reach Amar through the following ways:

E-Mail: amar@amarvyas.in Twitter: @amarauthor

Would you like to be informed about the release of Amar's upcoming books? Please visit www.amarvyas.in to subscribe to Amar's newsletter.

Printed in Great Britain
by Amazon.co.uk, Ltd.,
Marston Gate.